WILLIAM SHAKESPEARE was born in Stratford-upon-Avon in April, 1564, and his birth is traditionally celebrated on April 23. The facts of his life, known from surviving documents, are sparse. He was one of eight children born to John Shakespeare, a merchant of some standing in his community. William probably went to the King's New School in Stratford, but he had no university education. In November 1582, at the age of eighteen, he married Anne Hathaway, eight years his senior, who was pregnant with their first child, Susanna. She was born on May 26, 1583. Twins, a boy, Hamnet (who would die at age eleven), and a girl, Judith, were born in 1585. By 1592 Shakespeare had gone to London, working as an actor and already known as a playwright. A rival dramatist, Robert Greene, referred to him as "an upstart crow, beautified with our feathers." Shakespeare became a principal shareholder and playwright of the successful acting troupe the Lord Chamberlain's men (later, under James I, called the King's men). In 1599 the Lord Chamberlain's men built and occupied the Globe Theatre in Southwark near the Thames River. Here many of Shakespeare's plays were performed by the most famous actors of his time, including Richard Burbage, Will Kempe, and Robert Armin. In addition to his 37 plays, Shakespeare had a hand in others, including *Sir Thomas More* and *The Two Noble Kinsmen*, and he wrote poems, including *Venus and Adonis* and *The Rape of Lucrece*. His 154 sonnets were published, probably without his authorization, in 1609. In 1611 or 1612 he gave up his lodgings in London and devoted more and more of his time to retirement in Stratford, though he continued writing such plays as *The Tempest* and *Henry VIII* until about 1613. He died on April 23, 1616, and was buried in Holy Trinity Church, Stratford. No collected edition of his plays was published during his lifetime, but in 1623 two members of his acting company, John Heminges and Henry Condell, published the great collection now called the First Folio.

Bantam Shakespeare
The Complete Works—29 Volumes
Edited by David Bevington
With forewords by Joseph Papp on the plays

The Poems: Venus and Adonis, The Rape of Lucrece, The
Phoenix and Turtle, A Lover's Complaint,
the Sonnets

Antony and Cleopatra	*The Merchant of Venice*
As You Like It	*A Midsummer Night's Dream*
The Comedy of Errors	*Much Ado about Nothing*
Hamlet	*Othello*
Henry IV, Part One	*Richard II*
Henry IV, Part Two	*Richard III*
Henry V	*Romeo and Juliet*
Julius Caesar	*The Taming of the Shrew*
King Lear	*The Tempest*
Macbeth	*Twelfth Night*

Together in one volume:

Henry VI, Parts One, Two, and Three
King John and Henry VIII
*Measure for Measure, All's Well that Ends Well, and
Troilus and Cressida*
Three Early Comedies: Love's Labor's Lost, The Two
Gentlemen of Verona, The Merry
Wives of Windsor
Three Classical Tragedies: Titus Andronicus, Timon
of Athens, Coriolanus
The Late Romances: Pericles, Cymbeline, The Winter's
Tale, The Tempest

Two collections:

Four Comedies: The Taming of the Shrew, A Midsummer
Night's Dream, The Merchant of Venice,
Twelfth Night
Four Tragedies: Hamlet, Othello, King Lear, Macbeth

William Shakespeare

AS YOU LIKE IT

Edited by
David Bevington

David Scott Kastan,
James Hammersmith,
and Robert Kean Turner,
Associate Editors

With a Foreword by
Joseph Papp

BANTAM BOOKS
TORONTO / NEW YORK / LONDON / SYDNEY / AUCKLAND

AS YOU LIKE IT
*A Bantam Book / published by arrangement
with Scott, Foresman and Company*

PRINTING HISTORY
Scott Foresman edition published / January 1980
*Bantam edition, with newly edited text and substantially revised,
edited, and amplified notes, introductions, and other
materials, published / February 1988*
*Valuable advice on staging matters has been
provided by Richard Hosley.*
Collations checked by Eric Rasmussen.
Additional editorial assistance by Claire McEachern.

Bantam Classic edition / February 1988
All rights reserved.
Copyright © 1980, 1973, 1961, 1951 by Scott, Foresman and Company.
Foreword copyright © 1988 by New York Shakespeare Festival.
Cover art copyright © 1988 by Mark English.
This edition copyright © 1988 by Bantam Books.
*Revisions and annotations to Shakespeare text and its footnotes and
textual notes, Shakespeare's Sources essay and notes for the source,
and the play introduction copyright © 1988 by David Bevington.*
The Playhouse text copyright © 1988 by David Bevington.
*Performance history copyright © 1988
by David Bevington and David Scott Kastan.*
*Annotated bibliography copyright © 1988 by
David Scott Kastan and James Shapiro.*
Memorable Lines copyright © 1988 by Bantam Books.
*No part of this book may be reproduced or transmitted
in any form or by any means, electronic or mechanical,
including photocopying, recording, or by any information
storage and retrieval system, without permission
in writing from the publisher.*
For information address: Bantam Books.

Library of Congress Cataloging-in-Publication Data

Shakespeare, William, 1564–1616.
  As you like it / William Shakespeare; edited by David Bevington;
David Scott Kastan, James Hammersmith, and Robert Kean Turner,
associate editors; with a foreword by Joseph Papp.
    p.   cm.—(A Bantam classic)
  "Bantam edition with newly edited text and substantially revised,
edited, and amplified notes, introductions, and other materials"—
—T.p. verso.
  Bibliography: p.
  ISBN 0-553-21290-7
  I. Bevington, David M.   II. Title.
PR2803.A2B4 1988
822.3'3—dc19   87-24092
                                                                CIP

Published simultaneously in the United States and Canada

*Bantam Books are published by Bantam Books, a division of Bantam
Doubleday Dell Publishing Group, Inc. Its trademark, consisting of the
words "Bantam Books" and the portrayal of a rooster, is Registered in
U.S. Patent and Trademark Office and in other countries. Marca Regis-
trada. Bantam Books, 666 Fifth Avenue, New York, New York 10103.*

PRINTED IN THE UNITED STATES OF AMERICA

O   0 9 8 7 6 5 4 3 2 1

Contents

Foreword

It's hard to imagine, but Shakespeare wrote all of his plays with a quill pen, a goose feather whose hard end had to be sharpened frequently. How many times did he scrape the dull end to a point with his knife, dip it into the inkwell, and bring up, dripping wet, those wonderful words and ideas that are known all over the world?

In the age of word processors, typewriters, and ballpoint pens, we have almost forgotten the meaning of the word "blot." Yet when I went to school, in the 1930s, my classmates and I knew all too well what an inkblot from the metal-tipped pens we used would do to a nice clean page of a test paper, and we groaned whenever a splotch fell across the sheet. Most of us finished the school day with ink-stained fingers; those who were less careful also went home with ink-stained shirts, which were almost impossible to get clean.

When I think about how long it took me to write the simplest composition with a metal-tipped pen and ink, I can only marvel at how many plays Shakespeare scratched out with his goose-feather quill pen, year after year. Imagine him walking down one of the narrow cobblestoned streets of London, or perhaps drinking a pint of beer in his local alehouse. Suddenly his mind catches fire with an idea, or a sentence, or a previously elusive phrase. He is burning with impatience to write it down—but because he doesn't have a ballpoint pen or even a pencil in his pocket, he has to keep the idea in his head until he can get to his quill and parchment.

He rushes back to his lodgings on Silver Street, ignoring the vendors hawking brooms, the coaches clattering by, the piteous wails of beggars and prisoners. Bounding up the stairs, he snatches his quill and starts to write furiously, not even bothering to light a candle against the dusk. "To be, or not to be," he scrawls, "that is the—." But the quill point has gone dull, the letters have fattened out illegibly, and in the middle of writing one of the most famous passages in the history of dramatic literature, Shakespeare has to stop to sharpen his pen.

Taking a deep breath, he lights a candle now that it's dark, sits down, and begins again. By the time the candle has burned out and the noisy apprentices of his French Huguenot landlord have quieted down, Shakespeare has finished Act 3 of *Hamlet* with scarcely a blot.

Early the next morning, he hurries through the fog of a London summer morning to the rooms of his colleague Richard Burbage, the actor for whom the role of Hamlet is being written. He finds Burbage asleep and snoring loudly, sprawled across his straw mattress. Not only had the actor performed in *Henry V* the previous afternoon, but he had then gone out carousing all night with some friends who had come to the performance.

Shakespeare shakes his friend awake, until, bleary-eyed, Burbage sits up in his bed. "Dammit, Will," he grumbles, "can't you let an honest man sleep?" But the playwright, his eyes shining and the words tumbling out of his mouth, says, "Shut up and listen—tell me what you think of *this*!"

He begins to read to the still half-asleep Burbage, pacing around the room as he speaks. ". . . Whether 'tis nobler in the mind to suffer the slings and arrows of outrageous fortune—"

Burbage interrupts, suddenly wide awake, "That's excellent, very good, 'the slings and arrows of outrageous fortune,' yes, I think it will work quite well. . . ." He takes the parchment from Shakespeare and murmurs the lines to himself, slowly at first but with growing excitement.

The sun is just coming up, and the words of one of Shakespeare's most famous soliloquies are being uttered for the first time by the first actor ever to bring Hamlet to life. It must have been an exhilarating moment.

Shakespeare wrote most of his plays to be performed live by the actor Richard Burbage and the rest of the Lord Chamberlain's men (later the King's men). Today, however, our first encounter with the plays is usually in the form of the printed word. And there is no question that reading Shakespeare for the first time isn't easy. His plays aren't comic books or magazines or the dime-store detective novels I read when I was young. A lot of his sentences are complex. Many of his words are no longer used in our everyday speech. His profound thoughts are often condensed into poetry, which is not as straightforward as prose.

Yet when you hear the words spoken aloud, a lot of the language may strike you as unexpectedly modern. For Shakespeare's plays, like any dramatic work, weren't really meant to be read; they were meant to be spoken, seen, and performed. It's amazing how lines that are so troublesome in print can flow so naturally and easily when spoken.

I think it was precisely this music that first fascinated me. When I was growing up, Shakespeare was a stranger to me. I had no particular interest in him, for I was from a different cultural tradition. It never occurred to me that his plays might be more than just something to "get through" in school, like science or math or the physical education requirement we had to fulfill. My passions then were movies, radio, and vaudeville—certainly not Elizabethan drama.

I was, however, fascinated by words and language. Because I grew up in a home where Yiddish was spoken, and English was only a second language, I was acutely sensitive to the musical sounds of different languages and had an ear for lilt and cadence and rhythm in the spoken word. And so I loved reciting poems and speeches even as a very young child. In first grade I learned lots of short nature verses— "Who has seen the wind?," one of them began. My first foray into drama was playing the role of Scrooge in Charles Dickens's *A Christmas Carol* when I was eight years old. I liked summoning all the scorn and coldness I possessed and putting them into the words, "Bah, humbug!"

From there I moved on to longer and more famous poems and other works by writers of the 1930s. Then, in junior high school, I made my first acquaintance with Shakespeare through his play *Julius Caesar*. Our teacher, Miss McKay, assigned the class a passage to memorize from the opening scene of the play, the one that begins "Wherefore rejoice? What conquest brings he home?" The passage seemed so wonderfully theatrical and alive to me, and the experience of memorizing and reciting it was so much fun, that I went on to memorize another speech from the play on my own.

I chose Mark Antony's address to the crowd in Act 3,

scene 2, which struck me then as incredibly high drama. Even today, when I speak the words, I feel the same thrill I did that first time. There is the strong and athletic Antony descending from the raised pulpit where he has been speaking, right into the midst of a crowded Roman square. Holding the torn and bloody cloak of the murdered Julius Caesar in his hand, he begins to speak to the people of Rome:

> If you have tears, prepare to shed them now.
> You all do know this mantle. I remember
> The first time ever Caesar put it on;
> 'Twas on a summer's evening in his tent,
> That day he overcame the Nervii.
> Look, in this place ran Cassius' dagger through.
> See what a rent the envious Casca made.
> Through this the well-belovèd Brutus stabbed,
> And as he plucked his cursèd steel away,
> Mark how the blood of Caesar followed it,
> As rushing out of doors to be resolved
> If Brutus so unkindly knocked or no;
> For Brutus, as you know, was Caesar's angel.
> Judge, O you gods, how dearly Caesar loved him!
> This was the most unkindest cut of all . . .

I'm not sure now that I even knew Shakespeare had written a lot of other plays, or that he was considered "timeless," "universal," or "classic"—but I knew a good speech when I heard one, and I found the splendid rhythms of Antony's rhetoric as exciting as anything I'd ever come across.

Fifty years later, I still feel that way. Hearing good actors speak Shakespeare gracefully and naturally is a wonderful experience, unlike any other I know. There's a satisfying fullness to the spoken word that the printed page just can't convey. This is why seeing the plays of Shakespeare performed live in a theater is the best way to appreciate them. If you can't do that, listening to sound recordings or watching film versions of the plays is the next best thing.

But if you do start with the printed word, use the play as a script. Be an actor yourself and say the lines out loud. Don't worry too much at first about words you don't immediately understand. Look them up in the footnotes or a dictionary, but don't spend too much time on this. It is more profitable (and fun) to get the sense of a passage and sing it out. Speak naturally, almost as if you were talking to a friend, but be sure to enunciate the words properly. You'll be surprised at how much you understand simply by speaking the speech "trippingly on the tongue," as Hamlet advises the Players.

You might start, as I once did, with a speech from *Julius Caesar*, in which the tribune (city official) Marullus scolds the commoners for transferring their loyalties so quickly from the defeated and murdered general Pompey to the newly victorious Julius Caesar:

> Wherefore rejoice? What conquest brings he home?
> What tributaries follow him to Rome
> To grace in captive bonds his chariot wheels?
> You blocks, you stones, you worse than senseless
>   things!
> O you hard hearts, you cruel men of Rome,
> Knew you not Pompey? Many a time and oft
> Have you climbed up to walls and battlements,
> To towers and windows, yea, to chimney tops,
> Your infants in your arms, and there have sat
> The livelong day, with patient expectation,
> To see great Pompey pass the streets of Rome.

With the exception of one or two words like "wherefore" (which means "why," not "where"), "tributaries" (which means "captives"), and "patient expectation" (which means patient waiting), the meaning and emotions of this speech can be easily understood.

From here you can go on to dialogues or other more challenging scenes. Although you may stumble over unaccustomed phrases or unfamiliar words at first, and even fall flat when you're crossing some particularly rocky passages, pick yourself up and stay with it. Remember that it takes time to feel at home with anything new. Soon you'll come to recognize Shakespeare's unique sense of humor and way of saying things as easily as you recognize a friend's laughter.

And then it will just be a matter of choosing which one of Shakespeare's plays you want to tackle next. As a true fan of his, you'll find that you're constantly learning from his plays. It's a journey of discovery that you can continue for the rest of your life. For no matter how many times you read or see a particular play, there will always be something new there that you won't have noticed before.

Why do so many thousands of people get hooked on Shakespeare and develop a habit that lasts a lifetime? What can he really say to us today, in a world filled with inventions and problems he never could have imagined? And how do you get past his special language and difficult sentence structure to understand him?

The best way to answer these questions is to go see a live production. You might not know much about Shakespeare, or much about the theater, but when you watch actors performing one of his plays on the stage, it will soon become clear to you why people get so excited about a playwright who lived hundreds of years ago.

For the story—what's happening in the play—is the most accessible part of Shakespeare. In *A Midsummer Night's Dream*, for example, you can immediately understand the situation: a girl is chasing a guy who's chasing a girl who's chasing another guy. No wonder *A Midsummer Night's Dream* is one of the most popular of Shakespeare's plays: it's about one of the world's most popular pastimes— falling in love.

But the course of true love never did run smooth, as the young suitor Lysander says. Often in Shakespeare's comedies the girl whom the guy loves doesn't love him back, or she loves him but he loves someone else. In *The Two Gentlemen of Verona*, Julia loves Proteus, Proteus loves Sylvia, and Sylvia loves Valentine, who is Proteus's best friend. In the end, of course, true love prevails, but not without lots of complications along the way.

For in all of his plays—comedies, histories, and tragedies—Shakespeare is showing you human nature. His characters act and react in the most extraordinary ways—and sometimes in the most incomprehensible ways. People are always trying to find motivations for what a character does. They ask, "Why does Iago want to destroy Othello?"

The answer, to me, is very simple—because that's the way Iago is. That's just his nature. Shakespeare doesn't explain his characters; he sets them in motion—and away they go. He doesn't worry about whether they're likable or not. He's interested in interesting people, and his most fascinating characters are those who are unpredictable. If you lean back in your chair early on in one of his plays, thinking you've figured out what Iago or Shylock (in *The Merchant of Venice*) is up to, don't be too sure—because that great judge of human nature, Shakespeare, will surprise you every time.

He is just as wily in the way he structures a play. In *Macbeth*, a comic scene is suddenly introduced just after the bloodiest and most treacherous slaughter imaginable, of a guest and king by his host and subject, when in comes a drunk porter who has to go to the bathroom. Shakespeare is tickling your emotions by bringing a stand-up comic on-stage right on the heels of a savage murder.

It has taken me thirty years to understand even some of these things, and so I'm not suggesting that Shakespeare is immediately understandable. I've gotten to know him not through theory but through practice, the practice of the *living* Shakespeare—the playwright of the theater.

Of course the plays are a great achievement of dramatic literature, and they should be studied and analyzed in schools and universities. But you must always remember, when reading all the words *about* the playwright and his plays, that *Shakespeare's* words came first and that in the end there is nothing greater than a single actor on the stage speaking the lines of Shakespeare.

Everything important that I know about Shakespeare comes from the practical business of producing and directing his plays in the theater. The task of classifying, criticizing, and editing Shakespeare's printed works I happily leave to others. For me, his plays really do live on the stage, not on the page. That is what he wrote them for and that is how they are best appreciated.

Although Shakespeare lived and wrote hundreds of years ago, his name rolls off my tongue as if he were my brother. As a producer and director, I feel that there is a professional relationship between us that spans the centuries. As a human being, I feel that Shakespeare has enriched my understanding of life immeasurably. I hope you'll let him do the same for you.

❧

As You Like It is one of Shakespeare's best-written comedies, as full of lively speeches as the Forest of Arden is of living creatures. The one I enjoy most is not Jaques's famous speech beginning, "All the world's a stage, / And all the men and women merely players." Although this is well-deserving of its fame, I often respond to speeches that are less obviously philosophical and more actively theatrical, such as the speech Touchstone, the courtier-fool, has at the end of the play.

In this speech Touchstone delineates the several stages of a quarrel with a courtier, as follows: "the Retort Courteous," "the Quip Modest," "the Reply Churlish," "the Reproof Valiant," "the Countercheck Quarrelsome," "the Lie with Circumstance" and "the Lie Direct." Here we have a living example of the kind of brave, macho, chivalric exterior Elizabethans donned with words, doing their utmost to avoid any physical encounter that might provoke the drawing of swords. When an actor delivers this speech quickly and nimbly, it's a marvelously witty moment.

Another part of *As You Like It* that is as I like it is the deception Rosalind plays on Orlando, pretending to be a boy and telling him that she's going to teach him about love. At one point in their conversation he asks her how she can tell somebody's in love. Teasingly, she insists that Orlando couldn't possibly be in love because he doesn't have the marks of the lover: "A lean cheek, which you have not; a blue eye and sunken, which you have not; an unquestionable spirit, which you have not . . ." And on she goes, inventing an imaginary uncle who taught her all about love.

When Rosalind and Orlando first run across each other in the forest, she gives a wonderful discourse on Time, and how slowly it moves for someone in love waiting for his beloved. Within the play, this is Rosalind's way of playing the knave with Orlando. But it also has meaning for anyone who has ever been young and in love, watching the clock drag while waiting for that special person and then feeling the time fly by once you are together. Like so much else in Shakespeare, these lines that work so well within the play can also be applied to our own lives.

JOSEPH PAPP GRATEFULLY ACKNOWLEDGES THE HELP OF ELIZABETH KIRKLAND IN PREPARING THIS FOREWORD.

Introduction

As You Like It represents, together with *Much Ado about Nothing* and *Twelfth Night*, the summation of Shakespeare's achievement in festive, happy comedy during the years 1598–1601. *As You Like It* contains several motifs found in other Shakespearean comedies: the journey from a jaded court into a transforming silvan environment and back to a revitalized court (as in *A Midsummer Night's Dream*); hence, a contrasting of two worlds in the play, one presided over by a virtuous but exiled older brother and the other by a usurping younger brother (as in *The Tempest*); the heroine disguised as a man (as in *The Merchant of Venice*, *The Two Gentlemen of Verona*, *Cymbeline*, and *Twelfth Night*); and a structure of multiple plotting in which numerous groups of characters are thematically played off against one another (as in several of Shakespeare's comedies). What chiefly distinguishes this play from the others, however, is the nature and function of its pastoral setting—the Forest of Arden.

The Forest of Arden is seen in many perspectives. As a natural wilderness, it is probably most like the real forest Shakespeare knew near Stratford-upon-Avon in Warwickshire—a place capable of producing the vulgarity of an Audrey or the gentle simplicity of a Corin. It also owes something to the forest in Shakespeare's source, *Rosalynde*, based in turn on the forest of Ardennes in France. As an abode that is associated with Robin Hood, it is a mythic folk world compensating for social injustice, offering an alternative way of life to those persons in retreat from a society seemingly beyond repair. As the "golden world" (1.1.114), the forest evokes an even deeper longing for a mythological past age of innocence and plenty, when men shared some attributes of the giants and the gods. This myth has its parallel in the biblical Garden of Eden, before the human race experienced "the penalty of Adam" (2.1.5). Finally, in another of its aspects, the forest is Arcadia, a pastoral landscape embodied in an ancient and sophisticated literary tradition.

All but the first of these Ardens, compared and contrasted with one another, involve some idealization not only of nature and the natural landscape, but also of the human condition. These various Ardens place our real life in a complex perspective and force us to a fresh appraisal of our own ordinary existence. Duke Senior, for example, describes the forest environment as a corrective for the evils of society. He addresses his followers in the forest as "my co-mates and brothers in exile" (2.1.1), suggesting a kind of social equality that he could never know in the cramped formality of his previous official existence. The banished Duke and his followers have had to leave behind their lands and revenues in the grip of the usurping Frederick. No longer rich, though adequately provided with all of life's necessities, the Duke and his "merry men" live "like the old Robin Hood of England," and "fleet the time carelessly as they did in the golden world" (1.1.111–114). In this friendly society, a strong communal sense replaces the necessity for individual proprietorship. All comers are welcome, with food for all.

There are no luxuries in the forest, to be sure, but even this spare existence affords relief from the decadence of courtly life. "Sweet are the uses of adversity" (2.1.12), insists the Duke. He welcomes the cold of winter because, instead of flattering him as courtiers do, it teaches him the true condition of mankind and of himself. The forest is serenely impartial, neither malicious nor compassionate. Death, and even killing for food, are an inevitable part of forest existence. The Duke concedes that his presence in the forest means the slaughter of deer, who were the original inhabitants; Orlando and Adam find that death through starvation in the forest is all too real a possibility. The forest never stoops to the degrading perversity of man at his worst, but it is also incapable of charity and forgiveness.

Shakespeare's sources reflect the complexity of his vision of Arden. The original of the Orlando story, which Shakespeare may not have used directly, is *The Cook's Tale of Gamelyn*, found in a number of manuscripts of *The Canterbury Tales* and wrongly attributed to Chaucer. This hearty English romance glorifies the rebellious and even violent spirit of its Robin Hood hero, the neglected youngest son Gamelyn, who, aided by faithful old Adam the Spencer, evades his wicked eldest brother in a cunning and bloody escape. As king of the outlaws in Sherwood Forest, Gamelyn eventually triumphs over his eldest brother (now the sheriff) and sees him hanged. Here then originates the motif of refuge from social injustice in Arden, even though most of the actual violence has been omitted from Shakespeare's version. (A series of Robin Hood plays on a similar theme, beginning in 1598 with Anthony Munday's *The Downfall of Robert Earl of Huntingdon after called Robin Hood*, were being performed with great success by the Admiral's company, chief rivals of the Lord Chamberlain's company to which Shakespeare belonged.)

As You Like It is clearly indebted to Thomas Lodge's version of the Gamelyn story entitled *Rosalynde: Euphues' Golden Legacy* (published 1590), a prose narrative romance in the ornate Euphuistic style of the 1580s. (Lodge's Epistle to the Gentleman Readers, casually inviting them to be pleased with this story if they are so inclined—*"If you like it,* so"—probably gave Shakespeare a hint for the name of his own play.) Lodge accentuated the love story with its courtship in masquerade, provided some charming songs, and introduced the pastoral love motif involving Corin, Silvius, Phoebe, and Ganymede. Shakespeare's ordering of episode is generally close to that of Lodge. Pastoral literature, which had become a literary rage in the 1580s and early 1590s owing particularly to Edmund Spenser's *Shepheardes Calendar* (1579) and Philip Sidney's *Arcadia* (1590), traced its ancestry through such Renaissance continental writers as Jorge de Montemayor, Jacopo Sannazaro, and Giovanni Battista Guarini to the so-called Greek romances, and finally back to the eclogues of Virgil, Theocritus, and Bion. A literary mode that had begun originally as a realistic evocation of difficult country life had become, by the Renaissance, an elegant vehicle for the loftiest and most patrician sentiments in love, for philosophic debate, and even for extensive political analysis.

Shakespeare's alterations and additions give us insight into his method of construction and his thematic focus. Whereas Lodge cheerfully accepts the pastoral conventions of his day, Shakespeare exposes those conventions to some criticism and considerable irony. Alongside the mannered and literary Silvius and Phoebe, he places William and Audrey, as peasantlike a couple as ever drew milk from a cow's teat. The juxtaposition holds up to critical perspective the rival claims of the literary and natural worlds by examining the defects of each in relation to the strengths of the other. William and Audrey are Shakespeare's own creation, based presumably on observation and also on the dramatic convention of the rustic clown and wench as exemplified earlier in his Costard and Jaquenetta *(Love's Labor's Lost)*.

Equally original, and essential to the many-sided debate concerning the virtues of the court versus those of the country, are Touchstone and Jaques. Touchstone is a professional court fool, dressed in motley, a new comic type in Shakespeare, created apparently in response to the recent addition to the Lord Chamberlain's company of the brilliant actor Robert Armin. Jaques is also a new type, the malcontent satirist, reflecting the very latest literary vogue in the nondramatic poetry and drama for the private theater of George Chapman, John Marston, and Ben Jonson. (The private theaters, featuring boy actors, reopened in 1598–1599 after nearly a decade of enforced silence, and proceeded at once to specialize in satirical drama.) Touchstone and Jaques complement each other as critics and observers, one laughing at human folly with quizzical comic detachment and the other satirizing it with moralistic scorn. Once we have been exposed to this assortment of newly created characters, we can no longer view either pastoral life or pastoral love as simply as Lodge and other writers of the period portray them.

When *As You Like It* is compared with its chief source, Shakespeare can also be seen to have altered and considerably softened the characters of the wicked brothers Oliver and Frederick. Whereas Lodge's Saladyne is motivated by a greedy desire to seize his younger brother Rosader's property, Shakespeare's Oliver is envious of Orlando's natural goodness and popularity. As he confesses in soliloquy, Orlando is "so much in the heart of the world and especially of my own people . . . that I am altogether misprised" (1.1.159–161). In his warped way Oliver desires to be more like Orlando, and in the enchanted forest of Arden he eventually becomes so. Duke Frederick too is plainly envious of goodness. Trying to persuade his daughter Celia of the need for banishing Rosalind, he argues, "thou wilt show more bright and seem more virtuous / When she is gone"

(1.3.79–80). In a sense Frederick is ripe for conversion. Penitence and conciliation replace the vengeful conclusion of Lodge's novel, in which the nobles of France finally overthrow and execute the usurping king. Although Shakespeare's resolutions are sudden and inadequately explained, like all miracles they attest to the inexplicable power of goodness.

The court of Duke Frederick is "the envious court," identified by this fixed epithet. In it, brothers turn unnaturally against brothers: the younger Frederick usurps his older brother's throne, whereas the older Oliver denies the younger Orlando his birthright of education. In still another parallel, both Rosalind and Orlando find themselves mistrusted as the children of Frederick's political enemies, Duke Senior and Sir Rowland de Boys. A daughter and a son are held to be guilty by association. "Thou art thy father's daughter, there's enough" (1.3.56), Frederick curtly retorts in explaining Rosalind's exile. And to Orlando, triumphant in wrestling with Charles, Frederick asserts, "I would thou hadst been son to some man else" (1.2.214). Here again, Frederick plaintively reveals his attraction to goodness, even if at present this attraction is thwarted by tyrannous whim. Many of Frederick's entourage might also be better persons if they only knew how to escape the insincerities of their courtly life. Charles the wrestler, for example, places himself at Oliver's service, and yet he would happily avoid breaking Orlando's neck if to do so were consistent with self-interest. Even Le Beau, the giddy fop so delighted at first with the cruel sport of wrestling, takes Orlando aside at some personal risk to warn him of Duke Frederick's foul humor. Ideally, Le Beau would prefer to be a companion of Orlando's "in a better world than this" (1.2.275). The vision of a regenerative Utopia secretly abides in the heart of this courtly creature.

It is easier to anatomize the defects of a social order than to propound solutions. As have other Utopian visionaries (including Thomas More), Shakespeare uses playful debate to elicit complicated responses on the part of his audience. Which is preferable, the court or the country? Jaques and Touchstone are adept gadflies, incessantly pointing out contradictions and ironies. Jaques, the malcontent railer derived from literary satire, takes delight in being out of step with everyone. Seemingly his chief reason for having joined the others in the forest is to jibe at their motives for being there. To their song about the rejection of courtly ambition he mockingly supplies another verse, charging them with having left their wealth and ease out of mere willfulness (2.5.46–54). With ironic appropriateness, Jaques eventually decides to remain in the forest in the company of Frederick; Jaques cannot thrive on resolution and harmony. His humor is "melancholy," from which, as he observes, he draws consolation as a weasel sucks eggs (2.5.11–12). The others treat him as a sort of profane jester whose soured conceits add relish to their enjoyment of the forest life.

Despite his affectation, however, Jaques is serious and even excited in his defense of satire as a curative form of laughter (2.7.47–87). The appearance of Touchstone in the forest has reaffirmed in Jaques his profound commitment to a view of life as a meaningless process of decay governed by inexorable time. His function in such a life is to be mordant, unsparing. As literary satirist he must be free to awaken men's minds to their own folly. To the Duke's protestation that the satirist is merely self-indulgent and licentious, Jaques counters with a thoughtful and classically Horatian defense of satire as an art form devoted not to libelous attacks on individuals but to exposing types of folly. Any observer who feels himself individually portrayed merely condemns himself by confessing his resemblance to the type. This particular debate between the Duke and Jaques ends, appropriately, in a draw. The Duke's point is well taken, for Jaques's famous "Seven Ages of Man" speech, so often read out of context, occurs in a scene that also witnesses the rescue of Orlando and Adam from the forest. As though in answer to Jaques's acid depiction of covetous old age, we see old Adam's self-sacrifice and trust in Providence. Instead of "mere oblivion," we see charitable compassion prompting the Duke to aid Orlando and Orlando to aid Adam. Perhaps this vision seems of a higher spiritual order than that of Jaques. Nonetheless, without him the forest would be a dull and humorless place.

Touchstone's name suggests that he similarly offers a multiplicity of viewpoints. (A touchstone is a kind of stone used to test for gold and silver.) He shares with Jaques a skeptical view of life, but for Touchstone the inconsistency and absurdity of life are occasions for wit and humor rather than melancholy and cynicism. As a professional fool he observes that sane men are more foolish than he—as, for example, in their elaborate dueling code of the Retort Courteous and the Reply Churlish, leading finally to the Lie Circumstantial and the Lie Direct. He is fascinated by the games people make of their lives and is amused by their inability to be content with what they already have. Of the shepherd's life, he comments, "In respect that it is solitary, I like it very well; but in respect that it is private, it is a very vile life" (3.2.15–16). This paradox, though nonsensical, captures the restlessness of human striving for a life that can somehow combine the peaceful solitude of nature with the convenience and excitement of city life. Although Touchstone marries, even his marriage is a spoof of the institution rather than a serious attempt at commitment. Like all fools, who in Renaissance times were regarded as a breed apart, Touchstone exists outside the realm of ordinary human responses. There he can comment disinterestedly on human folly. He is prevented, however, from sharing fully in the human love and conciliation with which the play ends. He and Jaques are not touched by the play's regenerative magic; Jaques will remain in the forest, Touchstone will remain forever a childlike entertainer.

The regenerative power of Arden, as we have seen, is not the forest's alone. What saves Orlando is the human charity practiced by him and by the Duke, who, for all his love of the forest, longs to rejoin that human society where he has "with holy bell been knolled to church" (2.7.120). Civilization at its best is no less necessary to the human spirit than is the natural order of the forest. In love, also, perception and wisdom must be combined with nature's gifts. Orlando, when we first see him, is a young man of the finest natural qualities, but admittedly lacking experience in the nuances of complex human relationships. Nowhere does his lack of breeding betray him more unhappily than in his first encounter with Rosalind, following the wrestling match. In response to her unmistakable hints of favor he stands oxlike, tongue-tied. Later, however, in the forest, his first attempts at self-education in love lead him into an opposite danger: an excess of platitudinous manners parading in the guise of Petrarchism. (The Italian sonneteer Francis Petrarch has given to the language a name for the stereotypical literary mannerisms we associate with courtly love: the sighing and self-abasement of the young man, the chaste denial of love by the woman whom he worships, and the like.) Orlando's newfound self-abasement and idealization of his absent mistress are as unsatisfactory as his former naiveté. He must learn from Rosalind that a quest for true understanding in love avoids the extreme of pretentious mannerism as well as that of mere artlessness. Orlando as Petrarchan lover too much resembles Silvius, the lovesick young man, cowering before the imperious will of his coy mistress Phoebe. This stereotyped relationship, taken from the pages of fashionable pastoral romance, represents a posturing that Rosalind hopes to cure in Silvius and Phoebe even as she will also cure Orlando.

Rosalind is above all the realistic one, the plucky Shakespearean heroine showing her mettle in the world of men, emotionally more mature than her lover. Her concern is with a working and clear-sighted relationship in love, and to that end she daringly insists that Orlando learn something of woman's changeable mood. Above all, she must disabuse him of the dangerously misleading clichés of the Petrarchan love myth. When he protests he would die for love of Rosalind, she lectures him mockingly: "No, faith, die by attorney. The poor world is almost six thousand years old, and in all this time there was not any man died in his own person, videlicet, in a love cause." She debunks the legends of Troilus and Leander, youths supposed to have died for love who in fact met with more prosaic ends. "But these are all lies. Men have died from time to time, and worms have eaten them, but not for love" (4.1.89–102). When Orlando has been sufficiently tested as to patience, loyalty, and understanding, she unmasks herself to him and simultaneously unravels the plot of Silvius and Phoebe.

Rosalind's disguise name, Ganymede, taken from Jove's amorous cupbearer, has homosexual connotations. Shakespeare delicately exploits these overtones, both in Phoebe's pursuit of a young lady (but really a boy actor) in male attire, and in Orlando's courtship of Ganymede as though addressed to Rosalind. In this innocent titillation, found also in Shakespeare's source, there is no suggestion of deviate sexual practice. On the contrary, the point is that Orlando can speak frankly and personally to "Ganymede" as to a perfect friend, one to whom he can relate in platonically spiritual terms without the potentially distracting note of sexual attraction. Once this disinterested love has grown strong between them, the unmasking of Rosalind's sexual identity makes possible a physical union between them to confirm and express the spiritual. In these terms, the play's happy ending affirms marriage as an institution, not simply as the expected denouement. The procession to the altar is synchronous with the return to civilization's other institutions, made whole again not solely by the forest but by the power of goodness embodied in Rosalind, Orlando, Duke Senior, and the others who persevere.

As You Like It
in Performance

The forest in *As You Like It* is much more than a realistic theatrical setting: it is an idea, or really a number of ideas put in debate with one another, ideas about social justice, literary conventions, the uses of satire, the relationships between the sexes, and still other matters. Any attempt in the theater to present the forest too literally, allowing naturalistic spectacle to overwhelm the interplay of characters and ideas, is apt to diminish the play significantly. During its long history onstage, directors of *As You Like It* have demonstrated this point again and again.

Although the play seems to have flourished in Shakespeare's day, having been first performed at the newly opened Globe Theatre in 1599, *As You Like It* was ignored for the rest of the seventeenth century and then reappeared in 1723 at the Theatre Royal, Drury Lane, only in an adaptation that differs sharply from Shakespeare's play. Charles Johnson evidently felt, when he compiled *Love in a Forest*, that *As You Like It* needed generous infusions of material from other Shakespeare plays. "Pyramus and Thisbe" is purloined from *A Midsummer Night's Dream* as entertainment for Duke Senior, rather literally in response to Duke Senior's observation that "This wide and universal theater / Presents more woeful pageants than the scene / Wherein we play in" (2.7.136–138). Charles and Orlando fight with rapiers instead of wrestling and quarrel in language appropriated (or misappropriated) from the confrontation of Bolingbroke and Mowbray in *Richard II*. Jaques (played by Colley Cibber, who wanted as large a part as he could get) is allowed to speak in person his speech about the sobbing deer, rather than having the scene described by the First Lord. Audrey, William, Phoebe, and Corin disappear to make room for the added material, and Silvius's role is severely reduced. Jaques falls in love with Celia and woos her with some of Benedick's wit from *Much Ado about Nothing*. Oliver dies the instructive death of a villain, leaving his lands to Orlando, while "the fencer Charles" confesses that he was suborned by Oliver to impeach Orlando as a traitor.

The play more nearly as Shakespeare wrote it, but with changes still, was revived at Drury Lane in 1740, with Hannah Pritchard as Rosalind. Thomas Arne provided music for Amiens's two songs ("Under the greenwood tree" and "Blow, blow, thou winter wind"), and Celia (Kitty Clive) sang the "cuckoo" song from *Love's Labor's Lost*. In later years the song was often given to Rosalind. Throughout the century the play was chiefly the vehicle for leading actresses in the part of Rosalind—Hannah Pritchard, Ann Barry, Peg Woffington, Sarah Siddons—and for leading actors in the parts of Jaques and Touchstone, including Colley Cibber, James Quin, and Charles Macklin. *As You Like It* appeared more often at Drury Lane from 1776 to 1817 than any other Shakespeare play, missing only three seasons out of forty-one. Sir Oliver Mar-text was usually cut, along with Jaques's comment on the first encounter of Touchstone and Audrey, and so was much of Phoebe's dialogue; Hymen disappeared, and some of the play's best songs were eliminated or shortened. Jaques continued to describe in first person the episode of the sobbing deer, the tradition being fixed in print by actor-manager John Philip Kemble's acting edition in 1820 (and not reformed until actor-manager William Charles Macready restored the lines to the First Lord at Drury Lane in 1842). The play was performed as "opera" in 1824–1825, with numerous songs added from other plays and the sonnets, including "Full many a glorious morning" (sonnet 33), "Tell me where is fancy bred?" (*The Merchant of Venice*, 3.2.63), "Where the bee sucks" (*The Tempest*, 5.1.88), and, of course, the "cuckoo" song from *Love's Labor's Lost*. A number of these songs had already been borrowed for similar operatic versions of *A Midsummer Night's Dream, Twelfth Night, The Tempest, The Comedy of Errors, The Two Gentlemen of Verona,* and *The Merry Wives of Windsor,* and they were subsequently to be used in operas based on *The Taming of the Shrew* and *All's Well that Ends Well.*

The main contribution of the nineteenth century to this dressing up of *As You Like It* was to provide lavish settings that left little to the spectators' imagination. Macready delighted the eye with sets by the painter Clarkson Stanfield, elaborating each scene with such attention to detail that, as one contemporary critic marveled of Macready, "he has not *realized*, he has done more—he has *verified* the dramatist." The wrestling match in Act 1, scene 2, featured an arena of ropes and staves around which the courtiers stood, pressing eagerly forward and responding with shouts of applause (seconded by the audience) to every triumphant moment in the match. The pastoral scenes were graced with the accompaniment of distant sheep bells. Helen Faucit, Ada Rehan, Lily Langtry, and other famous actresses (though not Ellen Terry) played Rosalind in productions that gave special prominence to star performers. Texts were rearranged to accommodate the elaborate scenery: in Augustin Daly's production at the Lyceum Theatre in 1890, with Ada Rehan, Act 2 began with scene 3, the departure of Orlando and Adam for the forest, so that the action could proceed uninterruptedly thereafter in Arden. In his American production that had opened the previous December, Daly provided a "terrace and courtyard before the Duke's palace" with an arched gateway at the left, enabling a group of lords and ladies to go up on the terrace and watch the wrestling. In a production by John Hare and the Kendals (W. H. and Madge) at the St. James's Theatre in 1885, "the brook rippling among the sedges" appears to have been real water, losing itself among the leaves and what looked like real grass onstage, all arranged, according to the *Athenaeum*, so that it "renders easier the task of the imagination and enhances the pleasure of the spectator." The setting for Duke Frederick's court, executed by Lewis Wingfield, adopted the milieu of Charles VII's France, complete with elaborate headdresses and a plausible replica of the Château d'Amboise. The tradition of scenic elaboration continued into the early twentieth century, perhaps most notoriously in Oscar Asche's 1907 production at Her Majesty's Theatre, in which the Forest of Arden was recreated weekly with two thousand pots of ferns and cartloads of leaves.

Twentieth-century performance, on the other hand, has generally sought a more iconoclastic and theatrically self-aware idiom, even though occasionally, as in the 1936 film version with Laurence Olivier as a strikingly young and beautiful Orlando, one can still savor the saccharine tittering of sheltered young ladies that must have dominated many a Victorian production. New settings have been introduced: the eighteenth century of Watteau in Esmé Church's production at the Old Vic in 1937, the surreal world of Salvador Dali for a performance in Rome in 1950, leafless trees and a general atmosphere of hardship at Stratford-upon-Avon in 1961, and early Victorian England in New York in 1973. At Stratford-upon-Avon, Buzz Goodbody, in 1973, produced a modern-dress *As You Like It*, with Touchstone sporting a loud, checked suit, and Rosalind in jeans, while, four years later, Trevor Nunn set the play in Stuart England. Duke Frederick has more than once been portrayed as a Nazi, and Jaques as effeminate. Perhaps the most striking production of recent years was one by Cliford Williams in 1967 at the National Theatre. Williams employed an all-male cast, in Elizabethan dress, offering a new view of the transvestite disguisings and the explorations of the relationships between men and women that are so essential to the play. Whatever distortions these experiments may have introduced into the play in their quest for relevance, they have succeeded at least in challenging the complacent images of naturalistic production. Today, even when *As You Like It* is done in an appropriately Elizabethan setting, the production usually employs swift pacing and a suggestive use of scenery that calls upon the spectators to imagine for themselves what the forest is like.

Perhaps the BBC television *As You Like It* in 1978 best illustrates what is wrong with using realistic scenery in this play. The television camera can, and does, provide handsome locales throughout, in the style of the BBC's successful *Masterpiece Theatre:* we see a greensward lying before a real castle, a wrestling arena, and later, of course, a forest. But, as Duke Senior's fellow exiles sit around disconsolately listening to a song or the First Lord's description of Jaques, the forest seems disappointingly ordinary. The camera fails, on this occasion at least, to make anything magical out of a tree or shrub. In such an environment, the actors playing Corin, Silvius, and the rest, however proficient, look like their routine counterparts from central casting. The actors do not have to invoke a sense of place, for it is there even before they come on camera. One telling detail is the disappearance of stage magic from the presentation of Hymen, the god of marriage. In the theater, Hymen's identity is perfectly ambiguous: is he a god, in fact, or someone dressed for the part by the stage-managing Rosalind? In a realistically photographed setting, on the other hand, the director has to state his case, and so the BBC's Hymen is, or looks like, an effete young man who wears strange garlands in his hair and is otherwise rather underdressed for the occasion. Illusion is a paradoxical thing in drama: the more detail the director provides, the less imaginative the experience may be for the viewer.

Shakespeare's original performance certainly had to rely on the audience's participation in the making of illusion. Boy actors took the parts of the women, with the result that the device of male disguise for Rosalind (really a boy actor) calls attention to the way in which illusion is produced. The play is reflexive in other ways, as when Jaques refers to all the world as a stage and to men and women as merely players; his view is a sardonic one, but the playacting he describes is certainly pertinent to the managerial role of Rosalind. The marked contrasts between the court of Duke Frederick and the communal forest society of Duke Senior, so vital to the play's impact, is conveyed in Shakespeare's original stage conception not by elaborate sets but by actors on a bare stage, evoking through costuming, gesture, and speech the nature of two disparate worlds. Subsequent generations of Shakespearean idolaters have insisted on literalizing Shakespeare's evocative images, in the pictorial arts as in drama; Alderman John Boydell's famous Shakespeare art collection (illustrating the plays) of the early nineteenth century was particularly attentive to scenes not actually staged by Shakespeare at all, including the Seven Ages of Man, Jaques lying under a tree beside a brook, and Oliver asleep while a lion and a snake wait for him to awake. The literalizing that has been so much a part of Shakespearean illustration and production is no doubt a tribute to his genius as an imaginative artist, but the better tribute is to use a theatrical language of gesture and setting that invites the kind of involvement Shakespeare demanded of his first spectators.

The Playhouse

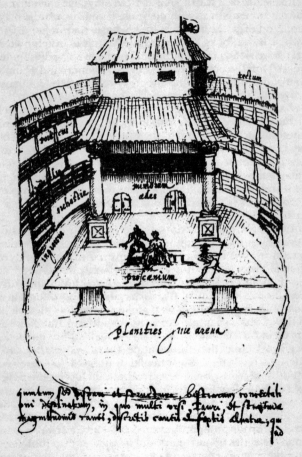

This early copy of a drawing by Johannes de Witt of the Swan Theatre in London (c. 1596), made by his friend Arend van Buchell, is the only surviving contemporary sketch of the interior of a public theater in the 1590s.

From other contemporary evidence, including the stage directions and dialogue of Elizabethan plays, we can surmise that the various public theaters where Shakespeare's plays were produced (the Theatre, the Curtain, the Globe) resembled the Swan in many important particulars, though there must have been some variations as well. The public playhouses were essentially round, or polygonal, and open to the sky, forming an acting arena approximately 70 feet in diameter; they did not have a large curtain with which to open and close a scene, such as we see today in opera and some traditional theater. A platform measuring approximately 43 feet across and 27 feet deep, referred to in the de Witt drawing as the *proscaenium*, projected into the yard, *planities sive arena*. The roof, *tectum*, above the stage and supported by two pillars, could contain machinery for ascents and descents, as were required in several of Shakespeare's late plays. Above this roof was a hut, shown in the drawing with a flag flying atop it and a trumpeter at its door announcing the performance of a play. The underside of the stage roof, called the heavens, was usually richly decorated with symbolic figures of the sun, the moon, and the constellations. The platform stage stood at a height of 5½ feet or so above the yard, providing room under the stage for underworldly effects. A trapdoor, which is not visible in this drawing, gave access to the space below.

The structure at the back of the platform (labeled *mimorum aedes*), known as the tiring-house because it was the actors' attiring (dressing) space, featured at least two doors, as shown here. Some theaters seem to have also had a discovery space, or curtained recessed alcove, perhaps between the two doors—in which Falstaff could have hidden from the sheriff (*1 Henry IV*, 2.4) or Polonius could have eavesdropped on Hamlet and his mother (*Hamlet*, 3.4). This discovery space probably gave the actors a means of access to and from the tiring-house. Curtains may also have been hung in front of the stage doors on occasion. The de Witt drawing shows a gallery above the doors that extends across the back and evidently contains spectators. On occasions when action "above" demanded the use of this space, as when Juliet appears at her "window" (*Romeo and Juliet*, 2.2 and 3.5), the gallery seems to have been used by the actors, but large scenes there were impractical.

The three-tiered auditorium is perhaps best described by Thomas Platter, a visitor to London in 1599 who saw on that occasion Shakespeare's *Julius Caesar* performed at the Globe:

> The playhouses are so constructed that they play on a raised platform, so that everyone has a good view. There are different galleries and places [*orchestra, sedilia, porticus*], however, where the seating is better and more comfortable and therefore more expensive. For whoever cares to stand below only pays one English penny, but if he wishes to sit, he enters by another door [*ingressus*] and pays another penny, while if he desires to sit in the most comfortable seats, which are cushioned, where he not only sees everything well but can also be seen, then he pays yet another English penny at another door. And during the performance food and drink are carried round the audience, so that for what one cares to pay one may also have refreshment.

Scenery was not used, though the theater building itself was handsome enough to invoke a feeling of order and hierarchy that lent itself to the splendor and pageantry onstage. Portable properties, such as thrones, stools, tables, and beds, could be carried or thrust on as needed. In the scene pictured here by de Witt, a lady on a bench, attended perhaps by her waiting-gentlewoman, receives the address of a male figure. If Shakespeare had written *Twelfth Night* by 1596 for performance at the Swan, we could imagine Malvolio appearing like this as he bows before the Countess Olivia and her gentlewoman, Maria.

AS YOU LIKE IT

[*Dramatis Personae*

DUKE SENIOR, *a banished duke*
DUKE FREDERICK, *his usurping brother*
ROSALIND, *daughter of Duke Senior, later disguised as* GANYMEDE
CELIA, *daughter of Duke Frederick, later disguised as* ALIENA

OLIVER,
JAQUES, } *sons of Sir Rowland de Boys*
ORLANDO,

AMIENS, } *lords attending Duke Senior*
JAQUES,

LE BEAU, *a courtier attending Duke Frederick*
CHARLES, *a wrestler in the court of Duke Frederick*

ADAM, *an aged servant of Oliver and then Orlando*
DENNIS, *a servant of Oliver*

TOUCHSTONE, *the* CLOWN *or* FOOL

CORIN, *an old shepherd*
SILVIUS, *a young shepherd, in love with Phoebe*
PHOEBE, *a shepherdess*
WILLIAM, *a country youth, in love with Audrey*
AUDREY, *a country wench*
SIR OLIVER MAR-TEXT, *a country vicar*

HYMEN, *god of marriage*

Lords and Attendants waiting on Duke Frederick and Duke Senior

SCENE: *Oliver's house; Duke Frederick's court; and the Forest of Arden*]

1.1

Enter Orlando and Adam.

ORLANDO As I remember, Adam, it was upon this fash-
icn bequeathed me by will but poor a thousand 2
crowns and, as thou sayst, charged my brother on 3
his blessing to breed me well; and there begins my 4
sadness. My brother Jaques he keeps at school, and 5
report speaks goldenly of his profit. For my part, he 6
keeps me rustically at home or, to speak more properly, stays me here at home unkept; for call you that 8
"keeping" for a gentleman of my birth, that differs not
from the stalling of an ox? His horses are bred better,
for besides that they are fair with their feeding, they 11
are taught their manage, and to that end riders dearly 12
hired. But I, his brother, gain nothing under him but
growth, for the which his animals on his dunghills are
as much bound to him as I. Besides this nothing that
he so plentifully gives me, the something that nature
gave me his countenance seems to take from me. He 17
lets me feed with his hinds, bars me the place of a 18
brother, and as much as in him lies, mines my gentil- 19
ity with my education. This is it, Adam, that grieves 20
me; and the spirit of my father, which I think is within
me, begins to mutiny against this servitude. I will no
longer endure it, though yet I know no wise remedy
how to avoid it.

Enter Oliver.

ADAM Yonder comes my master, your brother.

ORLANDO Go apart, Adam, and thou shalt hear how he 26
will shake me up.   [*Adam stands aside.*] 27

OLIVER Now, sir, what make you here?   28

1.1. Location: The garden of Oliver's house.
2 bequeathed i.e., he, my father, bequeathed. **but poor** merely **3 crowns**
coins worth five shillings **3–4 on his blessing** on pain of losing his
blessing **4 breed** bring up, educate **5 keeps at school** maintains at the
university **6 profit** i.e., progress **8 stays** detains. **unkept** not main-
tained properly **11 fair** in handsome shape **12 manage** gaits and move-
ments. **dearly** expensively **17 countenance** behavior, attitude **18 hinds**
farm hands. **bars me** excludes me from **19 as in him lies** as he is
able. **mines** undermines **20 education** i.e., lack of proper education
26 Go apart stand aside **27 shake me up** insult me **28 make** do. (But
Orlando takes it in the more usual sense.)

ORLANDO Nothing. I am not taught to make anything.

OLIVER What mar you then, sir?

ORLANDO Marry, sir, I am helping you to mar that 31
which God made, a poor unworthy brother of yours,
with idleness.

OLIVER Marry, sir, be better employed, and be naught 34
awhile.   35

ORLANDO Shall I keep your hogs and eat husks with 36
them? What prodigal portion have I spent, that I 37
should come to such penury?   38

OLIVER Know you where you are, sir?   39

ORLANDO O, sir, very well: here in your orchard.   40

OLIVER Know you before whom, sir?

ORLANDO Ay, better than him I am before knows me. 42
I know you are my eldest brother, and in the gentle 43
condition of blood you should so know me. The cour- 44
tesy of nations allows you my better, in that you are 45
the firstborn, but the same tradition takes not away
my blood, were there twenty brothers betwixt us. I
have as much of my father in me as you, albeit I confess your coming before me is nearer to his reverence. 49

OLIVER What, boy!   [He strikes Orlando.]

ORLANDO Come, come, elder brother, you are too
young in this.   [He seizes Oliver by the throat.] 52

OLIVER Wilt thou lay hands on me, villain?   53

ORLANDO I am no villain. I am the youngest son of Sir
Rowland de Boys; he was my father, and he is thrice
a villain that says such a father begot villains. Wert
thou not my brother, I would not take this hand from

---

31 Marry i.e., indeed. (Originally an oath by the Virgin Mary.) **34–35 be
naught awhile** (A mild malediction, like "go to the devil.") **36–38 Shall
. . . penury** (Alluding to the story of the Prodigal Son, in Luke 15:11–32,
who, having wasted his "portion" or inheritance, had to tend swine and
eat with them.) **39 where** i.e., in whose presence. (But Orlando sarcas-
tically takes the more literal meaning.) **40 orchard** garden **42 him** he
whom **43–44 in . . . blood** i.e., acknowledging the bond of our being of
gentle birth **44 know** acknowledge **44–45 courtesy of nations** recog-
nized custom (of primogeniture, whereby the eldest son inherits all the
land) **49 is nearer to his reverence** i.e., places you closer to the respect
that was due him **52 young** raw, inexperienced (at fighting) **53 villain**
i.e., worthless fellow. (But Orlando again plays on the literal meaning of
bondman or serf.)

thy throat till this other had pulled out thy tongue for
saying so. Thou hast railed on thyself.   59

ADAM Sweet masters, be patient! For your father's re- 60
membrance, be at accord.   61

OLIVER Let me go, I say.

ORLANDO I will not till I please. You shall hear me. My
father charged you in his will to give me good education. You have trained me like a peasant, obscuring 65
and hiding from me all gentlemanlike qualities. The 66
spirit of my father grows strong in me, and I will no
longer endure it; therefore allow me such exercises as
may become a gentleman, or give me the poor allottery 69
my father left me by testament; with that I will go buy
my fortunes.   [*He releases Oliver.*]

OLIVER And what wilt thou do? Beg when that is
spent? Well, sir, get you in. I will not long be troubled
with you; you shall have some part of your will. I pray
you, leave me.

ORLANDO I will no further offend you than becomes me
for my good.

OLIVER Get you with him, you old dog.

ADAM Is "old dog" my reward? Most true, I have lost
my teeth in your service. God be with my old master!
He would not have spoke such a word.
                              Exeunt Orlando [and] Adam.

OLIVER Is it even so? Begin you to grow upon me? I will 82
physic your rankness and yet give no thousand 83
crowns neither. Holla, Dennis!

      Enter Dennis.

DENNIS Calls your worship?

OLIVER Was not Charles, the Duke's wrestler, here to
speak with me?

DENNIS So please you, he is here at the door and im- 88
portunes access to you.

---

59 railed on thyself i.e., insulted your own blood   **60–61 your father's**
remembrance the memory of your father   **65 obscuring** i.e., obscuring
in me   **66 qualities** accomplishments   **69 allottery** share, portion
82 grow upon me i.e., take liberties with me   **83 physic** apply medicine
to.   **rankness** overgrowth, overweening   **88 So please you** if you please

OLIVER Call him in. [*Exit Dennis*.] 'Twill be a good way; and tomorrow the wrestling is.

    Enter Charles.

CHARLES Good morrow to your worship.   92
OLIVER Good Monsieur Charles, what's the new news at the new court?
CHARLES There's no news at the court, sir, but the old news: that is, the old Duke is banished by his younger brother the new Duke, and three or four loving lords have put themselves into voluntary exile with him, whose lands and revenues enrich the new Duke; therefore he gives them good leave to wander.
OLIVER Can you tell if Rosalind, the Duke's daughter, be banished with her father?
CHARLES O, no; for the Duke's daughter, her cousin, so loves her, being ever from their cradles bred together, that she would have followed her exile or have died to 105
stay behind her. She is at the court and no less be- 106
loved of her uncle than his own daughter, and never two ladies loved as they do.
OLIVER Where will the old Duke live?
CHARLES They say he is already in the Forest of Arden, and a many merry men with him; and there they live like the old Robin Hood of England. They say many young gentlemen flock to him every day and fleet the 113
time carelessly as they did in the golden world. 114
OLIVER What, you wrestle tomorrow before the new Duke?
CHARLES Marry, do I, sir; and I came to acquaint you with a matter. I am given, sir, secretly to understand that your younger brother Orlando hath a disposition to come in disguised against me to try a fall. Tomor- 120
row, sir, I wrestle for my credit, and he that escapes 121
me without some broken limb shall acquit him well. 122
Your brother is but young and tender, and for your love I would be loath to foil him, as I must for my 124

92 Good morrow good morning   **105–106 died to stay** died from staying   **113 fleet** pass   **114 carelessly** free from care.   **golden world** the primal age of innocence and ease from which man was thought to have degenerated. (See Ovid, *Metamorphoses* 1.)   **120 fall** bout   **121 credit** reputation   **122 shall** must   **124 foil** overthrow

own honor if he come in. Therefore, out of my love to
you, I came hither to acquaint you withal, that either 126
you might stay him from his intendment or brook 127
such disgrace well as he shall run into, in that it is a
thing of his own search and altogether against my will. 129
OLIVER   Charles, I thank thee for thy love to me, which
thou shalt find I will most kindly requite. I had myself
notice of my brother's purpose herein and have by
underhand means labored to dissuade him from it, but 133
he is resolute. I'll tell thee, Charles, it is the stubborn-
est young fellow of France, full of ambition, an envious emulator of every man's good parts, a secret and 136
villainous contriver against me his natural brother. 137
Therefore use thy discretion. I had as lief thou didst 138
break his neck as his finger. And thou wert best look
to 't; for if thou dost him any slight disgrace, or if he
do not mightily grace himself on thee, he will practice 141
against thee by poison, entrap thee by some treacherous device, and never leave thee till he hath ta'en thy
life by some indirect means or other; for I assure thee,
and almost with tears I speak it, there is not one so
young and so villainous this day living. I speak but
brotherly of him, but should I anatomize him to thee 147
as he is, I must blush and weep, and thou must look
pale and wonder.
CHARLES   I am heartily glad I came hither to you. If he
come tomorrow, I'll give him his payment. If ever he
go alone again, I'll never wrestle for prize more. And 152
so God keep your worship!
OLIVER   Farewell, good Charles. *Exit* [*Charles*]. Now
will I stir this gamester. I hope I shall see an end of 155
him; for my soul, yet I know not why, hates nothing
more than he. Yet he's gentle, never schooled and yet 157
learned, full of noble device, of all sorts enchantingly 158

126 withal with this   **127 stay** keep, deter.   **intendment** purpose, intent.   **brook** endure   **129 search** seeking   **133 underhand** indirect
136 emulator rival.   **parts** qualities   **137 contriver** plotter.   **natural** by
blood, legitimate   **138 lief** willingly   **141 grace . . . thee** distinguish
himself at your expense.   **practice** plot   **147 brotherly** i.e., with a reserve
proper to a brother.   **anatomize** lay open in detail, analyze   **152 go alone**
walk unassisted   **155 gamester** athlete, sportsman (here said sardoni-
cally)   **157 gentle** gentlemanly   **158 noble device** lofty aspiration.   **sorts**
classes of people.   **enchantingly** as if by the effect of enchantment

beloved, and indeed so much in the heart of the world
and especially of my own people, who best know him,
that I am altogether misprized. But it shall not be so   161
long; this wrestler shall clear all. Nothing remains but   162
that I kindle the boy thither, which now I'll go about.   163

Exit.

❖

1.2   *Enter Rosalind and Celia.*

CELIA   I pray thee, Rosalind, sweet my coz, be merry.   1

ROSALIND   Dear Celia, I show more mirth than I am
mistress of, and would you yet I were merrier? Unless
you could teach me to forget a banished father, you
must not learn me how to remember any extraordi-   5
nary pleasure.

CELIA   Herein I see thou lov'st me not with the full
weight that I love thee. If my uncle, thy banished father, had banished thy uncle, the Duke my father, so   9
thou hadst been still with me, I could have taught my
love to take thy father for mine. So wouldst thou, if the
truth of thy love to me were so righteously tempered   12
as mine is to thee.

ROSALIND   Well, I will forget the condition of my estate,   14
to rejoice in yours.

CELIA   You know my father hath no child but I, nor
none is like to have. And truly, when he dies, thou
shalt be his heir, for what he hath taken away from
thy father perforce I will render thee again in affec-   19
tion. By mine honor, I will, and when I break that
oath, let me turn monster. Therefore, my sweet Rose,
my dear Rose, be merry.

ROSALIND   From henceforth I will, coz, and devise
sports. Let me see, what think you of falling in love?

---

161 misprized despised   **162 clear all** solve everything   **163 kindle**
incite (to go).   **thither** i.e., to the wrestling match

1.2. Location: Duke Frederick's court. A place suitable for wrestling.
1 sweet my coz my sweet cousin   **5 learn** teach   **9 so** provided that
12 righteously tempered properly compounded   **14 condition of my**
estate state of my fortunes   **19 perforce** by force

CELIA Marry, I prithee, do, to make sport withal. But 25
love no man in good earnest, nor no further in sport
neither than with safety of a pure blush thou mayst in 27
honor come off again. 28

ROSALIND What shall be our sport, then?

CELIA Let us sit and mock the good huswife Fortune 30
from her wheel, that her gifts may henceforth be bestowed equally.

ROSALIND I would we could do so, for her benefits are
mightily misplaced, and the bountiful blind woman 34
doth most mistake in her gifts to women.

CELIA 'Tis true, for those that she makes fair she scarce 36
makes honest, and those that she makes honest she 37
makes very ill-favoredly. 38

ROSALIND Nay, now thou goest from Fortune's office to
Nature's. Fortune reigns in gifts of the world, not in 40
the lineaments of Nature. 41

Enter [Touchstone the] Clown.

CELIA No; when Nature hath made a fair creature, may
she not by Fortune fall into the fire? Though Nature
hath given us wit to flout at Fortune, hath not Fortune 44
sent in this fool to cut off the argument?

ROSALIND Indeed, there is Fortune too hard for Nature,
when Fortune makes Nature's natural the cutter-off of 47
Nature's wit.

CELIA Peradventure this is not Fortune's work neither
but Nature's, who perceiveth our natural wits too dull
to reason of such goddesses and hath sent this natural 51
for our whetstone; for always the dullness of the fool 52

---

25 sport entertainment   **27 pure** innocent   **28 come off** retire, escape
30 huswife one who manages household affairs, partially by spinning at
a spinning wheel. (Shakespeare conflates this wheel with the commonplace wheel of Fortune.) *Huswife* is used derogatorily here, with a
suggestion of "hussy."   **34 bountiful blind woman** i.e., Fortune
36 scarce rarely   **37 honest** chaste   **38 ill-favoredly** ugly   **40 gifts of
the world** e.g., riches and power   **41 lineaments** characteristics.
s.d. Touchstone a kind of stone used to test for gold and silver
44 flout mock, scoff   **47 natural** idiot, half-wit   **51 to reason of**
to think about   **52 whetstone** sharpener

is the whetstone of the wits.—How now, wit, whither 53
wander you?   54

TOUCHSTONE Mistress, you must come away to your father.

CELIA Were you made the messenger?

TOUCHSTONE No, by mine honor, but I was bid to come
for you.

ROSALIND Where learned you that oath, Fool?

TOUCHSTONE Of a certain knight that swore by his
honor they were good pancakes and swore by his 62
honor the mustard was naught. Now I'll stand to it 63
the pancakes were naught and the mustard was good,
and yet was not the knight forsworn.   65

CELIA How prove you that in the great heap of your
knowledge?

ROSALIND Ay, marry, now unmuzzle your wisdom.

TOUCHSTONE Stand you both forth now. Stroke your
chins, and swear by your beards that I am a knave.

CELIA By our beards, if we had them, thou art.

TOUCHSTONE By my knavery, if I had it, then I were;
but if you swear by that that is not, you are not forsworn. No more was this knight, swearing by his
honor, for he never had any; or if he had, he had
sworn it away before ever he saw those pancakes or
that mustard.

CELIA Prithee, who is 't that thou mean'st?

TOUCHSTONE One that old Frederick, your father, loves.

CELIA My father's love is enough to honor him. Enough,
speak no more of him; you'll be whipped for taxation 81
one of these days.

TOUCHSTONE The more pity that fools may not speak
wisely what wise men do foolishly.

CELIA By my troth, thou sayest true; for since the little 85
wit that fools have was silenced, the little foolery that 86
wise men have makes a great show. Here comes Monsieur Le Beau.

53–54 whither wander you (An allusion to the expression "wandering
wits.") **62 pancakes** fritters (which might be made of meat and so
require mustard) **63 naught** worthless. **stand to it** maintain, argue
65 forsworn perjured **81 taxation** censure, slander **85–86 since . . .
silenced** (Perhaps refers specifically to the Bishops' order of June 1599
banning satirical books.)

Enter Le Beau.

ROSALIND   With his mouth full of news.

CELIA   Which he will put on us as pigeons feed their 90
young.

ROSALIND   Then shall we be news-crammed.

CELIA   All the better; we shall be the more marketable.—*Bonjour*, Monsieur Le Beau. What's the 94
news?

LE BEAU   Fair princess, you have lost much good sport.

CELIA   Sport? Of what color?   97

LE BEAU   What color, madam? How shall I answer you?

ROSALIND   As wit and fortune will.

TOUCHSTONE   Or as the Destinies decrees.

CELIA   Well said; that was laid on with a trowel.   101

TOUCHSTONE   Nay, if I keep not my rank—   102

ROSALIND   Thou losest thy old smell.

LE BEAU   You amaze me, ladies. I would have told you 104
of good wrestling, which you have lost the sight of.

ROSALIND   Yet tell us the manner of the wrestling.

LE BEAU   I will tell you the beginning, and if it please
your ladyships you may see the end, for the best is
yet to do, and here, where you are, they are coming to 109
perform it.

CELIA   Well, the beginning, that is dead and buried.

LE BEAU   There comes an old man and his three sons—

CELIA   I could match this beginning with an old tale.

LE BEAU   Three proper young men, of excellent growth 114
and presence—

ROSALIND   With bills on their necks, "Be it known unto 116
all men by these presents."   117

LE BEAU   The eldest of the three wrestled with Charles,
the Duke's wrestler, which Charles in a moment threw
him and broke three of his ribs, that there is little hope
of life in him. So he served the second, and so the 121
third. Yonder they lie, the poor old man their father

---

90 put on force upon   **93–94 marketable** i.e., like animals that have
been crammed with food before being sent to market   **97 color** kind
101 with a trowel i.e., clumsily, bluntly   **102 rank** i.e., status as a wit.
(But Rosalind plays on the sense of "evil-smelling.")   **104 amaze** bewil-
der   **109 yet to do** still to come   **114 proper** handsome   **116 bills**
advertisements, proclamations   **117 these presents** this document
presented (with pun on *presence*)   **121 So** similarly

making such pitiful dole over them that all the behold- 123
ers take his part with weeping.

ROSALIND   Alas!

TOUCHSTONE   But what is the sport, monsieur, that the
ladies have lost?

LE BEAU   Why, this that I speak of.

TOUCHSTONE   Thus men may grow wiser every day. It
is the first time that ever I heard breaking of ribs was
sport for ladies.

CELIA   Or I, I promise thee.

ROSALIND   But is there any else longs to see this broken 133
music in his sides? Is there yet another dotes upon rib 134
breaking? Shall we see this wrestling, cousin?

LE BEAU   You must if you stay here, for here is the place
appointed for the wrestling, and they are ready to perform it.

CELIA   Yonder, sure, they are coming. Let us now stay
and see it.

*Flourish. Enter Duke [Frederick], Lords, Orlando,
Charles, and attendants.*

DUKE FREDERICK   Come on. Since the youth will not be
entreated, his own peril on his forwardness.   142

ROSALIND   Is yonder the man?

LE BEAU   Even he, madam.

CELIA   Alas, he is too young! Yet he looks successfully.   145

DUKE FREDERICK   How now, daughter and cousin? Are
you crept hither to see the wrestling?

ROSALIND   Ay, my liege, so please you give us leave.   148

DUKE FREDERICK   You will take little delight in it, I can
tell you, there is such odds in the man. In pity of the 150
challenger's youth I would fain dissuade him, but he 151
will not be entreated. Speak to him, ladies; see if you
can move him.

123 **dole** grief, lamentation   133 **any else** anyone else who
133–134 **broken music** (Literally, music arranged in parts for different
instruments; here applied to the breaking of ribs.)   142 **entreated . . .
forwardness** i.e., entreated to desist, let the risk be blamed upon his
own rashness   145 **successfully** i.e., as if he would be successful
148 **so . . . leave** if you will permit us   150 **odds** superiority.   **the man**
i.e., Charles   151 **fain** willingly

CELIA Call him hither, good Monsieur Le Beau.

DUKE FREDERICK Do so. I'll not be by. [*He steps aside.*]

LE BEAU Monsieur the challenger, the princess calls for you.

ORLANDO [*Approaching the ladies*] I attend them with all respect and duty.

ROSALIND Young man, have you challenged Charles the wrestler?

ORLANDO No, fair princess; he is the general challenger. I come but in, as others do, to try with him the strength of my youth.

CELIA Young gentleman, your spirits are too bold for your years. You have seen cruel proof of this man's strength. If you saw yourself with your eyes or knew 167 yourself with your judgment, the fear of your adven- 168 ture would counsel you to a more equal enterprise. We 169 pray you, for your own sake, to embrace your own safety and give over this attempt.

ROSALIND Do, young sir. Your reputation shall not therefore be misprized. We will make it our suit to the 173 Duke that the wrestling might not go forward.

ORLANDO I beseech you, punish me not with your hard thoughts, wherein I confess me much guilty to deny so fair and excellent ladies anything. But let your fair eyes and gentle wishes go with me to my trial; wherein if I be foiled, there is but one shamed that was never gracious; if killed, but one dead that is willing to 180 be so. I shall do my friends no wrong, for I have none to lament me; the world no injury, for in it I have nothing. Only in the world I fill up a place, which may 183 be better supplied when I have made it empty.

ROSALIND The little strength that I have, I would it were with you.

CELIA And mine, to eke out hers.

ROSALIND Fare you well. Pray heaven I be deceived 188 in you! 189

CELIA Your heart's desires be with you!

167–168 If . . . judgment i.e., if you saw yourself objectively, using your observation and your judgment **169 equal** i.e., where the odds are more equal **173 therefore** on that account. **misprized** despised **180 gracious** looked upon with favor **183 Only . . . I** in the world I merely **188–189 deceived in you** i.e., mistaken in fearing you will lose

CHARLES Come, where is this young gallant that is so desirous to lie with his mother earth?

ORLANDO Ready, sir, but his will hath in it a more modest working.   194

DUKE FREDERICK You shall try but one fall.

CHARLES No, I warrant Your Grace, you shall not entreat him to a second, that have so mightily persuaded him from a first.

ORLANDO You mean to mock me after; you should not have mocked me before. But come your ways.   200

ROSALIND Now Hercules be thy speed, young man!   201

CELIA I would I were invisible, to catch the strong fellow by the leg.   [Orlando and Charles] wrestle.

ROSALIND O excellent young man!

CELIA If I had a thunderbolt in mine eye, I can tell who should down.   Shout. [Charles is thrown.] 206

DUKE FREDERICK No more, no more.

ORLANDO Yes, I beseech Your Grace. I am not yet well 208
breathed.   209

DUKE FREDERICK
How dost thou, Charles?

LE BEAU   He cannot speak, my lord.

DUKE FREDERICK
Bear him away. What is thy name, young man?
                    [Exeunt some with Charles.]

ORLANDO Orlando, my liege, the youngest son of Sir Rowland de Boys.

DUKE FREDERICK
I would thou hadst been son to some man else.
The world esteemed thy father honorable,
But I did find him still mine enemy.   216
Thou shouldst have better pleased me with this deed
Hadst thou descended from another house.
But fare thee well; thou art a gallant youth.
I would thou hadst told me of another father.
                    Exit Duke [with train, and others. Rosalind
                    and Celia remain; Orlando stands
                    apart from them].

194 modest working decorous endeavor (than to lie with one's mother earth—an endeavor, Orlando implies, with sexual overtones) **200 come your ways** come on **201 Hercules be thy speed** may Hercules help you **206 down** fall **208–209 well breathed** warmed up **216 still** continually

CELIA [*To Rosalind*]
Were I my father, coz, would I do this?
ORLANDO [*To no one in particular*]
I am more proud to be Sir Rowland's son,
His youngest son, and would not change that calling   223
To be adopted heir to Frederick.
ROSALIND [*To Celia*]
My father loved Sir Rowland as his soul,
And all the world was of my father's mind.
Had I before known this young man his son,
I should have given him tears unto entreaties   228
Ere he should thus have ventured.
CELIA [*To Rosalind*]   Gentle cousin,
Let us go thank him and encourage him.
My father's rough and envious disposition   231
Sticks me at heart.—Sir, you have well deserved.   232
If you do keep your promises in love
But justly as you have exceeded all promise,   234
Your mistress shall be happy.
ROSALIND   Gentleman,   235
          [*Giving him a chain from her neck*]
Wear this for me, one out of suits with fortune,   236
That could give more, but that her hand lacks means.   237
[*To Celia*] Shall we go, coz?
CELIA   Ay. Fare you well, fair gentleman.
          [*Rosalind and Celia start to leave.*]
ORLANDO [*Aside*]
Can I not say, "I thank you"? My better parts
Are all thrown down, and that which here stands up
Is but a quintain, a mere lifeless block.   241
ROSALIND
He calls us back. My pride fell with my fortunes;
I'll ask him what he would.—Did you call, sir?   243
Sir, you have wrestled well and overthrown
More than your enemies.

223 calling position, status **228 unto** in addition to **231 envious**
malicious **232 Sticks** stabs **234 But justly** exactly **235 s.d. chain** (See
3.2.178, where Celia speaks of a chain given to Orlando by Rosalind.)
236 out . . . fortune (1) whose petitions to Fortune are rejected (2) not
wearing the livery of Fortune, not in her service **237 could** would be
disposed to **241 quintain** wooden figure used as a target in tilting
243 would wants

CELIA Will you go, coz?

ROSALIND   Have with you.—Fare you well.   247

                                   Exit [with Celia].

ORLANDO
  What passion hangs these weights upon my tongue?
  I cannot speak to her, yet she urged conference.   249
  O poor Orlando, thou art overthrown!
  Or Charles or something weaker masters thee.   251

          Enter Le Beau.

LE BEAU
  Good sir, I do in friendship counsel you
  To leave this place. Albeit you have deserved
  High commendation, true applause, and love,
  Yet such is now the Duke's condition   255
  That he misconsters all that you have done.   256
  The Duke is humorous. What he is indeed   257
  More suits you to conceive than I to speak of.

ORLANDO
  I thank you, sir. And, pray you, tell me this:
  Which of the two was daughter of the Duke
  That here was at the wrestling?

LE BEAU
  Neither his daughter, if we judge by manners,
  But yet indeed the taller is his daughter.   263
  The other is daughter to the banished Duke,
  And here detained by her usurping uncle
  To keep his daughter company, whose loves
  Are dearer than the natural bond of sisters.
  But I can tell you that of late this Duke
  Hath ta'en displeasure 'gainst his gentle niece,
  Grounded upon no other argument   270
  But that the people praise her for her virtues
  And pity her for her good father's sake;
  And, on my life, his malice 'gainst the lady
  Will suddenly break forth. Sir, fare you well.   274

247 **Have with you** I'll go with you   249 **urged conference** invited
conversation   251 **Or** either   255 **condition** state of mind, disposition
256 **misconsters** misconstrues   257 **humorous** temperamental, capricious   263 **taller** (Possibly a textual error for *smaller* or *lesser*, or else
an inconsistency on Shakespeare's part; at 1.3.113, Rosalind is shown to
be the taller.)   270 **argument** reason   274 **suddenly** very soon

Hereafter, in a better world than this,   275
I shall desire more love and knowledge of you.
ORLANDO
I rest much bounden to you. Fare you well.   277
                                    [*Exit Le Beau.*]
Thus must I from the smoke into the smother,   278
From tyrant Duke unto a tyrant brother.
But heavenly Rosalind!   *Exit.*

❖

1.3   *Enter Celia and Rosalind.*

CELIA   Why, cousin, why, Rosalind! Cupid have mercy!
  Not a word?
ROSALIND   Not one to throw at a dog.
CELIA   No, thy words are too precious to be cast away
  upon curs; throw some of them at me. Come, lame me 5
  with reasons.   6
ROSALIND   Then there were two cousins laid up, when
  the one should be lamed with reasons and the other
  mad without any.
CELIA   But is all this for your father?
ROSALIND   No, some of it is for my child's father. O,   11
  how full of briers is this working-day world!
CELIA   They are but burrs, cousin, thrown upon thee in
  holiday foolery. If we walk not in the trodden paths,
  our very petticoats will catch them.
ROSALIND   I could shake them off my coat; these burrs
  are in my heart.
CELIA   Hem them away.   18
ROSALIND   I would try, if I could cry "hem" and have   19
  him.
CELIA   Come, come, wrestle with thy affections.

---

275 world i.e., state of affairs   **277 bounden** indebted   **278 smoke into
the smother** i.e., out of the frying pan into the fire. (*Smother* means "a
dense suffocating smoke.")

1.3. Location: Duke Frederick's court.
5–6 lame . . . reasons i.e., throw some explanations (for your silence) at
me   **11 my child's father** one who might sire my children, i.e., Orlando   **18 Hem** cough (since you say they are in the chest)   **19 cry
"hem"** clear away with a "hem" or a cough (with a play on *him*)

ROSALIND   O, they take the part of a better wrestler than
myself!

CELIA   O, a good wish upon you! You will try in time,   24
in despite of a fall. But, turning these jests out of ser-   25
vice, let us talk in good earnest. Is it possible, on such   26
a sudden, you should fall into so strong a liking with
old Sir Rowland's youngest son?

ROSALIND   The Duke my father loved his father dearly.

CELIA   Doth it therefore ensue that you should love his
son dearly? By this kind of chase, I should hate him,   31
for my father hated his father dearly; yet I hate not   32
Orlando.

ROSALIND   No, faith, hate him not, for my sake.

CELIA   Why should I not? Doth he not deserve well?   35

Enter Duke [*Frederick*], *with lords.*

ROSALIND   Let me love him for that, and do you love
him because I do.—Look, here comes the Duke.

CELIA   With his eyes full of anger.

DUKE FREDERICK [*To Rosalind*]
Mistress, dispatch you with your safest haste   39
And get you from our court.

ROSALIND   Me, uncle?

DUKE FREDERICK   You, cousin.   40
Within these ten days if that thou be'st found
So near our public court as twenty miles,
Thou diest for it.

ROSALIND   I do beseech Your Grace
Let me the knowledge of my fault bear with me.
If with myself I hold intelligence   45
Or have acquaintance with mine own desires,
If that I do not dream or be not frantic—   47
As I do trust I am not—then, dear uncle,
Never so much as in a thought unborn   49
Did I offend Your Highness.

24–25 You . . . fall i.e., you'll undertake to wrestle with Orlando sooner
or later, despite the danger of your being thrown down. (Contains sexual
suggestion.)   **25–26 turning . . . service** i.e., dismissing this banter
31 chase argument that is pursued   **32 dearly** intensely   **35 deserve
well** i.e., well deserve to be hated. (But Rosalind interprets in the sense
of "deserve favor.")   **39 safest haste** speed necessary for your safety
40 cousin i.e., kinsman   **45 hold intelligence** am in communication
47 If that if.   **frantic** insane   **49 so much as** even

DUKE FREDERICK   Thus do all traitors.
  If their purgation did consist in words,   51
  They are as innocent as grace itself.
  Let it suffice thee that I trust thee not.

ROSALIND
  Yet your mistrust cannot make me a traitor.
  Tell me whereon the likelihood depends.

DUKE FREDERICK
  Thou art thy father's daughter, there's enough.

ROSALIND
  So was I when Your Highness took his dukedom;
  So was I when Your Highness banished him.
  Treason is not inherited, my lord;
  Or, if we did derive it from our friends,   60
  What's that to me? My father was no traitor.
  Then, good my liege, mistake me not so much
  To think my poverty is treacherous.

CELIA   Dear sovereign, hear me speak.

DUKE FREDERICK
  Ay, Celia, we stayed her for your sake,   65
  Else had she with her father ranged along.   66

CELIA
  I did not then entreat to have her stay;
  It was your pleasure and your own remorse.   68
  I was too young that time to value her,   69
  But now I know her. If she be a traitor,
  Why so am I. We still have slept together,   71
  Rose at an instant, learned, played, eat together,   72
  And wheresoe'er we went, like Juno's swans   73
  Still we went coupled and inseparable.

DUKE FREDERICK
  She is too subtle for thee; and her smoothness,
  Her very silence, and her patience
  Speak to the people, and they pity her.
  Thou art a fool. She robs thee of thy name,   78
  And thou wilt show more bright and seem more virtuous

51 purgation proof of innocence   **60 friends** relatives, kinsfolk
65 stayed kept   **66 ranged** roamed   **68 remorse** compassion   **69 that
time** then   **71 still** continually   **72 eat** ate, or have eaten   **73 Juno's
swans** i.e., yoked together (though according to Ovid it was Venus,
not Juno, who used swans to draw her chariot)   **78 name** reputation,
praise

When she is gone. Then open not thy lips.
Firm and irrevocable is my doom   81
Which I have passed upon her; she is banished.

CELIA
Pronounce that sentence then on me, my liege!
I cannot live out of her company.

DUKE FREDERICK
You are a fool. You, niece, provide yourself.   85
If you outstay the time, upon mine honor,
And in the greatness of my word, you die.   87

                                    Exit Duke [with Lords].

CELIA
O my poor Rosalind, whither wilt thou go?
Wilt thou change fathers? I will give thee mine.   89
I charge thee, be not thou more grieved than I am.

ROSALIND
I have more cause.

CELIA   Thou hast not, cousin.
Prithee, be cheerful. Know'st thou not the Duke
Hath banished me, his daughter?

ROSALIND   That he hath not.

CELIA
No, hath not? Rosalind lacks then the love
Which teacheth thee that thou and I am one.
Shall we be sundered? Shall we part, sweet girl?
No, let my father seek another heir.
Therefore devise with me how we may fly,
Whither to go, and what to bear with us.
And do not seek to take your change upon you,   100
To bear your griefs yourself and leave me out;
For, by this heaven, now at our sorrows pale,   102
Say what thou canst, I'll go along with thee.

ROSALIND   Why, whither shall we go?

CELIA
To seek my uncle in the Forest of Arden.

ROSALIND
Alas, what danger will it be to us,

---

81 doom sentence   **85 provide yourself** get ready   **87 in . . . word** i.e.,
upon my authority as Duke   **89 change** exchange   **100 change** change
of fortune   **102 pale** (Heaven is pale in sympathy with their plight.)

Maids as we are, to travel forth so far!
Beauty provoketh thieves sooner than gold.

CELIA
  I'll put myself in poor and mean attire   109
  And with a kind of umber smirch my face;   110
  The like do you. So shall we pass along
  And never stir assailants.

ROSALIND   Were it not better,
  Because that I am more than common tall,
  That I did suit me all points like a man?   114
  A gallant curtal ax upon my thigh,   115
  A boar spear in my hand, and—in my heart
  Lie there what hidden woman's fear there will—
  We'll have a swashing and a martial outside,   118
  As many other mannish cowards have
  That do outface it with their semblances.   120

CELIA
  What shall I call thee when thou art a man?

ROSALIND
  I'll have no worse a name than Jove's own page,
  And therefore look you call me Ganymede.   123
  But what will you be called?

CELIA
  Something that hath a reference to my state:
  No longer Celia, but Aliena.   126

ROSALIND
  But, cousin, what if we assayed to steal   127
  The clownish fool out of your father's court?
  Would he not be a comfort to our travel?

CELIA
  He'll go along o'er the wide world with me;
  Leave me alone to woo him. Let's away,   131
  And get our jewels and our wealth together,
  Devise the fittest time and safest way   133

---

109 mean lowly   **110 umber** brown pigment (to make them appear
tanned, as countrywomen would be)   **114 suit** dress   **115 curtal ax**
broad cutting sword   **118 swashing** swaggering, blustering
120 outface . . . semblances bluff their way through with mere appear-
ances   **123 Ganymede** Jupiter's cupbearer. (Used also in Lodge's *Rosalynde*.)   **126 Aliena** the estranged one   **127 assayed** tried   **131 woo**
persuade   **133 fittest** most appropriate

To hide us from pursuit that will be made
After my flight. Now go we in content   135
To liberty, and not to banishment.   *Exeunt.*

✤

---

135 content contentment

2.1   *Enter Duke Senior, Amiens, and two or three Lords, [dressed] like foresters.*

DUKE SENIOR
  Now, my co-mates and brothers in exile,
  Hath not old custom made this life more sweet   2
  Than that of painted pomp? Are not these woods
  More free from peril than the envious court?   4
  Here feel we not the penalty of Adam,   5
  The seasons' difference, as the icy fang   6
  And churlish chiding of the winter's wind,   7
  Which when it bites and blows upon my body
  Even till I shrink with cold, I smile and say,
  "This is no flattery; these are counselors
  That feelingly persuade me what I am."
  Sweet are the uses of adversity,   12
  Which, like the toad, ugly and venomous,   13
  Wears yet a precious jewel in his head;   14
  And this our life, exempt from public haunt,   15
  Finds tongues in trees, books in the running brooks,
  Sermons in stones, and good in everything.

AMIENS
  I would not change it. Happy is Your Grace
  That can translate the stubbornness of fortune
  Into so quiet and so sweet a style.

DUKE SENIOR
  Come, shall we go and kill us venison?
  And yet it irks me the poor dappled fools,   22
  Being native burghers of this desert city,   23
  Should in their own confines with forkèd heads   24
  Have their round haunches gored.

FIRST LORD   Indeed, my lord,

2.1. Location: The Forest of Arden.
2 old custom long experience   **4 envious** malicious   **5 feel we not** we
do not seriously suffer from. (*Not* is often emended to *but*.)   **penalty of
Adam** expulsion from Eden, bringing with it loss of innocence and *the
seasons' difference*, the change of seasons from summer to winter   **6 as**
such as   **7 churlish** rough   **12 uses** profits   **13–14 like . . . head** (Alludes to the widespread belief that the toad was a poisonous creature
but with a jewel embedded in its head that worked as an antidote.)
15 exempt cut off.   **haunt** society   **22 irks** grieves, vexes.   **fools** innocent creatures   **23 burghers** citizens.   **desert** uninhabited   **24 forkèd
heads** i.e., barbed hunting arrows

The melancholy Jaques grieves at that,
And in that kind swears you do more usurp   27
Than doth your brother that hath banished you.
Today my lord of Amiens and myself
Did steal behind him as he lay along   30
Under an oak whose antique root peeps out   31
Upon the brook that brawls along this wood,   32
To the which place a poor sequestered stag   33
That from the hunter's aim had ta'en a hurt
Did come to languish. And indeed, my lord,
The wretched animal heaved forth such groans
That their discharge did stretch his leathern coat
Almost to bursting, and the big round tears
Coursed one another down his innocent nose   39
In piteous chase. And thus the hairy fool,
Much markèd of the melancholy Jaques,   41
Stood on th' extremest verge of the swift brook,   42
Augmenting it with tears.

DUKE SENIOR   But what said Jaques?
Did he not moralize this spectacle?   44

FIRST LORD
O, yes, into a thousand similes.
First, for his weeping into the needless stream: 46
"Poor deer," quoth he, "thou mak'st a testament   47
As worldings do, giving thy sum of more   48
To that which had too much." Then, being there alone,
Left and abandoned of his velvet friends: 50
"'Tis right," quoth he, "thus misery doth part   51
The flux of company." Anon a careless herd,   52
Full of the pasture, jumps along by him
And never stays to greet him. "Ay," quoth Jaques,
"Sweep on, you fat and greasy citizens;
'Tis just the fashion. Wherefore do you look

---

27 kind regard, vein   **30 along** stretched out   **31 antique** ancient
32 brawls noisily flows   **33 sequestered** separated (from the herd)
39 Coursed followed   **41 markèd of** observed by   **42 extremest verge**
very edge   **44 moralize** draw out the hidden meaning of   **46 needless**
having no need (of more water)   **47 testament** will   **48 worldings** mortal
men; worldly men.   **sum of more** additional quantity   **50 velvet** i.e.,
prosperous. (Velvet was an appropriately rich dress for a courtier; the
term also alludes here to the velvet of the deers' antlers during rapid
growth.)   **51 'Tis right** i.e., that's how it goes.   **part** depart from   **52 flux
of company** stream of fellow creatures.   **Anon** soon.   **careless** carefree

Upon that poor and broken bankrupt there?"
Thus most invectively he pierceth through   58
The body of the country, city, court,
Yea, and of this our life, swearing that we
Are mere usurpers, tyrants, and what's worse,   61
To fright the animals and to kill them up   62
In their assigned and native dwelling place.

DUKE SENIOR
And did you leave him in this contemplation?

SECOND LORD
We did, my lord, weeping and commenting
Upon the sobbing deer.

DUKE SENIOR   Show me the place.
I love to cope him in these sullen fits,   67
For then he's full of matter.   68

FIRST LORD   I'll bring you to him straight.   *Exeunt.*

❖

2.2   *Enter Duke [Frederick], with Lords.*

DUKE FREDERICK
Can it be possible that no man saw them?
It cannot be. Some villains of my court
Are of consent and sufferance in this.   3

FIRST LORD
I cannot hear of any that did see her.
The ladies, her attendants of her chamber,
Saw her abed, and in the morning early
They found the bed untreasured of their mistress.

SECOND LORD
My lord, the roynish clown, at whom so oft   8
Your Grace was wont to laugh, is also missing.
Hisperia, the princess' gentlewoman,
Confesses that she secretly o'erheard
Your daughter and her cousin much commend
The parts and graces of the wrestler   13

58 **invectively** vehemently   61 **what's worse** anything worse   62 **up**
off   67 **cope** engage, encounter   68 **matter** substance, sentiment

2.2. Location: Duke Frederick's court.
3 **Are . . . this** have conspired in and permitted this   8 **roynish** scurvy,
coarse   13 **parts** good qualities

That did but lately foil the sinewy Charles,
And she believes wherever they are gone
That youth is surely in their company.

DUKE FREDERICK
  Send to his brother; fetch that gallant hither.   17
  If he be absent, bring his brother to me;   18
  I'll make him find him. Do this suddenly,   19
  And let not search and inquisition quail   20
  To bring again these foolish runaways.   *Exeunt.* 21

❖

2.3   *Enter Orlando and Adam, [meeting].*

ORLANDO Who's there?

ADAM
  What, my young master? O my gentle master,
  O my sweet master, O you memory   3
  Of old Sir Rowland! Why, what make you here?   4
  Why are you virtuous? Why do people love you?
  And wherefore are you gentle, strong, and valiant?   6
  Why would you be so fond to overcome   7
  The bonny prizer of the humorous Duke?   8
  Your praise is come too swiftly home before you.
  Know you not, master, to some kind of men
  Their graces serve them but as enemies?
  No more do yours. Your virtues, gentle master,   12
  Are sanctified and holy traitors to you.
  O, what a world is this, when what is comely
  Envenoms him that bears it!

ORLANDO
  Why, what's the matter?

ADAM   O unhappy youth,
  Come not within these doors! Within this roof
  The enemy of all your graces lives.
  Your brother—no, no brother; yet the son—

17, 18 his brother i.e., Oliver **18 he** i.e., Orlando **19 suddenly** speedily **20 inquisition** inquiry. **quail** fail, slacken **21 again** back

2.3. Location: Before Oliver's house.
3 memory memorial **4 what make you** what are you doing **6 wherefore** why **7 fond to** foolish as to **8 bonny prizer** sturdy champion or prizefighter. **humorous** temperamental **12 No more** no better

Yet not the son, I will not call him son
Of him I was about to call his father—
Hath heard your praises, and this night he means
To burn the lodging where you use to lie   23
And you within it. If he fail of that,
He will have other means to cut you off.
I overheard him and his practices.   26
This is no place, this house is but a butchery;   27
Abhor it, fear it, do not enter it.

ORLANDO
Why, whither, Adam, wouldst thou have me go?

ADAM
No matter whither, so you come not here.

ORLANDO
What, wouldst thou have me go and beg my food?
Or with a base and boisterous sword enforce   32
A thievish living on the common road?
This I must do, or know not what to do;
Yet this I will not do, do how I can.
I rather will subject me to the malice
Of a diverted blood and bloody brother.   37

ADAM
But do not so. I have five hundred crowns,
The thrifty hire I saved under your father,   39
Which I did store to be my foster nurse
When service should in my old limbs lie lame   41
And unregarded age in corners thrown.   42
Take that, and He that doth the ravens feed,   43
Yea, providently caters for the sparrow,   44
Be comfort to my age! Here is the gold;   [*Giving gold*]
All this I give you. Let me be your servant.
Though I look old, yet I am strong and lusty,   47
For in my youth I never did apply
Hot and rebellious liquors in my blood,
Nor did not with unbashful forehead woo   50
The means of weakness and debility;

23 **use** are accustomed   26 **practices** plots   27 **place** place for you, home.   **butchery** slaughterhouse   32 **boisterous** violent   37 **diverted blood** kinship diverted from the natural source   39 **thrifty . . . saved** wages I thriftily saved   41 **lie lame** i.e., be performed only lamely   42 **thrown** be thrown   43–44 **He . . . sparrow** (See Luke 12:6, 22–24, Psalms 147:9, Job 38:41, etc.)   47 **lusty** vigorous   50 **unbashful forehead** shameless countenance

Therefore my age is as a lusty winter,
Frosty but kindly. Let me go with you.
I'll do the service of a younger man
In all your business and necessities.

ORLANDO
O good old man, how well in thee appears
The constant service of the antique world,   57
When service sweat for duty, not for meed!   58
Thou art not for the fashion of these times,
Where none will sweat but for promotion,
And having that do choke their service up   61
Even with the having. It is not so with thee.   62
But, poor old man, thou prun'st a rotten tree,
That cannot so much as a blossom yield
In lieu of all thy pains and husbandry.   65
But come thy ways; we'll go along together,
And ere we have thy youthful wages spent,
We'll light upon some settled low content.   68

ADAM
Master, go on, and I will follow thee
To the last gasp, with truth and loyalty.
From seventeen years till now almost fourscore
Here livèd I, but now live here no more.
At seventeen years many their fortunes seek,
But at fourscore it is too late a week;   74
Yet fortune cannot recompense me better
Than to die well and not my master's debtor.

                                        Exeunt.

❖

2.4   *Enter Rosalind for Ganymede, Celia for Aliena,
          and Clown, alias Touchstone.*

ROSALIND   O Jupiter, how weary are my spirits!

---

57 constant faithful **58 sweat** sweated. **meed** reward **61–62 do choke
. . . having** i.e., cease serving once they have gained promotion **65 lieu of**
return for **68 low content** lowly contented state **74 week** i.e., time

2.4. Location: The Forest of Arden.
s.d. for i.e., disguised as

TOUCHSTONE   I care not for my spirits, if my legs were not weary.

ROSALIND   I could find in my heart to disgrace my man's apparel and to cry like a woman; but I must comfort the weaker vessel, as doublet and hose ought to show 6 itself courageous to petticoat. Therefore courage, good Aliena!

CELIA   I pray you, bear with me; I cannot go no further.

TOUCHSTONE   For my part, I had rather bear with you than bear you; yet I should bear no cross if I did bear 11 you, for I think you have no money in your purse.

ROSALIND   Well, this is the Forest of Arden.

TOUCHSTONE   Ay, now am I in Arden, the more fool I. When I was at home I was in a better place, but travelers must be content.

Enter Corin and Silvius.

ROSALIND   Ay, be so, good Touchstone.—Look you who comes here, a young man and an old in solemn talk.   [*They stand aside and listen.*]

CORIN
This is the way to make her scorn you still.

SILVIUS
O Corin, that thou knew'st how I do love her!

CORIN
I partly guess, for I have loved ere now.

SILVIUS
No, Corin, being old, thou canst not guess,
Though in thy youth thou wast as true a lover
As ever sighed upon a midnight pillow.
But if thy love were ever like to mine—
As sure I think did never man love so—
How many actions most ridiculous
Hast thou been drawn to by thy fantasy?   29

CORIN
Into a thousand that I have forgotten.

SILVIUS
O, thou didst then never love so heartily!

---

6 weaker vessel i.e., woman. (See 1 Peter 3:7.) **doublet and hose** close-fitting jacket and breeches; typical male attire **11 cross** (1) burden (2) coin having on it a figure of a cross **29 fantasy** love imaginings

If thou rememberest not the slightest folly
That ever love did make thee run into,
Thou hast not loved.
Or if thou hast not sat as I do now,
Wearing thy hearer in thy mistress' praise,   36
Thou hast not loved.
Or if thou hast not broke from company
Abruptly, as my passion now makes me,
Thou hast not loved.
O Phoebe, Phoebe, Phoebe!   *Exit.*

ROSALIND
Alas, poor shepherd! Searching of thy wound,   42
I have by hard adventure found mine own.   43

TOUCHSTONE And I mine. I remember, when I was in
love I broke my sword upon a stone and bid him take
that for coming a-night to Jane Smile; and I remember 46
the kissing of her batler and the cow's dugs that her 47
pretty chapped hands had milked; and I remember the
wooing of a peascod instead of her, from whom I took 49
two cods and, giving her them again, said with weep- 50
ing tears, "Wear these for my sake." We that are true
lovers run into strange capers; but as all is mortal in 52
nature, so is all nature in love mortal in folly. 53

ROSALIND Thou speak'st wiser than thou art ware of. 54

TOUCHSTONE Nay, I shall ne'er be ware of mine own
wit till I break my shins against it.

ROSALIND
Jove, Jove! This shepherd's passion
Is much upon my fashion.   58

TOUCHSTONE
And mine, but it grows something stale with me. 59

CELIA
I pray you, one of you question yond man

---

36 Wearing wearing out, or wearying **42 Searching of** probing **43 hard
adventure** bad luck **46 a-night** by night **47 batler** club or bat for beating clothes in process of washing. **dugs** udder **49 peascod** pea pod.
(Regarded as a lucky gift by rustic lovers.) **whom** i.e., which (referring
to the whole pea plant) **50 her** i.e., the pea plant **52 mortal** subject to
death **53 mortal** extreme **54 ware** aware (but Touchstone plays upon
the meaning "wary") **58 upon** after, according to **59 something**
somewhat

If he for gold will give us any food.
I faint almost to death.

TOUCHSTONE   Holla: you, clown!   62

ROSALIND
Peace, Fool! He's not thy kinsman.

CORIN   Who calls?

TOUCHSTONE
Your betters, sir.

CORIN   Else are they very wretched.

ROSALIND
Peace, I say.—Good even to you, friend.   65

CORIN
And to you, gentle sir, and to you all.

ROSALIND
I prithee, shepherd, if that love or gold
Can in this desert place buy entertainment,   68
Bring us where we may rest ourselves and feed.
Here's a young maid with travel much oppressed,
And faints for succor.

CORIN   Fair sir, I pity her   71
And wish, for her sake more than for mine own,
My fortunes were more able to relieve her;
But I am shepherd to another man
And do not shear the fleeces that I graze.   75
My master is of churlish disposition,   76
And little recks to find the way to heaven   77
By doing deeds of hospitality.
Besides, his cote, his flocks, and bounds of feed   79
Are now on sale, and at our sheepcote now,
By reason of his absence, there is nothing
That you will feed on. But what is, come see,
And in my voice most welcome shall you be.   83

ROSALIND
What is he that shall buy his flock and pasture?   84

---

62 clown yokel. (But Rosalind uses the word as it applies to Touchstone.)
65 even evening, i.e., afternoon **68 desert** uninhabited. **entertainment**
hospitality, provision **71 for succor** for lack of succor, i.e., food **75 do
. . . fleeces** i.e., do not obtain the profits from the flock **76 churlish**
niggardly, miserly **77 recks** cares, reckons **79 cote** cottage. **bounds of
feed** limits within which he has the right of pasturage **83 in my voice**
insofar as I have authority to speak **84 What** who

CORIN
That young swain that you saw here but erewhile, 85
That little cares for buying anything.

ROSALIND
I pray thee, if it stand with honesty, 87
Buy thou the cottage, pasture, and the flock,
And thou shalt have to pay for it of us. 89

CELIA
And we will mend thy wages. I like this place 90
And willingly could waste my time in it. 91

CORIN
Assuredly the thing is to be sold.
Go with me. If you like upon report
The soil, the profit, and this kind of life,
I will your very faithful feeder be 95
And buy it with your gold right suddenly. *Exeunt.* 96

❖

2.5 *Enter Amiens, Jaques, and others. [A table is set out.]*

Song.

AMIENS
Under the greenwood tree
Who loves to lie with me, 2
And turn his merry note 3
Unto the sweet bird's throat, 4
Come hither, come hither, come hither.
Here shall he see
No enemy
But winter and rough weather.

JAQUES More, more, I prithee, more.
AMIENS It will make you melancholy, Monsieur Jaques.
JAQUES I thank it. More, I prithee, more. I can suck mel-

---

85 erewhile a short time since **87 stand** be consistent **89 have to pay** have the money **90 mend** improve **91 waste** spend **95 feeder** servant **96 right suddenly** without delay

2.5. Location: The forest.
2 Who anyone who **3 turn** attune, adapt **4 throat** voice

ancholy out of a song as a weasel sucks eggs. More, I
prithee, more.

AMIENS   My voice is ragged. I know I cannot please you. 14

JAQUES   I do not desire you to please me, I do desire you
to sing. Come, more, another stanzo. Call you 'em
"stanzos"?

AMIENS   What you will, Monsieur Jaques.

JAQUES   Nay, I care not for their names; they owe me 19
nothing. Will you sing? 20

AMIENS   More at your request than to please myself.

JAQUES   Well then, if ever I thank any man, I'll thank you;
but that they call "compliment" is like th' encounter 23
of two dog-apes, and when a man thanks me heartily, 24
methinks I have given him a penny and he renders
me the beggarly thanks. Come, sing; and you that will 26
not, hold your tongues.

AMIENS   Well, I'll end the song.—Sirs, cover the while; 28
the Duke will drink under this tree.—He hath been all
this day to look you.   [*Food and drink are set out.*] 30

JAQUES   And I have been all this day to avoid him. He
is too disputable for my company. I think of as many 32
matters as he, but I give heaven thanks and make no
boast of them. Come, warble, come.

Song.

AMIENS [*Sings*]
       Who doth ambition shun
       And loves to live i' the sun,   36
       Seeking the food he eats
       And pleased with what he gets,
                        All together here.
   Come hither, come hither, come hither.
       Here shall he see
       No enemy
   But winter and rough weather.

14 **ragged** hoarse, rough   19–20 **they owe me nothing** (Jaques speaks of
names as of something valuable only when written as signatures to a
bond of indebtedness.)   23 **that** what.   **"compliment"** formal polite-
ness   24 **dog-apes** dog-faced baboons   26 **beggarly** effusive, like the
thanks of a beggar   28 **cover the while** set the table for a meal meanwhile   30 **to look** looking for   32 **disputable** inclined to dispute
36 **live i' the sun** dwell in the open air, without the cares of the court

JAQUES I'll give you a verse to this note that I made yes- 43
terday in despite of my invention.   44
AMIENS And I'll sing it.
JAQUES Thus it goes:

> If it do come to pass
> That any man turn ass,
> Leaving his wealth and ease,
> A stubborn will to please,
> Ducdame, ducdame, ducdame.   51
> Here shall he see
> Gross fools as he,
> An if he will come to me.

AMIENS What's that "ducdame"?
JAQUES 'Tis a Greek invocation, to call fools into a circle.
I'll go sleep, if I can; if I cannot, I'll rail against all the
firstborn of Egypt.   58
AMIENS And I'll go seek the Duke. His banquet is pre- 59
pared.   *Exeunt [separately].*

2.6 *Enter Orlando and Adam.*

ADAM Dear master, I can go no further. O, I die for

---

43 note tune **44 in . . . invention** although I lack imagination; or, without
even using my imagination **51 Ducdame** (Unexplained. One possible
suggestion is that it is a corruption of the gypsy words *dukrä mè*, meaning
"I foretell," "I tell fortunes or prophesy"; therefore, as the call of a gypsy
fortuneteller at fairs, it is a "Greek" [or sharper's] invocation. This also
renders the allusion to the firstborn of Egypt intelligible, since the firstborn Duke is banished and in the condition of a gypsy.) **58 firstborn of
Egypt** (In Exodus 12:28–33, the firstborn of Egypt are slain by the Lord to
achieve the release of the Jews. Perhaps Jaques ironically threatens to rail
against the firstborn because of their role in the exile of Moses and his
followers into the wilderness, which seems similar to the exile of Duke
Senior and his men in the forest; or perhaps he intends to rail against the
firstborn because of the "great cry" that was heard in Egypt following
their slaughter, a cry that would prevent sleep.) **59 banquet** wine and
dessert after dinner. (This repast, now prepared on stage, seemingly is
to remain there during the short following scene.)

**2.6. Location: The forest. The scene is continuous. By convention we
understand that Adam and Orlando are in a different part of the forest
and do not "see" the table left onstage.**

food! Here lie I down and measure out my grave.
Farewell, kind master.   [*He lies down.*]
ORLANDO Why, how now, Adam? No greater heart in
thee? Live a little, comfort a little, cheer thyself a little. 5
If this uncouth forest yield anything savage, I will ei- 6
ther be food for it or bring it for food to thee. Thy
conceit is nearer death than thy powers. For my sake 8
be comfortable; hold death awhile at the arm's end. I 9
will here be with thee presently, and if I bring thee not
something to eat, I will give thee leave to die; but if
thou diest before I come, thou art a mocker of my labor. Well said! Thou look'st cheerly, and I'll be with 13
thee quickly. Yet thou liest in the bleak air. Come, I 14
will bear thee to some shelter; and thou shalt not die
for lack of a dinner, if there live anything in this desert. [*He picks up Adam.*] Cheerly, good Adam! *Exeunt.*

2.7   *Enter Duke Senior and Lords, like outlaws.*

DUKE SENIOR
  I think he be transformed into a beast,
  For I can nowhere find him like a man.
FIRST LORD
  My lord, he is but even now gone hence.
  Here was he merry, hearing of a song.
DUKE SENIOR
  If he, compact of jars, grow musical,   5
  We shall have shortly discord in the spheres.   6
  Go, seek him, tell him I would speak with him.

      Enter Jaques.

FIRST LORD
  He saves my labor by his own approach.

5 comfort comfort yourself **6 uncouth** strange, wild **8 conceit**
thought, imagination **9 comfortable** comforted **13 Well said** well
done **14 Yet** still

2.7. Location: The forest; the scene is continuous. (A light repast, set out
for the Duke in 2.5, has remained onstage during 2.6.)
 5 compact of jars composed of discords **6 the spheres** the concentric
spheres of the Ptolemaic solar system (which, by their movement, were
thought to produce harmonious music)

DUKE SENIOR
Why, how now, monsieur, what a life is this,
That your poor friends must woo your company?
What, you look merrily!

JAQUES
A fool, a fool! I met a fool i' the forest,
A motley fool. A miserable world!   13
As I do live by food, I met a fool,
Who laid him down and basked him in the sun,
And railed on Lady Fortune in good terms,
In good set terms, and yet a motley fool.   17
"Good morrow, Fool," quoth I. "No, sir," quoth he,
"Call me not fool till heaven hath sent me fortune."   19
And then he drew a dial from his poke   20
And, looking on it with lackluster eye,
Says very wisely, "It is ten o'clock.
Thus we may see," quoth he, "how the world wags.   23
'Tis but an hour ago since it was nine,
And after one hour more 'twill be eleven;
And so from hour to hour we ripe and ripe,
And then from hour to hour we rot and rot,
And thereby hangs a tale." When I did hear
The motley fool thus moral on the time,   29
My lungs began to crow like Chanticleer   30
That fools should be so deep-contemplative,
And I did laugh sans intermission   32
An hour by his dial. O noble fool!
A worthy fool! Motley's the only wear.   34

DUKE SENIOR   What fool is this?

JAQUES
O worthy fool! One that hath been a courtier
And says if ladies be but young and fair
They have the gift to know it. And in his brain,
Which is as dry as the remainder biscuit   39

---

13 motley wearing motley, the parti-colored dress of the clown or professional jester   **17 set** carefully composed   **19 Call . . . fortune** (An
allusion to the proverb "Fortune favors fools.")   **20 dial** portable
sundial.   **poke** pouch or pocket   **23 wags** goes   **29 moral** moralize
30 crow i.e., laugh merrily.   **Chanticleer** a rooster   **32 sans** without
34 only wear only thing worth wearing   **39 dry** (According to Elizabethan physiology, a dry brain was marked by a strong memory but
a slow wit.)   **remainder** remaining

After a voyage, he hath strange places crammed　40
With observation, the which he vents
In mangled forms. O, that I were a fool!
I am ambitious for a motley coat.

DUKE SENIOR
Thou shalt have one.

JAQUES　　　　　　　　It is my only suit,　44
Provided that you weed your better judgments
Of all opinion that grows rank in them　46
That I am wise. I must have liberty
Withal, as large a charter as the wind,　48
To blow on whom I please, for so fools have.
And they that are most gallèd with my folly,　50
They most must laugh. And why, sir, must they so?
The "why" is plain as way to parish church:
He that a fool doth very wisely hit　53
Doth very foolishly, although he smart,　54
Not to seem senseless of the bob. If not,　55
The wise man's folly is anatomized　56
Even by the squandering glances of the fool.　57
Invest me in my motley; give me leave　58
To speak my mind, and I will through and through
Cleanse the foul body of th' infected world,
If they will patiently receive my medicine.

DUKE SENIOR
Fie on thee! I can tell what thou wouldst do.

JAQUES
What, for a counter, would I do but good?　63

DUKE SENIOR
Most mischievous foul sin, in chiding sin.
For thou thyself hast been a libertine,　65
As sensual as the brutish sting itself;　66

---

40 places (1) storage places (2) commonplaces, i.e., familiar ideas and quotations　**44 suit** (1) request (2) suit of clothes　**46 rank** wild　**48 charter** license, privilege　**50 gallèd** chafed, rubbed on a sore spot　**53 He . . . hit** he whom a fool wittily attacks　**54 Doth** acts.　**smart** feels the sting　**55 senseless of the bob** unaware of the jibe, taunt.　**If not** otherwise　**56 anatomized** dissected, revealed openly　**57 squandering glances** random hits　**58 Invest** dress　**63 counter** (Type of a thing of no intrinsic value, a metal disk used in counting.)　**65 libertine** one lacking moral restraint　**66 brutish sting** carnal impulse, appetite

And all th' embossèd sores and headed evils   67
That thou with license of free foot hast caught   68
Wouldst thou disgorge into the general world.   69
JAQUES   Why, who cries out on pride   70
That can therein tax any private party?   71
Doth it not flow as hugely as the sea,
Till that the weary very means do ebb?   73
What woman in the city do I name,
When that I say the city woman bears   75
The cost of princes on unworthy shoulders?   76
Who can come in and say that I mean her,
When such a one as she, such is her neighbor?
Or what is he of basest function   79
That says his bravery is not on my cost,   80
Thinking that I mean him, but therein suits   81
His folly to the mettle of my speech?   82
There then, how then? What then? Let me see wherein
My tongue hath wronged him. If it do him right,   84
Then he hath wronged himself. If he be free,   85
Why then my taxing like a wild goose flies,
Unclaimed of any man.—But who comes here?

Enter Orlando [with his sword drawn].

ORLANDO
Forbear, and eat no more.
JAQUES   Why, I have eat none yet.   88
ORLANDO
Nor shalt not, till necessity be served.
JAQUES
Of what kind should this cock come of?   90

67 embossèd swollen, tumid.   **headed evils** diseases and sores that have come to a head   **68 license . . . foot** the licentious freedom of a libertine   **69 disgorge** discharge, vomit   **70 pride** i.e., extravagance   **71 tax** blame, accuse.   **any private party** i.e., only some individual   **73 Till . . . ebb** until the ostentation finally subsides, having exhausted what fed it (?). (There are many conjectures, such as *wearer's very means*.)   **75 the city woman** the typical citizen's wife   **76 The cost of princes** i.e., clothes rich enough to adorn a prince   **79 basest function** lowest position in society   **80 That . . . cost** who says his finery is not bought at my expense (and is therefore none of my business)   **81 suits** (1) fits (2) dresses   **82 mettle** substance, contents   **84 right** justice (i.e., if I have described him accurately)   **85 wronged himself** (by calling attention to the accuracy of my description).   **free** i.e., blameless   **88 eat** eaten. (Pronounced "et.")   **90 cock** fighting cock (i.e., aggressive person)

DUKE SENIOR

Art thou thus boldened, man, by thy distress,
Or else a rude despiser of good manners,
That in civility thou seem'st so empty?

ORLANDO

You touched my vein at first. The thorny point   94
Of bare distress hath ta'en from me the show
Of smooth civility; yet am I inland bred   96
And know some nurture. But forbear, I say.   97
He dies that touches any of this fruit
Till I and my affairs are answerèd.   99

JAQUES

An you will not be answered with reason, I must die. 100

DUKE SENIOR

What would you have? Your gentleness shall force
More than your force move us to gentleness.

ORLANDO

I almost die for food, and let me have it!

DUKE SENIOR

Sit down and feed, and welcome to our table.

ORLANDO

Speak you so gently? Pardon me, I pray you.
I thought that all things had been savage here,
And therefore put I on the countenance
Of stern commandment. But whate'er you are
That in this desert inaccessible,
Under the shade of melancholy boughs,
Lose and neglect the creeping hours of time;
If ever you have looked on better days,
If ever been where bells have knolled to church,   113
If ever sat at any good man's feast,
If ever from your eyelids wiped a tear
And know what 'tis to pity and be pitied,
Let gentleness my strong enforcement be,
In the which hope I blush and hide my sword.

          [He sheathes his sword.]

DUKE SENIOR

True is it that we have seen better days,

---

94 vein condition, situation.   **at first** i.e., in what you first suggested
96 inland bred i.e., raised in civilized society, in the center of civilization
rather than on the outskirts   **97 nurture** education, training   **99 an-**
swerèd satisfied   **100 An** if   **113 knolled** rung

And have with holy bell been knolled to church,
And sat at good men's feasts, and wiped our eyes
Of drops that sacred pity hath engendered;
And therefore sit you down in gentleness,
And take upon command what help we have   124
That to your wanting may be ministered.   125

ORLANDO
Then but forbear your food a little while,
Whiles, like a doe, I go to find my fawn
And give it food. There is an old poor man
Who after me hath many a weary step
Limped in pure love. Till he be first sufficed,
Oppressed with two weak evils, age and hunger,   131
I will not touch a bit.

DUKE SENIOR   Go find him out,
And we will nothing waste till you return.   133

ORLANDO
I thank ye; and be blest for your good comfort!

                                             [*Exit.*]

DUKE SENIOR
Thou seest we are not all alone unhappy.
This wide and universal theater
Presents more woeful pageants than the scene
Wherein we play in.

JAQUES   All the world's a stage,
And all the men and women merely players.
They have their exits and their entrances,
And one man in his time plays many parts,
His acts being seven ages. At first the infant,
Mewling and puking in the nurse's arms.   143
Then the whining schoolboy, with his satchel
And shining morning face, creeping like snail
Unwillingly to school. And then the lover,
Sighing like furnace, with a woeful ballad
Made to his mistress' eyebrow. Then a soldier,
Full of strange oaths and bearded like the pard,   149
Jealous in honor, sudden, and quick in quarrel,   150

124 upon command for the asking   **125 wanting** need   **131 weak** causing
weakness   **133 waste** consume   **143 Mewling** crying   **149 bearded . . .
pard** having bristling mustaches like the panther's or leopard's whiskers
150 Jealous in honor quick to anger in matters of honor.   **sudden** rash

Seeking the bubble reputation
Even in the cannon's mouth. And then the justice,
In fair round belly with good capon lined,   153
With eyes severe and beard of formal cut,
Full of wise saws and modern instances;   155
And so he plays his part. The sixth age shifts
Into the lean and slippered pantaloon,   157
With spectacles on nose and pouch on side,
His youthful hose, well saved, a world too wide
For his shrunk shank; and his big manly voice,   160
Turning again toward childish treble, pipes
And whistles in his sound. Last scene of all,   162
That ends this strange eventful history,
Is second childishness and mere oblivion,   164
Sans teeth, sans eyes, sans taste, sans everything.

  Enter Orlando, with Adam.

DUKE SENIOR
 Welcome. Set down your venerable burden
 And let him feed.
ORLANDO I thank you most for him. [*He sets down Adam.*]
ADAM So had you need.
 I scarce can speak to thank you for myself.
DUKE SENIOR
 Welcome, fall to. I will not trouble you
 As yet to question you about your fortunes.
 Give us some music, and, good cousin, sing.
   [*They eat, while Orlando and Duke Senior*
          converse apart.]

   Song.

AMIENS
  Blow, blow, thou winter wind,
  Thou art not so unkind
   As man's ingratitude;
  Thy tooth is not so keen,

---

153 capon a rooster castrated to make the flesh more tender for eating
(and often presented to judges as a bribe) **155 saws** sayings. **modern
instances** commonplace illustrations **157 pantaloon** ridiculous, enfee-
bled old man. (A stock type in Italian comedy.) **160 shank** lower leg
162 his its **164 mere oblivion** total forgetfulness

Because thou art not seen,
　　Although thy breath be rude.   179
Heigh-ho, sing heigh-ho, unto the green holly.   180
Most friendship is feigning, most loving mere folly.
　　Then heigh-ho, the holly!
　　This life is most jolly.

Freeze, freeze, thou bitter sky,
That dost not bite so nigh   185
　　As benefits forgot;
Though thou the waters warp,   187
Thy sting is not so sharp
　　As friend remembered not.
Heigh-ho, sing heigh-ho, unto the green holly.
Most friendship is feigning, most loving mere folly.
　　Then heigh-ho, the holly!
　　This life is most jolly.

DUKE SENIOR
If that you were the good Sir Rowland's son,
As you have whispered faithfully you were
And as mine eye doth his effigies witness   196
Most truly limned and living in your face,   197
Be truly welcome hither. I am the duke
That loved your father. The residue of your fortune,   199
Go to my cave and tell me.—Good old man,
Thou art right welcome as thy master is.—
Support him by the arm. Give me your hand,
And let me all your fortunes understand.   *Exeunt.*   203

❖

179 **rude** rough   180 **holly** (An emblem of mirth.)   185 **nigh** near (to the heart)   187 **warp** freeze   196 **effigies** likeness, portrait   197 **limned** painted, portrayed   199 **The . . . fortune** the rest of your adventure
203 s.d. **Exeunt** (The table must be removed at this point.)

3.1 *Enter Duke [Frederick], Lords, and Oliver.*

DUKE FREDERICK
Not see him since? Sir, sir, that cannot be.
But were I not the better part made mercy,   2
I should not seek an absent argument   3
Of my revenge, thou present. But look to it: 4
Find out thy brother, wheresoe'er he is;
Seek him with candle; bring him dead or living   6
Within this twelvemonth, or turn thou no more   7
To seek a living in our territory.
Thy lands and all things that thou dost call thine
Worth seizure do we seize into our hands,
Till thou canst quit thee by thy brother's mouth   11
Of what we think against thee.

OLIVER
O, that Your Highness knew my heart in this!
I never loved my brother in my life.

DUKE FREDERICK
More villain thou.—Well, push him out of doors,
And let my officers of such a nature   16
Make an extent upon his house and lands.   17
Do this expediently, and turn him going.   *Exeunt.* 18

❖

3.2 *Enter Orlando [with a paper].*

ORLANDO
Hang there, my verse, in witness of my love;
  And thou, thrice-crownèd queen of night, survey   2
With thy chaste eye, from thy pale sphere above,

3.1. Location: Duke Frederick's court.
2 better greater. **made** made of **3 argument** subject (i.e., I would not seek revenge on Orlando) **4 thou present** i.e., with you here to feed my revenge **6 Seek . . . candle** (See Luke 15:8.) **7 turn** return **11 quit** acquit. **by . . . mouth** i.e., by Orlando's direct testimony **16 of such a nature** i.e., who attend to such duties **17 extent** writ of seizure
18 expediently expeditiously. **turn him going** send him packing

3.2. Location: The forest.
2 thrice-crownèd queen i.e., Diana in the three aspects of her divinity: as Luna or Cynthia, goddess of the moon; as Diana, goddess on earth; and as Hecate or Proserpina, goddess in the lower world

Thy huntress' name that my full life doth sway.   4
O Rosalind! These trees shall be my books,
  And in their barks my thoughts I'll character,   6
That every eye which in this forest looks
  Shall see thy virtue witnessed everywhere.
Run, run, Orlando, carve on every tree
The fair, the chaste, and unexpressive she.   *Exit.* 10

Enter Corin and [Touchstone the] Clown.

CORIN And how like you this shepherd's life, Master
  Touchstone?
TOUCHSTONE Truly, shepherd, in respect of itself, it is a 13
  good life; but in respect that it is a shepherd's life, it is
  naught. In respect that it is solitary, I like it very well; 15
  but in respect that it is private, it is a very vile life.
  Now in respect it is in the fields, it pleaseth me well;
  but in respect it is not in the court, it is tedious. As it
  is a spare life, look you, it fits my humor well; but as 19
  there is no more plenty in it, it goes much against my
  stomach. Hast any philosophy in thee, shepherd?
CORIN No more but that I know the more one sickens
  the worse at ease he is; and that he that wants money,
  means, and content is without three good friends; that
  the property of rain is to wet and fire to burn; that
  good pasture makes fat sheep and that a great cause
  of the night is lack of the sun; that he that hath learned
  no wit by nature nor art may complain of good breed- 28
  ing or comes of a very dull kindred.   29
TOUCHSTONE Such a one is a natural philosopher. Wast
  ever in court, shepherd?
CORIN No, truly.
TOUCHSTONE Then thou art damned.
CORIN Nay, I hope.
TOUCHSTONE Truly, thou art damned, like an ill-roasted
  egg, all on one side.
CORIN For not being at court? Your reason.

---

4 Thy huntress' i.e., Rosalind's, who is here thought of as a chaste
huntress accompanying Diana, patroness of the hunt. **sway** control
6 character inscribe **10 unexpressive** inexpressible **13 in respect of
itself** considered in and for itself **15 naught** vile, wicked **19 spare**
frugal. **humor** temperament **28 wit** wisdom. **art** study
28–29 complain . . . breeding lament the lack of good breeding

TOUCHSTONE   Why, if thou never wast at court, thou
never sawst good manners; if thou never sawst good 39
manners, then thy manners must be wicked; and 40
wickedness is sin, and sin is damnation. Thou art in
a parlous state, shepherd. 42

CORIN   Not a whit, Touchstone. Those that are good
manners at the court are as ridiculous in the country
as the behavior of the country is most mockable at the
court. You told me you salute not at the court but you 46
kiss your hands; that courtesy would be uncleanly, if 47
courtiers were shepherds.

TOUCHSTONE   Instance, briefly; come, instance. 49

CORIN   Why, we are still handling our ewes, and their 50
fells you know are greasy. 51

TOUCHSTONE   Why, do not your courtier's hands sweat?
And is not the grease of a mutton as wholesome as the
sweat of a man? Shallow, shallow. A better instance, I
say; come.

CORIN   Besides, our hands are hard.

TOUCHSTONE   Your lips will feel them the sooner. Shallow again. A more sounder instance, come.

CORIN   And they are often tarred over with the surgery 59
of our sheep; and would you have us kiss tar? The
courtier's hands are perfumed with civet. 61

TOUCHSTONE   Most shallow man! Thou worms' meat, in 62
respect of a good piece of flesh indeed! Learn of the 63
wise, and perpend: civet is of a baser birth than tar, the 64
very uncleanly flux of a cat. Mend the instance, shep- 65
herd.

CORIN   You have too courtly a wit for me. I'll rest.

TOUCHSTONE   Wilt thou rest damned? God help thee,
shallow man! God make incision in thee! Thou art 69
raw. 70

39, 40 manners (1) etiquette (2) morals   **42 parlous** perilous   **46–47 but
you kiss** without kissing   **49 Instance** proof   **50 still** always   **51 fells**
skins with the wool, or fleeces   **59 tarred over** anointed with tar on
their cuts and sores   **61 civet** (A perfume derived from the civet cat, as
Touchstone points out.)   **62 worms' meat** food for worms, i.e., subject
to decay of the flesh   **63 respect of** comparison with   **64 perpend**
reflect, consider   **65 flux** secretion.   **Mend** improve   **69 incision** a cut,
perhaps for the purpose of letting blood (here, to let out folly); or for
seasoning as raw meat is scored and salted before cooking   **70 raw**
inexperienced (with a play on "sore," requiring surgery)

CORIN   Sir, I am a true laborer: I earn that I eat, get that 71
  I wear, owe no man hate, envy no man's happiness,
  glad of other men's good, content with my harm, and 73
  the greatest of my pride is to see my ewes graze and
  my lambs suck.

TOUCHSTONE   That is another simple sin in you, to bring
  the ewes and the rams together and to offer to get your 77
  living by the copulation of cattle; to be bawd to a bell- 78
  wether, and to betray a she-lamb of a twelvemonth to
  a crooked-pated old cuckoldly ram, out of all reason- 80
  able match. If thou beest not damned for this, the devil
  himself will have no shepherds; I cannot see else how
  thou shouldst scape.   83

CORIN   Here comes young Master Ganymede, my new
  mistress's brother.

  Enter Rosalind [with a paper, reading].

ROSALIND
      "From the east to western Ind,   86
      No jewel is like Rosalind.
      Her worth, being mounted on the wind,
      Through all the world bears Rosalind.
      All the pictures fairest lined   90
      Are but black to Rosalind.   91
      Let no face be kept in mind
      But the fair of Rosalind."

TOUCHSTONE   I'll rhyme you so eight years together,   94
  dinners and suppers and sleeping hours excepted. It   95
  is the right butter-women's rank to market.   96

ROSALIND   Out, Fool!

TOUCHSTONE   For a taste:
      If a hart do lack a hind,
      Let him seek out Rosalind.
      If the cat will after kind,   101

---

71 that what   **73 content . . . harm** patient with my ill fortune   **77 offer**
undertake   **78 cattle** livestock   **80 crooked-pated** with crooked horns.
cuckoldly i.e., horned like a cuckold, or husband of an unfaithful
wife.   **out of** contrary to   **83 scape** escape   **86 Ind** Indies   **90 lined**
drawn   **91 black** dark-complexioned. (Thought to be ugly.)   **94 together**
without stop   **95–96 It is . . . market** i.e., the rhymes, all alike, follow
each other precisely like a line of butter-women or dairywomen jogging
along to market   **101 after kind** follow its natural instinct

So be sure will Rosalind.
Wintered garments must be lined,   103
So must slender Rosalind.
They that reap must sheaf and bind;   105
Then to cart with Rosalind.   106
Sweetest nut hath sourest rind;
Such a nut is Rosalind.
He that sweetest rose will find
Must find love's prick and Rosalind.   110

This is the very false gallop of verses. Why do you 111
infect yourself with them?

ROSALIND   Peace, you dull fool! I found them on a tree.

TOUCHSTONE   Truly, the tree yields bad fruit.

ROSALIND   I'll graft it with you, and then I shall graft it 115
with a medlar. Then it will be the earliest fruit i' the 116
country; for you'll be rotten ere you be half ripe, and
that's the right virtue of the medlar.   118

TOUCHSTONE   You have said; but whether wisely or no,
let the forest judge.

Enter Celia, with a writing.

ROSALIND   Peace, here comes my sister, reading. Stand
aside.

CELIA [*Reads*]
    "Why should this a desert be?
        For it is unpeopled? No!
    Tongues I'll hang on every tree,
        That shall civil sayings show: 126
    Some, how brief the life of man
        Runs his erring pilgrimage,   128
    That the stretching of a span   129
        Buckles in his sum of age;   130

---

103 Wintered prepared for winter   **105 sheaf and bind** tie in a bundle
106 to cart (1) onto the harvest cart (2) onto the cart used to carry
delinquent women through the streets, exposing them to public ridi-
cule   **110 prick** thorn. (With bawdy suggestion, as elsewhere in Touchstone's verses: *will after kind*, etc.)   **111 false gallop** canter   **115 you**
(with a pun on *yew*)   **116 medlar** a fruit like a small brown-skinned
apple that is eaten when it starts to decay (with a pun on *meddler*)
118 right virtue true quality   **126 civil sayings** maxims of civilized
life   **128 his erring** its wandering   **129 That . . . span** so that the dis-
tance across an open-spread hand   **130 Buckles in** encompasses

> Some, of violated vows
>   Twixt the souls of friend and friend;
> But upon the fairest boughs,
>   Or at every sentence end,
> Will I 'Rosalinda' write,
>   Teaching all that read to know
> The quintessence of every sprite   137
>   Heaven would in little show.   138
> Therefore heaven Nature charged
>   That one body should be filled
> With all graces wide-enlarged.   141
>   Nature presently distilled
> Helen's cheek, but not her heart,   143
>   Cleopatra's majesty,
> Atalanta's better part,   145
>   Sad Lucretia's modesty.   146
> Thus Rosalind of many parts
>   By heavenly synod was devised,   148
> Of many faces, eyes, and hearts,
>   To have the touches dearest prized.   150
> Heaven would that she these gifts should have,
> And I to live and die her slave."

ROSALIND O most gentle Jupiter, what tedious homily 153
of love have you wearied your parishioners withal,
and never cried, "Have patience, good people!"

CELIA How now? Back, friends. Shepherd, go off a lit- 156
tle. Go with him, sirrah. 157

137 quintessence highest perfection. (Literally, the fifth essence or ele-
ment of the medieval alchemists, purer even than fire.) **sprite** spirit
138 in little in small space, i.e., in one person, Rosalind. (Alludes probably
to the idea of man as the microcosm; the heavenly bodies would be
composed of quintessence, which is here thought of as the supreme
quality of a person.) **141 wide-enlarged** widely distributed (i.e., that had
been spread through the world but now are concentrated in Rosalind)
143 Helen's . . . heart i.e., the beauty of Helen of Troy but not her false
heart **145 Atalanta's better part** i.e., her fleetness of foot, not her scorn-
fulness and greed. (She refused to marry any man who was unable to
defeat her in a foot race and, when challenged by Hippomenes, lost to
him because Hippomenes dropped in her way three apples of the Hes-
perides.) **146 Lucretia** honorable Roman lady raped by Tarquin (whose
story Shakespeare tells in *The Rape of Lucrece*) **148 synod** assembly
150 touches traits **153 Jupiter** (Often emended to *pulpiter*.) **156 Back**
i.e., move back, away. (Addressed to Corin and Touchstone.) **157 sirrah**
(Form of address to inferiors; here, Touchstone.)

TOUCHSTONE   Come, shepherd, let us make an honorable retreat, though not with bag and baggage, yet   159
with scrip and scrippage.   *Exit [with Corin].*   160

CELIA   Didst thou hear these verses?

ROSALIND   O, yes, I heard them all, and more too, for
some of them had in them more feet than the verses
would bear.

CELIA   That's no matter. The feet might bear the verses.

ROSALIND   Ay, but the feet were lame and could not
bear themselves without the verse and therefore stood   167
lamely in the verse.

CELIA   But didst thou hear without wondering how thy
name should be hanged and carved upon these trees?

ROSALIND   I was seven of the nine days out of the won-   171
der before you came; for look here what I found on a   172
palm tree. I was never so berhymed since Pythagoras'   173
time, that I was an Irish rat, which I can hardly re-   174
member.

CELIA   Trow you who hath done this?   176

ROSALIND   Is it a man?

CELIA   And a chain that you once wore about his neck.   178
Change you color?

ROSALIND   I prithee, who?

CELIA   O Lord, Lord, it is a hard matter for friends to   181
meet; but mountains may be removed with earth-   182
quakes and so encounter.   183

ROSALIND   Nay, but who is it?

CELIA   Is it possible?

ROSALIND   Nay, I prithee now with most petitionary ve-
hemence, tell me who it is.

CELIA   O wonderful, wonderful, and most wonderful
wonderful! And yet again wonderful, and after that,

159 bag and baggage i.e., equipment appropriate to a retreating army
160 scrip and scrippage shepherd's pouch and its contents   **167 without** (1) without the help of (2) outside   **171–172 seven . . . wonder** (A
reference to the common phrase "a nine days' wonder.")   **173 Pythagoras** Greek philosopher credited with the doctrine of the transmigration
of souls   **174 that** when.   **Irish rat** (Refers to a current belief that Irish
enchanters could rhyme rats and other animals to death.)   **176 Trow
you** have you any idea   **178 And a chain** i.e., and with a chain
181–183 friends . . . encounter (A playful inversion of the proverb,
"Friends may meet, but mountains never greet." Celia appears to be
teasing Rosalind's eagerness to meet Orlando.)   **removed with** moved by

out of all whooping!   190

ROSALIND Good my complexion! Dost thou think, 191
though I am caparisoned like a man, I have a doublet 192
and hose in my disposition? One inch of delay more
is a South Sea of discovery. I prithee, tell me who is it 194
quickly, and speak apace. I would thou couldst stam-
mer, that thou mightst pour this concealed man out of
thy mouth, as wine comes out of a narrow-mouthed
bottle, either too much at once or none at all. I prithee,
take the cork out of thy mouth that I may drink thy
tidings.

CELIA So you may put a man in your belly.   201

ROSALIND Is he of God's making? What manner of 202
man? Is his head worth a hat, or his chin worth a
beard?

CELIA Nay, he hath but a little beard.

ROSALIND Why, God will send more, if the man will be
thankful. Let me stay the growth of his beard, if thou 207
delay me not the knowledge of his chin.

CELIA It is young Orlando, that tripped up the wrestler's
heels and your heart both in an instant.

ROSALIND Nay, but the devil take mocking. Speak sad 211
brow and true maid.   212

CELIA I' faith, coz, 'tis he.

ROSALIND Orlando?

CELIA Orlando.

ROSALIND Alas the day, what shall I do with my doublet and hose? What did he when thou sawst him?
What said he? How looked he? Wherein went he? 218
What makes he here? Did he ask for me? Where re- 219
mains he? How parted he with thee? And when shalt
thou see him again? Answer me in one word.

CELIA You must borrow me Gargantua's mouth first; 222

190 out . . . whooping beyond all whooping, i.e., power to utter
191 Good my complexion O my (feminine) temperament, my woman's
curiosity 192 caparisoned bedecked. (Usually said of a horse.) 194 a
South Sea of discovery i.e., as tedious as the long delays on exploratory
voyages to the South Seas 201 belly (1) stomach (2) womb 202 of
God's making i.e., a real man, not of his tailor's making 207 stay wait
for 211–212 sad . . . maid seriously and truthfully 218 Wherein went
he in what clothes was he dressed 219 makes does 222 Gargantua's
mouth (Gargantua is the giant of popular literature who, in Rabelais's
novel, swallowed five pilgrims in a salad.)

'tis a word too great for any mouth of this age's size.
To say ay and no to these particulars is more than to 224
answer in a catechism.   225

ROSALIND   But doth he know that I am in this forest and
in man's apparel? Looks he as freshly as he did the
day he wrestled?

CELIA   It is as easy to count atomies as to resolve the 229
propositions of a lover. But take a taste of my finding 230
him, and relish it with good observance. I found him 231
under a tree, like a dropped acorn.

ROSALIND   It may well be called Jove's tree, when it 233
drops forth such fruit.

CELIA   Give me audience, good madam.

ROSALIND   Proceed.

CELIA   There lay he, stretched along, like a wounded
knight.

ROSALIND   Though it be pity to see such a sight, it well
becomes the ground.   240

CELIA   Cry "holla" to thy tongue, I prithee; it curvets 241
unseasonably. He was furnished like a hunter.   242

ROSALIND   O, ominous! He comes to kill my heart.   243

CELIA   I would sing my song without a burden. Thou 244
bring'st me out of tune.   245

ROSALIND   Do you not know I am a woman? When I
think, I must speak. Sweet, say on.

     Enter Orlando and Jaques.

CELIA   You bring me out.—Soft, comes he not here?

ROSALIND   'Tis he. Slink by, and note him.
                   [They stand aside and listen.]

JAQUES   I thank you for your company, but, good faith,
I had as lief have been myself alone.

ORLANDO   And so had I; but yet, for fashion's sake, I
thank you too for your society.

224–225 To . . . catechism to give even yes and no answers to these questions would take longer than to go through the catechism (i.e., the formal
questioning used in the Church to teach the principles of faith)
229 atomies motes, specks of dirt   **230 propositions** questions   **231 relish
it** heighten its pleasant taste.   **observance** attention   **233 Jove's tree** the
oak   **240 becomes** adorns   **241 holla** stop.   **curvets** prances
242 furnished equipped, dressed   **243 heart** (with pun on *hart*)
244 burden undersong, bass part   **244–245 Thou bring'st** you put

JAQUES   God b' wi' you. Let's meet as little as we can.   254

ORLANDO   I do desire we may be better strangers.

JAQUES   I pray you, mar no more trees with writing love songs in their barks.

ORLANDO   I pray you, mar no more of my verses with reading them ill-favoredly.   259

JAQUES   Rosalind is your love's name?

ORLANDO   Yes, just.   261

JAQUES   I do not like her name.

ORLANDO   There was no thought of pleasing you when she was christened.

JAQUES   What stature is she of?

ORLANDO   Just as high as my heart.

JAQUES   You are full of pretty answers. Have you not been acquainted with goldsmiths' wives, and conned   268
them out of rings?   269

ORLANDO   Not so; but I answer you right painted cloth,   270
from whence you have studied your questions.

JAQUES   You have a nimble wit; I think 'twas made of Atalanta's heels. Will you sit down with me? And we   273
two will rail against our mistress the world and all our misery.

ORLANDO   I will chide no breather in the world but my-   276
self, against whom I know most faults.

JAQUES   The worst fault you have is to be in love.

ORLANDO   'Tis a fault I will not change for your best virtue. I am weary of you.

JAQUES   By my troth, I was seeking for a fool when I found you.

ORLANDO   He is drowned in the brook. Look but in, and you shall see him.

JAQUES   There I shall see mine own figure.

ORLANDO   Which I take to be either a fool or a cipher.   286

JAQUES   I'll tarry no longer with you. Farewell, good Seigneur Love.

254 God b' wi' you God be with you, i.e., good-bye   **259 ill-favoredly**
unsympathetically   **261 just** just so   **268 conned** memorized   **269 rings**
(Verses or "posies" were often inscribed in rings.)   **270 right** true, perfect.   **painted cloth** canvas painted with pictures and mottoes (frequently
scriptural), hence a ready source of commonplaces   **273 Atalanta's heels**
(See above, l. 145, note.)   **276 breather** living being   **286 cipher** (1) nonentity (2) figure

ORLANDO I am glad of your departure. Adieu, good
Monsieur Melancholy.   [*Exit Jaques.*]

ROSALIND [*Aside to Celia*] I will speak to him like a
saucy lackey and under that habit play the knave with 292
him.—Do you hear, forester?

ORLANDO Very well. What would you?

ROSALIND I pray you, what is 't o'clock?

ORLANDO You should ask me what time o' day. There's
no clock in the forest.

ROSALIND Then there is no true lover in the forest, else
sighing every minute and groaning every hour would
detect the lazy foot of Time as well as a clock.   300

ORLANDO And why not the swift foot of Time? Had not
that been as proper?

ROSALIND By no means, sir. Time travels in divers
paces with divers persons. I'll tell you who Time ambles withal, who Time trots withal, who Time gallops 305
withal, and who he stands still withal.

ORLANDO I prithee, who doth he trot withal?

ROSALIND Marry, he trots hard with a young maid be- 308
tween the contract of her marriage and the day it is
solemnized. If the interim be but a se'nnight, Time's 310
pace is so hard that it seems the length of seven year.

ORLANDO Who ambles Time withal?

ROSALIND With a priest that lacks Latin and a rich man
that hath not the gout, for the one sleeps easily because he cannot study and the other lives merrily because he feels no pain, the one lacking the burden of
lean and wasteful learning, the other knowing no bur- 317
den of heavy tedious penury. These Time ambles
withal.

ORLANDO Who doth he gallop withal?

ROSALIND With a thief to the gallows, for though he go 321
as softly as foot can fall, he thinks himself too soon 322
there.

ORLANDO Who stays it still withal?

ROSALIND With lawyers in the vacation; for they sleep
between term and term, and then they perceive not 326
how Time moves.

292 habit guise   **300 detect** reveal   **305 withal** with   **308 hard** slowly,
with uneven pace   **310 se'nnight** week   **317 wasteful** making one waste
away   **321–322 go as softly** walk as slowly   **326 term** court session

ORLANDO   Where dwell you, pretty youth?

ROSALIND   With this shepherdess, my sister; here in the
skirts of the forest, like fringe upon a petticoat.

ORLANDO   Are you native of this place?

ROSALIND   As the coney that you see dwell where she is   332
kindled.   333

ORLANDO   Your accent is something finer than you
could purchase in so removed a dwelling.   335

ROSALIND   I have been told so of many. But indeed an
old religious uncle of mine taught me to speak, who   337
was in his youth an inland man, one that knew court-   338
ship too well, for there he fell in love. I have heard him   339
read many lectures against it, and I thank God I am
not a woman, to be touched with so many giddy of-   341
fences as he hath generally taxed their whole sex
withal.

ORLANDO   Can you remember any of the principal evils
that he laid to the charge of women?

ROSALIND   There were none principal; they were all like
one another as halfpence are, every one fault seeming
monstrous till his fellow fault came to match it.

ORLANDO   I prithee, recount some of them.

ROSALIND   No, I will not cast away my physic but on
those that are sick. There is a man haunts the forest
that abuses our young plants with carving "Rosalind"
on their barks, hangs odes upon hawthorns, and ele-
gies on brambles, all, forsooth, deifying the name of
Rosalind. If I could meet that fancymonger, I would   355
give him some good counsel, for he seems to have the
quotidian of love upon him.   357

ORLANDO   I am he that is so love-shaked. I pray you, tell
me your remedy.

ROSALIND   There is none of my uncle's marks upon you.
He taught me how to know a man in love, in which
cage of rushes I am sure you are not prisoner.   362

ORLANDO   What were his marks?

332 **coney** rabbit   333 **kindled** littered, born   335 **purchase** acquire.
removed remote   337 **religious** i.e., member of a religious order
338 **inland** from a center of civilization   338–339 **courtship** (1) wooing
(2) knowledge of courtly manners   341 **touched** tainted   355 **fancymonger** dealer or advertiser of love   357 **quotidian** fever recurring
daily. (See *love-shaked*, l. 358).   362 **cage of rushes** i.e., flimsy prison

ROSALIND   A lean cheek, which you have not; a blue eye 364
and sunken, which you have not; an unquestionable 365
spirit, which you have not; a beard neglected, which
you have not—but I pardon you for that, for simply 367
your having in beard is a younger brother's revenue. 368
Then your hose should be ungartered, your bonnet un- 369
banded, your sleeve unbuttoned, your shoe untied, 370
and everything about you demonstrating a careless
desolation. But you are no such man; you are rather
point-device in your accoutrements, as loving your- 373
self, than seeming the lover of any other.

ORLANDO   Fair youth, I would I could make thee believe
I love.

ROSALIND   Me believe it? You may as soon make her
that you love believe it, which I warrant she is apter
to do than to confess she does. That is one of the
points in the which women still give the lie to their 380
consciences. But in good sooth, are you he that hangs 381
the verses on the trees wherein Rosalind is so
admired?

ORLANDO   I swear to thee, youth, by the white hand of
Rosalind, I am that he, that unfortunate he.

ROSALIND   But are you so much in love as your rhymes
speak?

ORLANDO   Neither rhyme nor reason can express how
much.

ROSALIND   Love is merely a madness and, I tell you, 390
deserves as well a dark house and a whip as madmen 391
do; and the reason why they are not so punished and
cured is that the lunacy is so ordinary that the whip-
pers are in love too. Yet I profess curing it by counsel.

ORLANDO   Did you ever cure any so?

ROSALIND   Yes, one, and in this manner. He was to
imagine me his love, his mistress; and I set him every
day to woo me. At which time would I, being but a

---

364 blue eye i.e., having dark circles   **365 unquestionable** unwilling to
converse   **367–368 simply . . . revenue** what beard you have is like a
younger brother's inheritance (i.e., small)   **369–370 bonnet unbanded** hat
lacking a band around the crown   **373 point-device** faultless, correct
380 still continually   **381 good sooth** honest truth   **390 merely** utterly
391 dark . . . whip (The common treatment of lunatics.)

moonish youth, grieve, be effeminate, changeable, 399
longing and liking, proud, fantastical, apish, shallow,
inconstant, full of tears, full of smiles; for every passion
something and for no passion truly anything, as boys
and women are for the most part cattle of this color;
would now like him, now loathe him; then entertain
him, then forswear him; now weep for him, then spit
at him; that I drave my suitor from his mad humor of 406
love to a living humor of madness, which was to for- 407
swear the full stream of the world and to live in a nook
merely monastic. And thus I cured him; and this way 409
will I take upon me to wash your liver as clean as a 410
sound sheep's heart, that there shall not be one spot of
love in 't.

ORLANDO   I would not be cured, youth.

ROSALIND   I would cure you, if you would but call me
Rosalind and come every day to my cote and woo me. 415

ORLANDO   Now by the faith of my love, I will. Tell me
where it is.

ROSALIND   Go with me to it, and I'll show it you; and
by the way you shall tell me where in the forest you 419
live. Will you go?

ORLANDO   With all my heart, good youth.

ROSALIND   Nay, you must call me Rosalind.—Come, sister, will you go?   *Exeunt.*

❖

3.3   *Enter [Touchstone the] Clown, Audrey; and
        Jaques [apart].*

TOUCHSTONE   Come apace, good Audrey. I will fetch up 1
your goats, Audrey. And how, Audrey, am I the man 2
yet? Doth my simple feature content you?   3

AUDREY   Your features, Lord warrant us! What features?

---

399 **moonish** changeable   406 **drave** drove   406–407 **mad . . . madness**
mad fancy of love to a real madness   409 **merely** utterly   410 **liver** (Supposed seat of the emotions, especially love.)   415 **cote** cottage   419 **by** on

3.3. Location: The forest.
1 **apace** quickly   2 **And how** i.e., what do you say   3 **simple feature**
plain appearance. (But Audrey does not understand.)

TOUCHSTONE I am here with thee and thy goats, as the
most capricious poet, honest Ovid, was among the 6
Goths.   7

JAQUES [*Aside*] O knowledge ill-inhabited, worse than 8
Jove in a thatched house!   9

TOUCHSTONE When a man's verses cannot be under- 10
stood, nor a man's good wit seconded with the for- 11
ward child, understanding, it strikes a man more dead 12
than a great reckoning in a little room. Truly, I would 13
the gods had made thee poetical.

AUDREY I do not know what "poetical" is. Is it honest
in deed and word? Is it a true thing?

TOUCHSTONE No, truly; for the truest poetry is the most
feigning, and lovers are given to poetry, and what 18
they swear in poetry may be said as lovers they do 19
feign.

AUDREY Do you wish then that the gods had made me
poetical?

TOUCHSTONE I do, truly; for thou swear'st to me thou
art honest. Now, if thou wert a poet, I might have 24
some hope thou didst feign.   25

AUDREY Would you not have me honest?

TOUCHSTONE No, truly, unless thou wert hard-favored; 27
for honesty coupled to beauty is to have honey a sauce 28
to sugar.

JAQUES [*Aside*] A material fool!   30

AUDREY Well, I am not fair, and therefore I pray the
gods make me honest.

6 capricious witty, fanciful. (Derived from Latin *caper*, male goat; hence,
"goatish, lascivious.") **7 Goths** (with pun on *goats;* the two words were
pronounced alike) **8 ill-inhabited** ill-lodged **9 Jove . . . house** (An allusion to Ovid's *Metamorphoses* 8, containing the story of Jupiter and
Mercury lodging disguised in the humble cottage of Baucis and Phile-
mon.) **10–11 verses . . . understood** (Ovid's verses were misunderstood by
the barbaric Goths among whom he lived in exile, just as Touchstone's
wit is misunderstood by Audrey.) **11 seconded with** supported by
11–12 forward precocious **13 great . . . room** exorbitant charge for
refreshment or lodging in a cramped tavern room. (Some scholars see in
this passage an allusion to the death of Christopher Marlowe, who was
stabbed by Ingram Frysar at an inn in Deptford in a quarrel over a tavern
reckoning, May 30, 1593.) **18 feigning** inventive, imaginative. (But Touchstone plays on the sense of "false, lying.") **19 may be said** i.e., it may be
said **24 honest** chaste **25 feign** (1) pretend (2) desire **27 hard-favored**
ugly **28 honesty** chastity **30 material** full of sense

TOUCHSTONE Truly, and to cast away honesty upon a
foul slut were to put good meat into an unclean dish. 34

AUDREY I am not a slut, though I thank the gods I am
foul.

TOUCHSTONE Well, praised be the gods for thy foulness!
Sluttishness may come hereafter. But be it as it may
be, I will marry thee, and to that end I have been with
Sir Oliver Mar-text, the vicar of the next village, who 40
hath promised to meet me in this place of the forest
and to couple us.

JAQUES [*Aside*] I would fain see this meeting. 43

AUDREY Well, the gods give us joy!

TOUCHSTONE Amen. A man may, if he were of a fearful
heart, stagger in this attempt; for here we have no 46
temple but the wood, no assembly but horn-beasts. 47
But what though? Courage! As horns are odious, they 48
are necessary. It is said, "Many a man knows no end 49
of his goods." Right! Many a man has good horns and 50
knows no end of them. Well, that is the dowry of his 51
wife; 'tis none of his own getting. Horns? Even so. 52
Poor men alone? No, no, the noblest deer hath them
as huge as the rascal. Is the single man therefore 54
blessed? No; as a walled town is more worthier than a
village, so is the forehead of a married man more honorable than the bare brow of a bachelor; and by how
much defense is better than no skill, by so much is a 58
horn more precious than to want. 59

Enter Sir Oliver Mar-text.

Here comes Sir Oliver. Sir Oliver Mar-text, you are well
met. Will you dispatch us here under this tree, or shall 61
we go with you to your chapel?

SIR OLIVER Is there none here to give the woman?

34 foul ugly   **40 Sir** (Courtesy title for a clergyman.)   **43 fain** gladly
46 stagger hesitate   **47 horn-beasts** (Alludes to the joke about cuckolds
having horns.)   **48 what though** what though it be so.   **As** though
49 necessary unavoidable   **49–50 knows . . . goods** thinks there will be
no end to his wealth   **51 knows . . . them** i.e., doesn't realize he has
pointed horns on his brow.   **dowry** marriage gift   **52 getting** (1) obtain-
ing (2) begetting (since his wife's children will not be his)   **54 rascal**
deer that are lean and out of season   **58 defense** the art of self-
defense   **59 than to want** i.e., than to be without a horn   **61 dispatch us**
finish off our business

TOUCHSTONE I will not take her on gift of any man.

SIR OLIVER   Truly, she must be given, or the marriage is
   not lawful.

JAQUES [*Advancing*]   Proceed, proceed. I'll give her.

TOUCHSTONE   Good even, good Master What-ye-call-'t.
   How do you, sir? You are very well met. God 'ild you 69
   for your last company. I am very glad to see you. Even
   a toy in hand here, sir.—Nay, pray be covered.   71

JAQUES   Will you be married, motley?

TOUCHSTONE   As the ox hath his bow, sir, the horse his 73
   curb, and the falcon her bells, so man hath his desires; 74
   and as pigeons bill, so wedlock would be nibbling.   75

JAQUES   And will you, being a man of your breeding,
   be married under a bush like a beggar? Get you to   77
   church, and have a good priest that can tell you what   78
   marriage is. This fellow will but join you together as   79
   they join wainscot; then one of you will prove a
   shrunk panel and, like green timber, warp, warp.

TOUCHSTONE [*Aside*]   I am not in the mind but I were 82
   better to be married of him than of another, for he is   83
   not like to marry me well; and not being well married,
   it will be a good excuse for me hereafter to leave my
   wife.

JAQUES   Go thou with me, and let me counsel thee.

TOUCHSTONE   Come, sweet Audrey. We must be married, or we must live in bawdry. Farewell, good Master Oliver; not

           "O sweet Oliver,   91
            O brave Oliver,
       Leave me not behind thee";
but

           "Wind away,   95
            Begone, I say,

---

69 'ild you yield you, reward you   **71 a toy in hand** a trifle to be attended to.   **be covered** put on your hat, i.e., no need to show respect.
(Perhaps said to Audrey, or perhaps to Jaques, who may have removed
his hat in deference to the ceremony.)   **73 bow** yoke   **74 curb** chain or
strap under the horse's jaw used to control it.   **bells** (attached to a
falcon's leg to warn its prey)   **75 bill** peck   **77 under a bush** i.e., by a
"hedge-priest," an uneducated clergyman   **78–79 tell . . . is** expound
the obligations of marriage   **82–83 I am . . . better** I do not know but
that it would be better for me   **83 of** by   **91–97 O . . . thee** (Phrases
from a current ballad.)   **95 Wind** wander

I will not to wedding with thee."

        [Exeunt Jaques, Touchstone, and Audrey.]

SIR OLIVER 'Tis no matter. Ne'er a fantastical knave of 98
them all shall flout me out of my calling.   *Exit.*

❖

3.4   *Enter Rosalind and Celia.*

ROSALIND Never talk to me; I will weep.

CELIA Do, I prithee, but yet have the grace to consider
that tears do not become a man.

ROSALIND But have I not cause to weep?

CELIA As good cause as one would desire; therefore
weep.

ROSALIND His very hair is of the dissembling color.   7

CELIA Something browner than Judas's. Marry, his 8
kisses are Judas's own children.   9

ROSALIND I' faith, his hair is of a good color.

CELIA An excellent color. Your chestnut was ever the 11
only color.

ROSALIND And his kissing is as full of sanctity as the
touch of holy bread.   14

CELIA He hath bought a pair of cast lips of Diana. A 15
nun of winter's sisterhood kisses not more religiously; 16
the very ice of chastity is in them.

ROSALIND But why did he swear he would come this
morning, and comes not?

CELIA Nay, certainly, there is no truth in him.

ROSALIND Do you think so?

CELIA Yes, I think he is not a pickpurse nor a horse-
stealer, but for his verity in love, I do think him as

---

98 fantastical affected

3.4. Location: The forest.
7 the dissembling color i.e., reddish, traditionally the color of Judas's
hair **8 Something** somewhat **9 Judas's own children** i.e., false, betray-
ing **11 Your chestnut** i.e., this chestnut color that people talk about
14 holy bread ordinary leavened bread which was blessed after the Eu-
charist and distributed to those who had not communed **15 cast** cast
off, discarded, once belonging to; or, cast, molded. **Diana** goddess of
chastity **16 of winter's sisterhood** i.e., devoted to barrenness and cold

    concave as a covered goblet or a worm-eaten nut.   24

ROSALIND Not true in love?

CELIA Yes, when he is in, but I think he is not in.

ROSALIND You have heard him swear downright he was.

CELIA "Was" is not "is." Besides, the oath of a lover is no stronger than the word of a tapster; they are both the confirmer of false reckonings. He attends here in 31 the forest on the Duke your father.

ROSALIND I met the Duke yesterday and had much question with him. He asked me of what parentage I 34 was. I told him, of as good as he; so he laughed and let me go. But what talk we of fathers, when there is such 36 a man as Orlando?

CELIA O, that's a brave man! He writes brave verses, 38 speaks brave words, swears brave oaths, and breaks them bravely, quite traverse, athwart the heart of his 40 lover, as a puny tilter, that spurs his horse but on 41 one side, breaks his staff like a noble goose. But all's 42 brave that youth mounts and folly guides. Who comes here?

     Enter Corin.

CORIN
Mistress and master, you have oft inquired
After the shepherd that complained of love
Who you saw sitting by me on the turf,
Praising the proud disdainful shepherdess
That was his mistress.

CELIA   Well, and what of him?

CORIN
If you will see a pageant truly played
Between the pale complexion of true love   51
And the red glow of scorn and proud disdain,

---

24 concave hollow.   **covered goblet** i.e., an empty goblet. (The cover is on only when the goblet is empty.)   **31 false reckonings** (Tapsters, or bar-keeps, were notorious for inflating bills.)   **34 question** conversation **36 what** why   **38 brave** fine, excellent   **40 traverse** across, awry. (A term from tilting, indicating a poorly aimed thrust.)   **41 puny** inexperienced. (Literally, junior.)   **but** only   **42 noble goose** i.e., a goose-headed young nobleman   **51 pale complexion** (Sighing was believed to draw the blood from the heart.)

Go hence a little, and I shall conduct you,
If you will mark it.

ROSALIND   O, come, let us remove!   54
The sight of lovers feedeth those in love.
Bring us to this sight, and you shall say
I'll prove a busy actor in their play.   *Exeunt.*

❧

3.5   *Enter Silvius and Phoebe.*

SILVIUS
Sweet Phoebe, do not scorn me, do not, Phoebe!
Say that you love me not, but say not so
In bitterness. The common executioner,
Whose heart th' accustomed sight of death makes hard,
Falls not the ax upon the humbied neck   5
But first begs pardon. Will you sterner be   6
Than he that dies and lives by bloody drops?   7

     Enter Rosalind, Celia, and Corin [behind].

PHOEBE
I would not be thy executioner;
I fly thee, for I would not injure thee.
Thou tell'st me there is murder in mine eye.
'Tis pretty, sure, and very probable,   11
That eyes, that are the frail'st and softest things,
Who shut their coward gates on atomies,   13
Should be called tyrants, butchers, murderers!
Now I do frown on thee with all my heart,
And if mine eyes can wound, now let them kill thee.
Now counterfeit to swoon; why now fall down,
Or if thou canst not, O, for shame, for shame,
Lie not, to say mine eyes are murderers!
Now show the wound mine eye hath made in thee.
Scratch thee but with a pin, and there remains

---

54 will mark wish to see

3.5. Location: The forest.
5 Falls lets fall   **6 But first begs** without first begging   **7 dies and lives**
i.e., makes his living his life long   **11 sure** surely   **13 gates on atomies**
i.e., eyelids to protect against specks of dirt

Some scar of it; lean upon a rush,   22
The cicatrice and capable impressure   23
Thy palm some moment keeps; but now mine eyes,
Which I have darted at thee, hurt thee not,
Nor, I am sure, there is no force in eyes
That can do hurt.

SILVIUS   O dear Phoebe,
If ever—as that ever may be near—
You meet in some fresh cheek the power of fancy,   29
Then shall you know the wounds invisible
That love's keen arrows make.

PHOEBE   But till that time
Come not thou near me; and when that time comes,
Afflict me with thy mocks, pity me not,
As till that time I shall not pity thee.

ROSALIND [*Advancing*]
And why, I pray you? Who might be your mother,
That you insult, exult, and all at once,   36
Over the wretched? What though you have no beauty—   37
As, by my faith, I see no more in you   38
Than without candle may go dark to bed—   39
Must you be therefore proud and pitiless?
Why, what means this? Why do you look on me?
I see no more in you than in the ordinary   42
Of nature's sale-work.—'Od's my little life,   43
I think she means to tangle my eyes too!   44
No, faith, proud mistress, hope not after it.
'Tis not your inky brows, your black silk hair,
Your bugle eyeballs, nor your cheek of cream   47
That can entame my spirits to your worship.—   48
You foolish shepherd, wherefore do you follow her,
Like foggy south, puffing with wind and rain?   50
You are a thousand times a properer man   51
Than she a woman. 'Tis such fools as you

22 rush a marsh plant   **23 cicatrice** mark, impression.   **capable impressure** perceptible impression   **29 fancy** love   **36 all at once** i.e., all in a breath   **37 no** i.e., no more   **38–39 I see . . . bed** i.e., your beauty is not so brilliant that it will suffice to light you to bed in the dark   **42 ordinary** common run   **43 sale-work** ready-made products, i.e., not of the best quality, not distinctive.   **'Od's** may God save   **44 tangle** ensnare   **47 bugle** black and glassy   **48 to your worship** to worship of you   **50 south** south wind (from which came fog and rain; i.e., Silvius' sighs and tears)   **51 properer** handsomer

That makes the world full of ill-favored children.
'Tis not her glass, but you, that flatters her,   54
And out of you she sees herself more proper   55
Than any of her lineaments can show her.—   56
But, mistress, know yourself. Down on your knees
And thank heaven, fasting, for a good man's love!
For I must tell you friendly in your ear,
Sell when you can, you are not for all markets.
Cry the man mercy, love him, take his offer;   61
Foul is most foul, being foul to be a scoffer.—   62
So take her to thee, shepherd. Fare you well.

PHOEBE
Sweet youth, I pray you, chide a year together.   64
I had rather hear you chide than this man woo.

ROSALIND [To Phoebe]   He's fallen in love with your foulness, [To Silvius] and she'll fall in love with my anger.
If it be so, as fast as she answers thee with frowning
looks, I'll sauce her with bitter words. [To Phoebe.] Why 69
look you so upon me?

PHOEBE   For no ill will I bear you.

ROSALIND
I pray you, do not fall in love with me,
For I am falser than vows made in wine.   73
Besides, I like you not. [To Silvius.] If you will know my
  house,
'Tis at the tuft of olives here hard by.—
Will you go, sister?—Shepherd, ply her hard.—   76
Come, sister.—Shepherdess, look on him better,
And be not proud. Though all the world could see,   78
None could be so abused in sight as he.   79
Come, to our flock.   Exit [with Celia and Corin].

PHOEBE
Dead shepherd, now I find thy saw of might,   81
"Who ever loved that loved not at first sight?"   82

54 glass mirror   55 out of you i.e., with you as her mirror   56 lineaments
features   61 Cry . . . mercy beg the man's pardon   62 Foul . . . scoffer i.e.,
ugliness is most ugly when it is rough and abusive. (Plays on two meanings
of foul.)   64 together continuously   69 sauce rebuke   73 in wine while
drunk   76 ply her hard i.e., woo her energetically   78 could see i.e., could
look at you   79 abused in sight deceived through the eyes   81 Dead shepherd i.e., Christopher Marlowe, who died in 1593.   saw saying.   of might
forceful, convincing   82 Who . . . sight (From Marlowe's Hero and Leander,
Sestiad 1, 176, first published in 1598.)

SILVIUS
  Sweet Phoebe—
PHOEBE   Ha, what sayst thou, Silvius?
SILVIUS   Sweet Phoebe, pity me.
PHOEBE
  Why, I am sorry for thee, gentle Silvius.
SILVIUS
  Wherever sorrow is, relief would be.   86
  If you do sorrow at my grief in love,
  By giving love, your sorrow and my grief
  Were both extermined.   89
PHOEBE
  Thou hast my love. Is not that neighborly?   90
SILVIUS
  I would have you.
PHOEBE   Why, that were covetousness.   91
  Silvius, the time was that I hated thee,
  And yet it is not that I bear thee love;   93
  But since that thou canst talk of love so well,
  Thy company, which erst was irksome to me,   95
  I will endure, and I'll employ thee too.
  But do not look for further recompense
  Than thine own gladness that thou art employed.
SILVIUS
  So holy and so perfect is my love,
  And I in such a poverty of grace,   100
  That I shall think it a most plenteous crop
  To glean the broken ears after the man
  That the main harvest reaps. Loose now and then
  A scattered smile, and that I'll live upon.
PHOEBE
  Know'st thou the youth that spoke to me erewhile?   105
SILVIUS
  Not very well, but I have met him oft,
  And he hath bought the cottage and the bounds   107

---

86 Wherever . . . be i.e., whenever one experiences sorrow, one ought to
wish to offer relief **89 Were both extermined** would both be banished,
ended **90 Is . . . neighborly** i.e., I love you as one is supposed to love
one's neighbor or fellow Christian (as distinguished from conjugal
love) **91 covetousness** (The tenth commandment forbids coveting
anything that is your neighbor's.) **93 yet it is not** it (the time) is not yet
come **95 erst** formerly **100 poverty of grace** (i.e., love, his divinity, has
been ungracious to him) **105 erewhile** before **107 bounds** pastures

That the old carlot once was master of.   108

PHOEBE
Think not I love him, though I ask for him;
'Tis but a peevish boy—yet he talks well—
But what care I for words? Yet words do well
When he that speaks them pleases those that hear.
It is a pretty youth—not very pretty—
But sure he's proud—and yet his pride becomes him.
He'll make a proper man. The best thing in him
Is his complexion; and faster than his tongue
Did make offense, his eye did heal it up.
He is not very tall—yet for his years he's tall.
His leg is but so-so—and yet 'tis well.
There was a pretty redness in his lip,
A little riper and more lusty red
Than that mixed in his cheek; 'twas just the difference
Betwixt the constant red and mingled damask.   123
There be some women, Silvius, had they marked him
In parcels as I did, would have gone near   125
To fall in love with him; but for my part   126
I love him not nor hate him not; and yet
I have more cause to hate him than to love him.
For what had he to do to chide at me?   129
He said mine eyes were black and my hair black
And, now I am remembered, scorned at me.   131
I marvel why I answered not again.   132
But that's all one; omittance is no quittance.   133
I'll write to him a very taunting letter,
And thou shalt bear it. Wilt thou, Silvius?

SILVIUS
Phoebe, with all my heart.

PHOEBE   I'll write it straight;   136
The matter's in my head and in my heart.
I will be bitter with him and passing short.   138
Go with me, Silvius.   *Exeunt.*

❖

108 **carlot** churl, countryman   123 **mingled damask** mingled red and
white, i.e., the color of the damask rose   125 **In parcels** piece by piece,
in detail.   **gone near** come close   126 **fall** falling   129 **what . . . do**
what business had he   131 **am remembered** remember, recollect
132 **again** back   133 **But . . . quittance** i.e., but just the same, my failure
to answer him doesn't mean I won't do so later   136 **straight** immediately   138 **passing short** exceedingly curt

4.1 *Enter Rosalind and Celia, and Jaques.*

JAQUES I prithee, pretty youth, let me be better acquainted with thee.

ROSALIND They say you are a melancholy fellow.

JAQUES I am so; I do love it better than laughing.

ROSALIND Those that are in extremity of either are 5
abominable fellows and betray themselves to every
modern censure worse than drunkards. 7

JAQUES Why, 'tis good to be sad and say nothing.

ROSALIND Why then 'tis good to be a post.

JAQUES I have neither the scholar's melancholy, which
is emulation, nor the musician's, which is fantastical, 11
nor the courtier's, which is proud, nor the soldier's,
which is ambitious, nor the lawyer's, which is politic, 13
nor the lady's, which is nice, nor the lover's, which is 14
all these; but it is a melancholy of mine own, compounded of many simples, extracted from many ob- 16
jects, and indeed the sundry contemplation of my 17
travels, in which my often rumination wraps me in a
most humorous sadness. 19

ROSALIND A traveler! By my faith, you have great reason to be sad. I fear you have sold your own lands to
see other men's. Then to have seen much and to have
nothing is to have rich eyes and poor hands.

JAQUES Yes, I have gained my experience.

Enter Orlando.

ROSALIND And your experience makes you sad. I had
rather have a fool to make me merry than experience
to make me sad—and to travel for it too! 27

ORLANDO Good day and happiness, dear Rosalind!

JAQUES Nay, then, God b' wi' you, an you talk in blank 29
verse.

ROSALIND Farewell, Monsieur Traveler. Look you lisp 31

4.1. Location: The forest.
5 are . . . of go to extremes in **7 modern censure** common judgment
11 emulation envy. **fantastical** extravagantly fanciful **13 politic**
calculated **14 nice** fastidious **16 simples** ingredients (usually herbs)
of a drug **16–17 objects** i.e., objects of my observation **17 sundry**
various, collected **19 humorous** moody **27 travel** (with a pun on
travail, labor) **29 an** if **31 Look** be sure. (Said ironically.)

and wear strange suits, disable all the benefits of your 32
own country, be out of love with your nativity, and 33
almost chide God for making you that countenance
you are, or I will scarce think you have swam in a 35
gondola.   [*Exit Jaques.*] 36
Why, how now, Orlando, where have you been all
this while? You a lover? An you serve me such another
trick, never come in my sight more.

ORLANDO   My fair Rosalind, I come within an hour of
my promise.

ROSALIND   Break an hour's promise in love? He that will
divide a minute into a thousand parts and break but
a part of the thousandth part of a minute in the affairs
of love, it may be said of him that Cupid hath clapped 45
him o' the shoulder, but I'll warrant him heart-whole. 46

ORLANDO   Pardon me, dear Rosalind.

ROSALIND   Nay, an you be so tardy, come no more in
my sight. I had as lief be wooed of a snail.   49

ORLANDO   Of a snail?

ROSALIND   Ay, of a snail; for though he comes slowly,
he carries his house on his head—a better jointure, I 52
think, than you make a woman. Besides, he brings his
destiny with him.

ORLANDO   What's that?

ROSALIND   Why, horns, which such as you are fain to 56
be beholding to your wives for. But he comes armed in 57
his fortune and prevents the slander of his wife.   58

ORLANDO   Virtue is no horn maker, and my Rosalind is
virtuous.

ROSALIND   And I am your Rosalind.

CELIA   It pleases him to call you so; but he hath a Rosalind of a better leer than you.   63

ROSALIND   Come, woo me, woo me, for now I am in a
holiday humor and like enough to consent. What

32 disable depreciate, disparage   **33 nativity** i.e., place of birth
35–36 swam . . . gondola ridden in a gondola, i.e., been in Venice, where
almost all travelers go   **45–46 clapped . . . shoulder** i.e., accosted or
arrested him   **49 lief** willingly   **52 jointure** marriage settlement
56 horns (1) snails' horns (2) cuckold's horns, signs of an unfaithful
wife.   **fain** willing   **57 beholding** beholden, indebted   **57–58 armed . . .
fortune** i.e., with the horns of a cuckold, which it was his fate to earn
58 prevents forestalls, anticipates   **63 of . . . leer** better-looking

would you say to me now, an I were your very, very
Rosalind?

ORLANDO I would kiss before I spoke.

ROSALIND Nay, you were better speak first, and when
you were graveled for lack of matter, you might take 70
occasion to kiss. Very good orators, when they are out, 71
they will spit; and for lovers lacking—God warrant us!— 72
matter, the cleanliest shift is to kiss. 73

ORLANDO How if the kiss be denied?

ROSALIND Then she puts you to entreaty, and there begins new matter.

ORLANDO Who could be out, being before his beloved
mistress?

ROSALIND Marry, that should you, if I were your
mistress, or I should think my honesty ranker than 80
my wit.

ORLANDO What, of my suit? 82

ROSALIND Not out of your apparel, and yet out of your
suit. Am not I your Rosalind?

ORLANDO I take some joy to say you are, because I
would be talking of her.

ROSALIND Well, in her person I say I will not have you.

ORLANDO Then in mine own person I die.

ROSALIND No, faith, die by attorney. The poor world is 89
almost six thousand years old, and in all this time 90
there was not any man died in his own person, vide- 91
licet, in a love cause. Troilus had his brains dashed out 92
with a Grecian club, yet he did what he could to die 93

---

70 graveled stuck, at a standstill. (Literally, run aground on a shoal.)
71 out i.e., at a loss through forgetfulness or confusion **72 warrant**
defend **73 cleanliest shift** cleverest device **80 honesty** chastity.
ranker even more corrupt. (Rosalind playfully interprets *being out
before one's mistress*, l. 77–78, as not being inside her, not having sex
with her; she says her lover will have to stay out, and thus will not
obtain his suit, l. 84.) **82 of my suit** (Orlando means "out of my suit,"
at a loss for words in my wooing; but Rosalind puns on the meaning
"suit of clothes"; to be out of apparel would be to be undressed.)
89 attorney proxy **90 six . . . old** (A common figure in biblical calcula-
tion.) **91–92 videlicet** namely **92 Troilus** hero of the story of Troilus
and Cressida in which he remains faithful to her but she is faithless in
love **92–93 had . . . club** (Troilus was slain by Achilles; Rosalind's
account of his death is calculatedly unromantic.)

before, and he is one of the patterns of love. Leander, 94
he would have lived many a fair year though Hero
had turned nun, if it had not been for a hot midsummer night; for, good youth, he went but forth to
wash him in the Hellespont and being taken with the
cramp was drowned; and the foolish chroniclers of that
age found it was—Hero of Sestos. But these are all 100
lies. Men have died from time to time, and worms
have eaten them, but not for love.

ORLANDO   I would not have my right Rosalind of this 103
mind, for I protest her frown might kill me.

ROSALIND   By this hand, it will not kill a fly. But come,
now I will be your Rosalind in a more coming-on dis- 106
position, and ask me what you will, I will grant it.

ORLANDO   Then love me, Rosalind.

ROSALIND   Yes, faith, will I, Fridays and Saturdays
and all.

ORLANDO   And wilt thou have me?

ROSALIND   Ay, and twenty such.

ORLANDO   What sayest thou?

ROSALIND   Are you not good?

ORLANDO   I hope so.

ROSALIND   Why then, can one desire too much of a good
thing? Come, sister, you shall be the priest and marry
us. Give me your hand, Orlando. What do you say,
sister?

ORLANDO   Pray thee, marry us.

CELIA   I cannot say the words.

ROSALIND   You must begin, "Will you, Orlando—"

CELIA   Go to. Will you, Orlando, have to wife this Rosa- 123
lind?

ORLANDO   I will.

ROSALIND   Ay, but when?

ORLANDO   Why now, as fast as she can marry us.

ROSALIND   Then you must say, "I take thee, Rosalind,
for wife."

94 Leander hero of the story of Hero and Leander, who lost his life swim-
ming the Hellespont to visit his sweetheart. (Rosalind's account of the
cramp is more undercutting of romantic idealism.)   **100 found it was**
arrived at the verdict that the cause (of his death) was   **103 right** real
106 coming-on compliant   **123 Go to** (An exclamation of mild impatience.)

ORLANDO   I take thee, Rosalind, for wife.

ROSALIND   I might ask you for your commission; but I 131
do take thee, Orlando, for my husband. There's a girl
goes before the priest, and certainly a woman's 133
thought runs before her actions.

ORLANDO   So do all thoughts; they are winged.

ROSALIND   Now tell me how long you would have her
after you have possessed her.

ORLANDO   For ever and a day.

ROSALIND   Say "a day," without the "ever." No, no, Orlando, men are April when they woo, December when
they wed. Maids are May when they are maids, but
the sky changes when they are wives. I will be more
jealous of thee than a Barbary cock-pigeon over his 143
hen, more clamorous than a parrot against rain, more 144
newfangled than an ape, more giddy in my desires 145
than a monkey. I will weep for nothing, like Diana in 146
the fountain, and I will do that when you are disposed 147
to be merry; I will laugh like a hyena, and that when
thou art inclined to sleep.

ORLANDO   But will my Rosalind do so?

ROSALIND   By my life, she will do as I do.

ORLANDO   O, but she is wise.

ROSALIND   Or else she could not have the wit to do this;
the wiser, the waywarder. Make the doors upon a 154
woman's wit, and it will out at the casement; shut
that, and 'twill out at the keyhole; stop that, 'twill fly
with the smoke out at the chimney.

ORLANDO   A man that had a wife with such a wit, he
might say, "Wit, whither wilt?"   159

---

131 ask . . . commission ask you what authority you have for taking her
(since no one is here to give the bride away)   **133 goes before** (who) anticipates   **143 Barbary cock-pigeon** an ornamental pigeon originally from the
Barbary (north) coast of Africa. (Following Pliny, the cock-pigeon's jealousy
was often contrasted with the mildness of the hen.)   **144 against** before, in
expectation of   **145 newfangled** infatuated with novelty   **146 for nothing**
for no apparent reason   **146–147 Diana in the fountain** (Diana frequently
appeared as the centerpiece of fountains. Stow's *Survey of London* describes the setting up of a fountain with a Diana in green marble in the
year 1596.)   **154 Make** make fast, shut   **159 Wit, whither wilt** wit, where
are you going. (A common Elizabethan expression implying that one is
talking fantastically, with a wildly wandering wit.)

ROSALIND   Nay, you might keep that check for it till you   160
met your wife's wit going to your neighbor's bed.

ORLANDO   And what wit could wit have to excuse that?

ROSALIND   Marry, to say she came to seek you there.
You shall never take her without her answer, unless
you take her without her tongue. O, that woman that
cannot make her fault her husband's occasion, let her   166
never nurse her child herself, for she will breed it like
a fool!

ORLANDO   For these two hours, Rosalind, I will leave
thee.

ROSALIND   Alas, dear love, I cannot lack thee two hours!

ORLANDO   I must attend the Duke at dinner. By two
o'clock I will be with thee again.

ROSALIND   Ay, go your ways, go your ways; I knew
what you would prove. My friends told me as much,
and I thought no less. That flattering tongue of yours
won me. 'Tis but one cast away, and so, come, death!   177
Two o'clock is your hour?

ORLANDO   Ay, sweet Rosalind.

ROSALIND   By my troth, and in good earnest, and so
God mend me, and by all pretty oaths that are not
dangerous, if you break one jot of your promise or
come one minute behind your hour, I will think you
the most pathetical break-promise, and the most hol-   184
low lover, and the most unworthy of her you call Rosalind, that may be chosen out of the gross band of the   186
unfaithful. Therefore beware my censure and keep
your promise.

ORLANDO   With no less religion than if thou wert indeed   189
my Rosalind. So adieu.

ROSALIND   Well, Time is the old justice that examines all
such offenders, and let Time try. Adieu.   192

                                        Exit [*Orlando*].

CELIA   You have simply misused our sex in your love   193

---

160 **check** retort   166 **make . . . occasion** i.e., turn a defense of her own
conduct into an accusation against her husband   177 **but one cast away**
only one woman jilted   184 **pathetical** pitiable, miserable   186 **gross
band** whole troop   189 **religion** strict fidelity   192 **try** determine
193 **simply misused** absolutely slandered

prate. We must have your doublet and hose plucked 194
over your head and show the world what the bird 195
hath done to her own nest. 196

ROSALIND   O coz, coz, coz, my pretty little coz, that thou
didst know how many fathom deep I am in love! But
it cannot be sounded; my affection hath an unknown 199
bottom, like the Bay of Portugal.

CELIA   Or rather, bottomless, that as fast as you pour
affection in, it runs out.

ROSALIND   No, that same wicked bastard of Venus, that 203
was begot of thought, conceived of spleen, and born of 204
madness, that blind rascally boy that abuses every- 205
one's eyes because his own are out, let him be judge
how deep I am in love. I'll tell thee, Aliena, I cannot be
out of the sight of Orlando. I'll go find a shadow and 208
sigh till he come.

CELIA   And I'll sleep.   *Exeunt.*

❖

4.2   *Enter Jaques and Lords [dressed as] Foresters.*

JAQUES   Which is he that killed the deer?

FIRST LORD   Sir, it was I.

JAQUES   Let's present him to the Duke, like a Roman
conqueror, and it would do well to set the deer's horns
upon his head for a branch of victory. Have you no 5
song, Forester, for this purpose?

SECOND LORD   Yes, sir.

JAQUES   Sing it. 'Tis no matter how it be in tune, so it
make noise enough.   *Music.*

Song.

SECOND LORD
What shall he have that killed the deer?

194–196 We . . . nest i.e., we must expose you for what you are, a
woman, and show everyone how a woman has defamed her own kind
just as a foul bird proverbially fouls its own nest   **199 sounded** measured for depth   **203 bastard of Venus** i.e., Cupid, son of Venus and
Mercury rather than Vulcan, Venus' husband   **204 thought** fancy.
spleen i.e., impulse   **205 abuses** deceives   **208 shadow** shady spot

4.2. Location: The forest.
5 branch wreath

His leather skin and horns to wear.
Then sing him home; the rest shall bear   12
    This burden.   13
Take thou no scorn to wear the horn;   14
It was a crest ere thou wast born.
    Thy father's father wore it,
    And thy father bore it.
The horn, the horn, the lusty horn
Is not a thing to laugh to scorn.   *Exeunt.*

❖

4.3   *Enter Rosalind and Celia.*

ROSALIND How say you now? Is it not past two o'clock?
And here much Orlando!   2
CELIA I warrant you, with pure love and troubled   3
brain, he hath ta'en his bow and arrows and is gone
forth—to sleep.

    Enter Silvius [with a letter].

Look who comes here.
SILVIUS
My errand is to you, fair youth.
My gentle Phoebe bid me give you this.
                    [He gives the letter.]
I know not the contents, but as I guess
By the stern brow and waspish action
Which she did use as she was writing of it,
It bears an angry tenor. Pardon me,
I am but as a guiltless messenger.
ROSALIND *[Examining the letter]*
Patience herself would startle at this letter
And play the swaggerer. Bear this, bear all!
She says I am not fair, that I lack manners;
She calls me proud, and that she could not love me

12–13 bear This burden (1) sing this refrain (2) wear the horns that all
cuckolds must wear **14 Take . . . scorn** be not ashamed. (Alludes to
joke about cuckold's horns.)

4.3. Location: The forest.
2 much (Said ironically: A fat lot we see of Orlando!) **3 warrant** assure

Were man as rare as phoenix. 'Od's my will!   18
Her love is not the hare that I do hunt.
Why writes she so to me? Well, shepherd, well,
This is a letter of your own device.

SILVIUS
No, I protest, I know not the contents.
Phoebe did write it.

ROSALIND   Come, come, you are a fool,
And turned into the extremity of love.   24
I saw her hand; she has a leathern hand,   25
A freestone-colored hand. I verily did think   26
That her old gloves were on, but 'twas her hands;
She has a huswife's hand—but that's no matter.   28
I say she never did invent this letter;
This is a man's invention and his hand.

SILVIUS   Sure it is hers.

ROSALIND
Why, 'tis a boisterous and a cruel style,
A style for challengers. Why, she defies me,
Like Turk to Christian. Women's gentle brain
Could not drop forth such giant-rude invention,
Such Ethiop words, blacker in their effect   36
Than in their countenance. Will you hear the letter?

SILVIUS
So please you, for I never heard it yet;
Yet, heard too much of Phoebe's cruelty.

ROSALIND
She Phoebes me. Mark how the tyrant writes.   *Read.* 40
    "Art thou god to shepherd turned,
    That a maiden's heart hath burned?"
Can a woman rail thus?

SILVIUS   Call you this railing?

ROSALIND   *Read.*
    "Why, thy godhead laid apart,   45
    Warr'st thou with a woman's heart?"

18 phoenix a fabulous bird of Arabia, the only one of its kind, which
lived five hundred years, died in flames, and was reborn of its own
ashes.   **'Od's my will** God's is my will, or, may God save my will
24 turned brought   **25 leathern** leathery   **26 freestone-colored** sand-
stone-colored, brownish-yellow   **28 hand** handwriting (with play on the
ordinary meaning)   **36 Ethiop** i.e., black   **40 Phoebes** i.e., treats cru-
elly   **45 thy . . . apart** having laid aside your godhead (for human shape)

Did you ever hear such railing?
　　"Whiles the eye of man did woo me,
　　That could do no vengeance to me."   49
Meaning me a beast.   50
　　"If the scorn of your bright eyne
　　Have power to raise such love in mine,
　　Alack, in me what strange effect
　　Would they work in mild aspect!   54
　　Whiles you chid me, I did love;   55
　　How then might your prayers move!
　　He that brings this love to thee
　　Little knows this love in me;
　　And by him seal up thy mind,   59
　　Whether that thy youth and kind   60
　　Will the faithful offer take
　　Of me and all that I can make,
　　Or else by him my love deny,
　　And then I'll study how to die."

SILVIUS　Call you this chiding?

CELIA　Alas, poor shepherd!

ROSALIND　Do you pity him? No, he deserves no pity.—
Wilt thou love such a woman? What, to make thee an
instrument and play false strains upon thee? Not to be   69
endured! Well, go your way to her, for I see love hath
made thee a tame snake, and say this to her: that if she   71
love me, I charge her to love thee; if she will not, I will
never have her unless thou entreat for her. If you be a
true lover, hence, and not a word; for here comes more
company.   *Exit Silvius.*

　　Enter Oliver.

OLIVER
Good morrow, fair ones. Pray you, if you know,
Where in the purlieus of this forest stands   77
A sheepcote fenced about with olive trees?

---

49 vengeance mischief, harm　**50 Meaning me** i.e., implying that I am
54 in mild aspect i.e., if they looked on me mildly. (Suggests also astro-
logical influence.)　**55 chid** chided　**59 by . . . mind** i.e., send your
thoughts in a letter via Silvius　**60 youth and kind** youthful nature
69 instrument (1) tool (2) musical instrument　**71 tame snake** i.e.,
pathetic wretch　**77 purlieus** tracts of land on the border of a forest

CELIA
  West of this place, down in the neighbor bottom;   79
  The rank of osiers by the murmuring stream   80
  Left on your right hand brings you to the place.   81
  But at this hour the house doth keep itself;
  There's none within.

OLIVER
  If that an eye may profit by a tongue,
  Then should I know you by description,
  Such garments and such years: "The boy is fair,
  Of female favor, and bestows himself   87
  Like a ripe sister; the woman, low   88
  And browner than her brother." Are not you
  The owner of the house I did inquire for?

CELIA
  It is no boast, being asked, to say we are.

OLIVER
  Orlando doth commend him to you both,
  And to that youth he calls his Rosalind
  He sends this bloody napkin. Are you he?   94
              [*He produces a bloody handkerchief.*]

ROSALIND
  I am. What must we understand by this?

OLIVER
  Some of my shame, if you will know of me
  What man I am, and how, and why, and where
  This handkerchief was stained.

CELIA   I pray you, tell it.

OLIVER
  When last the young Orlando parted from you
  He left a promise to return again
  Within an hour, and, pacing through the forest,
  Chewing the food of sweet and bitter fancy,   102
  Lo, what befell! He threw his eye aside,
  And mark what object did present itself:
  Under an old oak, whose boughs were mossed with age
  And high top bald with dry antiquity,
  A wretched ragged man, o'ergrown with hair,
  Lay sleeping on his back. About his neck

79 neighbor bottom neighboring dell   **80 rank of osiers** row of willows
81 Left left behind, passed   **87 favor** features.   **bestows** behaves   **88 ripe**
mature or elder   **94 napkin** handkerchief   **102 fancy** love

A green and gilded snake had wreathed itself,
Who with her head nimble in threats approached
The opening of his mouth; but suddenly,
Seeing Orlando, it unlinked itself   112
And with indented glides did slip away   113
Into a bush, under which bush's shade
A lioness, with udders all drawn dry,   115
Lay couching, head on ground, with catlike watch,
When that the sleeping man should stir; for 'tis   117
The royal disposition of that beast
To prey on nothing that doth seem as dead.
This seen, Orlando did approach the man
And found it was his brother, his elder brother.

CELIA
O, I have heard him speak of that same brother,
And he did render him the most unnatural   123
That lived amongst men.

OLIVER   And well he might so do,
For well I know he was unnatural.

ROSALIND
But to Orlando: did he leave him there,
Food to the sucked and hungry lioness?

OLIVER
Twice did he turn his back and purposed so;
But kindness, nobler ever than revenge,
And nature, stronger than his just occasion,   130
Made him give battle to the lioness,
Who quickly fell before him; in which hurtling   132
From miserable slumber I awaked.

CELIA
Are you his brother?

ROSALIND   Was 't you he rescued?

CELIA
Was 't you that did so oft contrive to kill him?

OLIVER
'Twas I; but 'tis not I. I do not shame   136
To tell you what I was, since my conversion
So sweetly tastes, being the thing I am.

112 **unlinked** uncoiled   113 **indented** zigzag   115 **udders . . . dry** (It
would therefore be fierce with hunger.)   117 **When** for the moment
123 **render him** describe him as   130 **just occasion** fair chance (of revenge)   132 **hurtling** clatter, tumult   136 **do not shame** am not ashamed

ROSALIND
  But for the bloody napkin?
OLIVER   By and by.   139
  When from the first to last betwixt us two
  Tears our recountments had most kindly bathed,   141
  As how I came into that desert place,
  In brief, he led me to the gentle Duke,
  Who gave me fresh array and entertainment,   144
  Committing me unto my brother's love;
  Who led me instantly unto his cave,
  There stripped himself, and here upon his arm
  The lioness had torn some flesh away,
  Which all this while had bled; and now he fainted
  And cried, in fainting, upon Rosalind.
  Brief, I recovered him, bound up his wound,   151
  And, after some small space, being strong at heart,
  He sent me hither, stranger as I am,
  To tell this story, that you might excuse
  His broken promise, and to give this napkin
  Dyed in his blood unto the shepherd youth
  That he in sport doth call his Rosalind.
                            [*Rosalind swoons.*]
CELIA
  Why, how now, Ganymede, sweet Ganymede!
OLIVER
  Many will swoon when they do look on blood.
CELIA
  There is more in it.—Cousin Ganymede!
OLIVER   Look, he recovers.
ROSALIND   I would I were at home.
CELIA   We'll lead you thither.—
  I pray you, will you take him by the arm?
                            [*They help Rosalind up.*]
OLIVER   Be of good cheer, youth. You a man? You lack
  a man's heart.
ROSALIND   I do so, I confess it. Ah, sirrah, a body would   167
  think this was well counterfeited. I pray you, tell your
  brother how well I counterfeited. Heigh-ho!
OLIVER   This was not counterfeit. There is too great tes-

139 **for** as regards   141 **recountments** relating of events (to one another)   144 **array** attire.   **entertainment** hospitality, provision
151 **Brief** in brief.   **recovered** revived   167 **a body** anybody, one

timony in your complexion that it was a passion of 171
earnest. 172

ROSALIND Counterfeit, I assure you.

OLIVER Well then, take a good heart and counterfeit to
be a man.

ROSALIND So I do; but i' faith, I should have been a
woman by right.

CELIA Come, you look paler and paler. Pray you, draw
homewards.—Good sir, go with us.

OLIVER
That will I, for I must bear answer back
How you excuse my brother, Rosalind.

ROSALIND I shall devise something. But, I pray you,
commend my counterfeiting to him. Will you go?

Exeunt.

❖

171–172 **a passion of earnest** a genuine swoon, genuine emotion

5.1   *Enter [Touchstone the] Clown and Audrey.*

TOUCHSTONE   We shall find a time, Audrey. Patience, gentle Audrey.

AUDREY   Faith, the priest was good enough, for all the 3
old gentleman's saying. 4

TOUCHSTONE   A most wicked Sir Oliver, Audrey, a most vile Mar-text. But Audrey, there is a youth here in the forest lays claim to you.

AUDREY   Ay, I know who 'tis. He hath no interest in me 8
in the world. Here comes the man you mean.

Enter William.

TOUCHSTONE   It is meat and drink to me to see a clown. 10
By my troth, we that have good wits have much to
answer for. We shall be flouting; we cannot hold. 12

WILLIAM   Good even, Audrey.

AUDREY   God gi' good even, William. 14

WILLIAM   And good even to you, sir.

[*He removes his hat.*]

TOUCHSTONE   Good even, gentle friend. Cover thy head, cover thy head; nay, prithee, be covered. How old are you, friend?

WILLIAM   Five-and-twenty, sir.

TOUCHSTONE   A ripe age. Is thy name William?

WILLIAM   William, sir.

TOUCHSTONE   A fair name. Wast born i' the forest here?

WILLIAM   Ay, sir, I thank God.

TOUCHSTONE   "Thank God"—a good answer. Art rich?

WILLIAM   Faith, sir, so-so.

TOUCHSTONE   "So-so" is good, very good, very excellent good; and yet it is not, it is but so-so. Art thou wise?

WILLIAM   Ay, sir, I have a pretty wit.

TOUCHSTONE   Why, thou sayst well. I do now remember a saying, "The fool doth think he is wise, but the

---

5.1. Location: The forest.
3–4 the old gentleman's i.e., Jaques's **8 interest in** claim to **10 clown**
i.e., country yokel **12 shall** must. **flouting** scoffing, expressing contempt. **hold** i.e., hold back, hold our tongues **14 God gi' good even**
God give you good evening, i.e., afternoon

wise man knows himself to be a fool." The heathen 31
philosopher, when he had a desire to eat a grape, 32
would open his lips when he put it into his mouth, 33
meaning thereby that grapes were made to eat and lips 34
to open. You do love this maid? 35

WILLIAM I do, sir.

TOUCHSTONE Give me your hand. Art thou learned?

WILLIAM No, sir.

TOUCHSTONE Then learn this of me: to have is to have.
For it is a figure in rhetoric that drink, being poured 40
out of a cup into a glass, by filling the one doth empty 41
the other. For all your writers do consent that *ipse* is 42
he. Now, you are not *ipse*, for I am he.

WILLIAM Which he, sir?

TOUCHSTONE He, sir, that must marry this woman.
Therefore, you clown, abandon—which is in the vul-
gar "leave"—the society—which in the boorish is "company"—of this female—which in the common is
"woman"; which together is, abandon the society of this
female, or, clown, thou perishest; or, to thy better understanding, diest; or, to wit, I kill thee, make thee
away, translate thy life into death, thy liberty into
bondage. I will deal in poison with thee, or in basti- 53
nado, or in steel; I will bandy with thee in faction, I 54
will o'errun thee with policy; I will kill thee a hundred 55
and fifty ways. Therefore tremble, and depart.

AUDREY Do, good William.

WILLIAM God rest you merry, sir.   *Exit.* 58

     Enter Corin.

CORIN Our master and mistress seeks you. Come,
away, away!

TOUCHSTONE Trip, Audrey, trip, Audrey! I attend, I at- 61
tend.   *Exeunt.*

31–35 The heathen . . . open (This is probably Touchstone's way of
telling William, whose mouth is no doubt gaping like a rustic's, that the
grape, i.e., Audrey, is not for his lips.) **40–42 drink . . . other** i.e., both
Touchstone and William cannot possess Audrey **42 your writers** i.e.,
the authorities. **ipse** he himself. (Latin.) **53–54 bastinado** beating with
a cudgel **54 bandy** contend. **in faction** factiously **55 o'errun . . .
policy** overwhelm you with craft, cunning **58 God . . . merry** (Common
salutation at parting.) **61 Trip** go nimbly

5.2   *Enter Orlando [with his wounded arm in a*
           scarf] and Oliver.

ORLANDO   Is 't possible that on so little acquaintance
you should like her? That but seeing you should love
her? And loving woo? And, wooing, she should
grant? And will you persevere to enjoy her?

OLIVER   Neither call the giddiness of it in question, the 5
poverty of her, the small acquaintance, my sudden
wooing, nor her sudden consenting; but say with me,
"I love Aliena"; say with her that she loves me; consent
with both that we may enjoy each other. It shall be to
your good; for my father's house and all the revenue
that was old Sir Rowland's will I estate upon you, and 11
here live and die a shepherd.

      Enter Rosalind.

ORLANDO   You have my consent. Let your wedding be
tomorrow. Thither will I invite the Duke and all 's con- 14
tented followers. Go you and prepare Aliena; for look
you, here comes my Rosalind.

ROSALIND   God save you, brother.   17

OLIVER   And you, fair sister.   [*Exit.*] 18

ROSALIND   O my dear Orlando, how it grieves me to
see thee wear thy heart in a scarf!   20

ORLANDO   It is my arm.

ROSALIND   I thought thy heart had been wounded with
the claws of a lion.

ORLANDO   Wounded it is, but with the eyes of a lady.

ROSALIND   Did your brother tell you how I counterfeited
to swoon when he showed me your handkerchief?

ORLANDO   Ay, and greater wonders than that.

ROSALIND   O, I know where you are. Nay, 'tis true.   28
There was never anything so sudden but the fight of

5.2. Location: The forest.
5 giddiness sudden speed   **11 estate** settle as an estate, bestow   **14 all**
's all his   **17 brother** i.e., brother-in-law to be   **18 sister** (Rosalind is
still dressed as a man, but Oliver evidently adopts the fiction that
"Ganymede" is Orlando's Rosalind.)   **20 wear . . . scarf** (Perhaps she
suggests that Orlando has been wearing his heart on his sleeve; literally,
she refers to the scarf or bandage for his wounded arm.)   **28 where you
are** i.e., what you mean

two rams and Caesar's thrasonical brag of "I came, 30
saw, and overcame." For your brother and my sister
no sooner met but they looked, no sooner looked but
they loved, no sooner loved but they sighed, no sooner
sighed but they asked one another the reason, no
sooner knew the reason but they sought the remedy;
and in these degrees have they made a pair of stairs to 36
marriage which they will climb incontinent, or else be 37
incontinent before marriage. They are in the very
wrath of love, and they will together. Clubs cannot 39
part them.

ORLANDO They shall be married tomorrow, and I will
bid the Duke to the nuptial. But O, how bitter a thing
it is to look into happiness through another man's
eyes! By so much the more shall I tomorrow be at the
height of heart-heaviness, by how much I shall think
my brother happy in having what he wishes for.

ROSALIND Why then tomorrow I cannot serve your
turn for Rosalind?

ORLANDO I can live no longer by thinking.

ROSALIND I will weary you then no longer with idle
talking. Know of me then, for now I speak to some
purpose, that I know you are a gentleman of good con- 52
ceit. I speak not this that you should bear a good opin- 53
ion of my knowledge, insomuch I say I know you are; 54
neither do I labor for a greater esteem than may in
some little measure draw a belief from you, to do 56
yourself good and not to grace me. Believe then, if you 57
please, that I can do strange things. I have, since I was
three years old, conversed with a magician, most pro- 59
found in his art and yet not damnable. If you do love 60
Rosalind so near the heart as your gesture cries it out, 61
when your brother marries Aliena, shall you marry
her. I know into what straits of fortune she is driven;

---

30 thrasonical boastful. (From Thraso, the boaster in Terence's
Eunuchus.) **36 degrees** (Plays on the original meaning, "steps.") **pair**
flight **37 incontinent** immediately (followed by a pun on the meaning
"unchaste or sexually unrestrained") **39 wrath** impetuosity, ardor
52-53 conceit intelligence, understanding **54 insomuch** inasmuch as
56 belief i.e., confidence in my ability **57 grace me** bring favor on
myself **59 conversed** associated **60 not damnable** not a practicer of
forbidden or black magic, worthy of damnation **61 gesture** bearing.
cries it out proclaims

and it is not impossible to me, if it appear not incon- 64
venient to you, to set her before your eyes tomorrow, 65
human as she is, and without any danger. 66

ORLANDO Speak'st thou in sober meanings? 67

ROSALIND By my life I do, which I tender dearly, 68
though I say I am a magician. Therefore, put you in 69
your best array; bid your friends; for if you will be
married tomorrow, you shall, and to Rosalind, if you
will.

Enter Silvius and Phoebe.

Look, here comes a lover of mine and a lover of hers.

PHOEBE
Youth, you have done me much ungentleness,
To show the letter that I writ to you.

ROSALIND
I care not if I have. It is my study 76
To seem despiteful and ungentle to you.
You are there followed by a faithful shepherd;
Look upon him, love him; he worships you.

PHOEBE
Good shepherd, tell this youth what 'tis to love.

SILVIUS
It is to be all made of sighs and tears;
And so am I for Phoebe.

PHOEBE   And I for Ganymede.

ORLANDO   And I for Rosalind.

ROSALIND   And I for no woman.

SILVIUS
It is to be all made of faith and service;
And so am I for Phoebe.

PHOEBE   And I for Ganymede.

ORLANDO   And I for Rosalind.

ROSALIND   And I for no woman.

SILVIUS
It is to be all made of fantasy, 91

64–65 **inconvenient** inappropriate   66 **human** i.e., the real Rosalind.   **danger**
i.e., the danger to the soul from one's involvement in magic or witchcraft
67 **in sober meanings** seriously   68 **tender dearly** value highly   69 **though
. . . magician** (According to Elizabethan antiwitchcraft statutes, some forms
of witchcraft were punishable by death; Rosalind thus endangers her life by
what she has said.)   76 **study** conscious endeavor   91 **fantasy** imagination

All made of passion and all made of wishes,
All adoration, duty, and observance,   93
All humbleness, all patience, and impatience,
All purity, all trial, all observance;   95
And so am I for Phoebe.

PHOEBE   And so am I for Ganymede.

ORLANDO   And so am I for Rosalind.

ROSALIND   And so am I for no woman.

PHOEBE [*To Rosalind*]
    If this be so, why blame you me to love you?   100

SILVIUS [*To Phoebe*]
    If this be so, why blame you me to love you?

ORLANDO
    If this be so, why blame you me to love you?

ROSALIND   Why do you speak too, "Why blame you me
    to love you?"

ORLANDO   To her that is not here, nor doth not hear.

ROSALIND   Pray you, no more of this; 'tis like the howl-
    ing of Irish wolves against the moon. [*To Silvius.*] I
    will help you, if I can. [*To Phoebe.*] I would love you, if
    I could.—Tomorrow meet me all together. [*To Phoebe.*] I
    will marry you, if ever I marry woman, and I'll be mar-
    ried tomorrow. [*To Orlando.*] I will satisfy you, if ever
    I satisfied man, and you shall be married tomorrow.
    [*To Silvius.*] I will content you, if what pleases you
    contents you, and you shall be married tomorrow. [*To
    Orlando.*] As you love Rosalind, meet. [*To Silvius.*] As
    you love Phoebe, meet. And as I love no woman, I'll
    meet. So fare you well. I have left you commands.

SILVIUS   I'll not fail, if I live.

PHOEBE   Nor I.

ORLANDO   Nor I.   *Exeunt.*

✦

5.3   *Enter [Touchstone the] Clown and Audrey.*

TOUCHSTONE   Tomorrow is the joyful day, Audrey; to-
    morrow will we be married.

93 observance devotion, respect   **95 observance** (Perhaps a composi-
tor's error, repeated from two lines previous; many editors emend to
obedience.)   **100 to love you** for loving you

5.3. Location: The forest.

AUDREY I do desire it with all my heart; and I hope it is
no dishonest desire to desire to be a woman of the 4
world. Here come two of the banished Duke's pages. 5

Enter two Pages.

FIRST PAGE Well met, honest gentleman.
TOUCHSTONE By my troth, well met. Come, sit, sit, and
a song.   [*They sit.*]
SECOND PAGE We are for you. Sit i' the middle 9
FIRST PAGE Shall we clap into 't roundly, without hawk- 10
ing or spitting or saying we are hoarse, which are the 11
only prologues to a bad voice? 12
SECOND PAGE I' faith, i' faith, and both in a tune, like 13
two gypsies on a horse. 14

Song.

BOTH PAGES
      It was a lover and his lass,
        With a hey, and a ho, and a hey-nonny-no,
      That o'er the green cornfield did pass 17
        In the springtime, the only pretty ring time, 18
      When birds do sing, hey ding a ding, ding,
      Sweet lovers love the spring.

      Between the acres of the rye, 21
        With a hey, and a ho, and a hey-nonny-no,
      These pretty country folks would lie
        In the springtime, the only pretty ring time,
      When birds do sing, hey ding a ding, ding,
      Sweet lovers love the spring.

      This carol they began that hour,
        With a hey, and a ho, and a hey-nonny-no,
      How that a life was but a flower
        In the springtime, the only pretty ring time,

4 dishonest immodest **4–5 woman of the world** married woman; also,
one who advances herself socially **9 We are for you** i.e., fine, we're
ready **10 clap . . . roundly** begin at once and with spirit **10–11 hawking** clearing the throat **12 only** common, customary **13 in a tune** (1) in
unison (2) keeping time **14 on a** on one **17 cornfield** field of grain
18 ring time time most apt for marriage **21 Between the acres** i.e., on
unplowed strips between the fields

When birds do sing, hey ding a ding, ding,
Sweet lovers love the spring.

And therefore take the present time,
    With a hey, and a ho, and a hey-nonny-no,
For love is crownèd with the prime   35
    In the springtime, the only pretty ring time,
When birds do sing, hey ding a ding, ding,
Sweet lovers love the spring.

TOUCHSTONE   Truly, young gentlemen, though there
    was no great matter in the ditty, yet the note was very   40
    untunable.   41
FIRST PAGE   You are deceived, sir; we kept time, we lost
    not our time.
TOUCHSTONE   By my troth, yes; I count it but time lost
    to hear such a foolish song. God b' wi' you, and God
    mend your voices! Come, Audrey.   *Exeunt.*

❖

5.4   *Enter Duke Senior, Amiens, Jaques, Orlando,
          Oliver, [and] Celia.*

DUKE SENIOR
    Dost thou believe, Orlando, that the boy
    Can do all this that he hath promisèd?
ORLANDO
    I sometimes do believe and sometimes do not,
    As those that fear they hope and know they fear.   4

        Enter Rosalind, Silvius, and Phoebe.

ROSALIND
    Patience once more, whiles our compact is urged.   5
    [*To the Duke.*] You say, if I bring in your Rosalind,
    You will bestow her on Orlando here?
DUKE SENIOR
    That would I, had I kingdoms to give with her.

35 **prime** spring   **40 matter** sense, meaning.   **note** music
41 untunable untuneful, discordant

5.4. Location: The forest.
4 they hope i.e., that they merely hope   **5 urged** put forward

ROSALIND [*To Orlando*]
  And you say you will have her when I bring her?
ORLANDO
  That would I, were I of all kingdoms king.
ROSALIND [*To Phoebe*]
  You say you'll marry me, if I be willing?
PHOEBE
  That will I, should I die the hour after.
ROSALIND
  But if you do refuse to marry me,
  You'll give yourself to this most faithful shepherd?
PHOEBE   So is the bargain.
ROSALIND [*To Silvius*]
  You say that you'll have Phoebe if she will?
SILVIUS
  Though to have her and death were both one thing.
ROSALIND
  I have promised to make all this matter even.   18
  Keep you your word, O Duke, to give your daughter;
  You yours, Orlando, to receive his daughter;
  Keep you your word, Phoebe, that you'll marry me,
  Or else, refusing me, to wed this shepherd;
  Keep your word, Silvius, that you'll marry her
  If she refuse me; and from hence I go
  To make these doubts all even.
                     Exeunt Rosalind and Celia.
DUKE SENIOR
  I do remember in this shepherd boy
  Some lively touches of my daughter's favor.   27
ORLANDO
  My lord, the first time that I ever saw him
  Methought he was a brother to your daughter.
  But, my good lord, this boy is forest-born
  And hath been tutored in the rudiments
  Of many desperate studies by his uncle,   32
  Whom he reports to be a great magician,
  Obscurèd in the circle of this forest.   34

---

18 even smooth   **27 lively** lifelike.   **favor** appearance   **32 desperate**
dangerous   **34 Obscurèd** hidden (with a possible allusion to the magic
circle that protected the magician from the devil during incantation)

Enter [Touchstone the] Clown and Audrey.

JAQUES   There is, sure, another flood toward, and these 35
couples are coming to the ark. Here comes a pair of
very strange beasts, which in all tongues are called
fools.

TOUCHSTONE   Salutation and greeting to you all!

JAQUES   Good my lord, bid him welcome. This is the
motley-minded gentleman that I have so often met in
the forest. He hath been a courtier, he swears.

TOUCHSTONE   If any man doubt that, let him put me to
my purgation. I have trod a measure; I have flattered a 44
lady; I have been politic with my friend, smooth with
mine enemy; I have undone three tailors; I have had 46
four quarrels and like to have fought one.   47

JAQUES   And how was that ta'en up?   48

TOUCHSTONE   Faith, we met and found the quarrel was
upon the seventh cause.

JAQUES   How seventh cause?—Good my lord, like this
fellow.

DUKE SENIOR   I like him very well.

TOUCHSTONE   God 'ild you, sir, I desire you of the like. 54
I press in here, sir, amongst the rest of the country
copulatives, to swear and to forswear, according as 56
marriage binds and blood breaks. A poor virgin, sir, 57
an ill-favored thing, sir, but mine own; a poor humor 58
of mine, sir, to take that that no man else will. Rich
honesty dwells like a miser, sir, in a poor house, as 60
your pearl in your foul oyster.   61

DUKE SENIOR   By my faith, he is very swift and senten- 62
tious.   63

TOUCHSTONE   According to the fool's bolt, sir, and such 64
dulcet diseases.   65

---

35 toward coming on   **44 purgation** proof, trial.   **measure** slow, stately
dance   **46 undone** ruined, bankrupted (by refusing to pay massive debts
owed them)   **47 like** been likely, came close   **48 ta'en up** settled, made
up   **54 'ild** yield, reward.   **I . . . like** I wish the same to you. (A polite
phrase used to reply to a compliment.)   **56 copulatives** i.e., people about
to copulate within marriage   **57 blood breaks** passion drives one to
violate the marriage vows (with a suggestion of breaking the maiden-
head)   **58 humor** whim   **60 honesty** chastity   **61 your pearl** i.e., the pearl
that one hears about   **62 swift** quick-witted   **62–63 sententious** pithy
64 fool's bolt (Alluding to the proverb "A fool's bolt [arrow] is soon
shot.")   **65 dulcet diseases** pleasant afflictions, entertaining yet sharp

JAQUES   But for the seventh cause. How did you find
the quarrel on the seventh cause?

TOUCHSTONE   Upon a lie seven times removed—bear
your body more seeming, Audrey—as thus, sir. I did 69
dislike the cut of a certain courtier's beard. He sent me 70
word, if I said his beard was not cut well, he was in
the mind it was: this is called the Retort Courteous. If I
sent him word again it was not well cut, he would
send me word he cut it to please himself: this is called
the Quip Modest. If again it was not well cut, he dis- 75
abled my judgment: this is called the Reply Churlish. If 76
again it was not well cut, he would answer I spake
not true: this is called the Reproof Valiant. If again it
was not well cut, he would say I lie: this is called the
Countercheck Quarrelsome. And so to the Lie Circum- 80
stantial and the Lie Direct.

JAQUES   And how oft did you say his beard was not
well cut?

TOUCHSTONE   I durst go no further than the Lie Circumstantial, nor he durst not give me the Lie Direct; and
so we measured swords and parted. 86

JAQUES   Can you nominate in order now the degrees of
the lie?

TOUCHSTONE   O sir, we quarrel in print, by the book, as 89
you have books for good manners. I will name you the
degrees. The first, the Retort Courteous; the second,
the Quip Modest; the third, the Reply Churlish; the
fourth, the Reproof Valiant; the fifth, the Countercheck Quarrelsome; the sixth, the Lie with Circumstance; the seventh, the Lie Direct. All these you may
avoid but the Lie Direct; and you may avoid that too,
with an If. I knew when seven justices could not take 97
up a quarrel, but when the parties were met them- 98
selves, one of them thought but of an If, as, "If you
said so, then I said so"; and they shook hands and
swore brothers. Your If is the only peacemaker; much 101
virtue in If.

---

69 seeming seemly   **70 dislike** express dislike of   **75–76 disabled** dis-
paraged   **80 Countercheck** rebuff   **86 measured swords** (i.e., as in the
mere preliminary to a duel)   **89 quarrel . . . book** (Touchstone is travesty-
ing books on the general subject of honor and arms, which dealt with
occasions and circumstances of the duel.)   **97–98 take up** settle
101 swore brothers pledged themselves to act as brothers

JAQUES   Is not this a rare fellow, my lord? He's as good
  at anything and yet a fool.
DUKE SENIOR   He uses his folly like a stalking-horse, and   105
  under the presentation of that he shoots his wit.   106

> *Enter Hymen, Rosalind, and Celia. Still music.*
> *[Rosalind and Celia are no longer disguised.]*

HYMEN
> Then is there mirth in heaven,
> When earthly things made even
>   Atone together.   109
> Good Duke, receive thy daughter;
> Hymen from heaven brought her,
>   Yea, brought her hither,
> That thou mightst join her hand with his
> Whose heart within his bosom is.

ROSALIND [*To the Duke*]
  To you I give myself, for I am yours.
  [*To Orlando.*] To you I give myself, for I am yours.
DUKE SENIOR
  If there be truth in sight, you are my daughter.
ORLANDO
  If there be truth in sight, you are my Rosalind.
PHOEBE
  If sight and shape be true,
  Why then, my love adieu!
ROSALIND [*To the Duke*]
  I'll have no father, if you be not he.
  [*To Orlando.*] I'll have no husband, if you be not he.
  [*To Phoebe.*] Nor ne'er wed woman, if you be not she.
HYMEN
> Peace, ho! I bar confusion.
> 'Tis I must make conclusion
>   Of these most strange events.
> Here's eight that must take hands
> To join in Hymen's bands,
>   If truth holds true contents.   129

105 **stalking-horse** a real or artificial horse under cover of which the
hunter approached his game   106 **presentation** semblance.   **s.d. Hymen**
Roman god of faithful marriage.   **Still** soft   109 **Atone** are at one   129 **If
. . . contents** if truth be true, i.e., if the newly revealed realities truly satisfy

[*To Orlando and Rosalind.*]
    You and you no cross shall part.   130
[*To Oliver and Celia.*]
    You and you are heart in heart.
[*To Phoebe.*]
    You to his love must accord   132
    Or have a woman to your lord.   133
[*To Touchstone and Audrey.*]
    You and you are sure together,   134
    As the winter to foul weather.
[*To All.*]
    Whiles a wedlock hymn we sing,
    Feed yourselves with questioning,   137
    That reason wonder may diminish   138
    How thus we met, and these things finish.

Song.

    Wedding is great Juno's crown,   140
      O blessèd bond of board and bed!
    'Tis Hymen peoples every town;
      High wedlock then be honorèd.   143
    Honor, high honor, and renown,
      To Hymen, god of every town!

DUKE SENIOR [*To Celia*]
    O my dear niece, welcome thou art to me!
    Even daughter welcome in no less degree.   147
PHOEBE [*To Silvius*]
    I will not eat my word, now thou art mine;
    Thy faith my fancy to thee doth combine.   149

    Enter Second Brother [*Jaques de Boys*].

JAQUES DE BOYS
    Let me have audience for a word or two.
    I am the second son of old Sir Rowland,
    That bring these tidings to this fair assembly.

130 cross disagreement   **132 his** i.e., Silvius's.   **accord** agree   **133 to**
for.   **lord** i.e., husband   **134 sure** closely united   **137 Feed** satisfy
138 reason understanding   **140 Juno's** (Juno was Roman queen of the
gods, presiding, in the Renaissance view, over faithful wedlock.)
143 High solemn   **147 Even . . . degree** i.e., you are as welcome as
my daughter and to no less extent   **149 combine** unite

Duke Frederick, hearing how that every day
Men of great worth resorted to this forest,
Addressed a mighty power, which were on foot   155
In his own conduct, purposely to take   156
His brother here and put him to the sword;
And to the skirts of this wild wood he came,
Where, meeting with an old religious man,
After some question with him, was converted   160
Both from his enterprise and from the world,
His crown bequeathing to his banished brother,
And all their lands restored to them again
That were with him exiled. This to be true
I do engage my life.
DUKE SENIOR   Welcome, young man.   165
Thou offer'st fairly to thy brothers' wedding: 166
To one his lands withheld and to the other   167
A land itself at large, a potent dukedom.   168
First, in this forest let us do those ends   169
That here were well begun and well begot;   170
And after, every of this happy number
That have endured shrewd days and nights with us   172
Shall share the good of our returnèd fortune,
According to the measure of their states.   174
Meantime, forget this new-fall'n dignity   175
And fall into our rustic revelry.
Play, music! And you brides and bridegrooms all,
With measure heaped in joy, to the measures fall.   178
JAQUES
Sir, by your patience. If I heard you rightly,   179
The Duke hath put on a religious life
And thrown into neglect the pompous court.   181
JAQUES DE BOYS   He hath.

---

155 Addressed prepared. **power** army **156 In . . . conduct** under his own command **160 question** conversation **165 engage** pledge **166 Thou offer'st fairly** you contribute handsomely **167 the other** i.e., Orlando **168 A land . . . large** i.e., an entire dukedom. (As husband of Rosalind, Orlando will eventually inherit as Duke.) **169 do those ends** accomplish those purposes **170 begot** conceived **172 shrewd** hard, trying **174 states** status, rank **175 new-fall'n** newly acquired **178 With . . . joy** (1) with joyful steps (2) with joy generously bestowed. **measures** dances **179 by your patience** by your leave, i.e., let the music wait a moment **181 pompous** ceremonious

JAQUES

  To him will I. Out of these convertites   183
  There is much matter to be heard and learned.   184
  [*To the Duke.*] You to your former honor I bequeath;
  Your patience and your virtue well deserves it.
  [*To Orlando.*] You to a love that your true faith doth
    merit;
  [*To Oliver.*] You to your land and love and great allies;
  [*To Silvius.*] You to a long and well-deservèd bed;
  [*To Touchstone.*] And you to wrangling, for thy loving
    voyage
  Is but for two months victualed. So, to your pleasures.   191
  I am for other than for dancing measures.

DUKE SENIOR   Stay, Jaques, stay.

JAQUES

  To see no pastime I. What you would have
  I'll stay to know at your abandoned cave.   *Exit.*

DUKE SENIOR

  Proceed, proceed. We'll begin these rites,
  As we do trust they'll end, in true delights.
              [*They dance.*] *Exeunt* [*all but Rosalind*].

---

183 convertites converts   **184 matter** sound sense   **191 victualed**
provisioned

[Epilogue]

ROSALIND It is not the fashion to see the lady the epilogue; but it is no more unhandsome than to see the 2
lord the prologue. If it be true that good wine needs 3
no bush, 'tis true that a good play needs no epilogue. 4
Yet to good wine they do use good bushes, and good
plays prove the better by the help of good epilogues.
What a case am I in then, that am neither a good epilogue nor cannot insinuate with you in the behalf of a 8
good play! I am not furnished like a beggar; therefore 9
to beg will not become me. My way is to conjure you, 10
and I'll begin with the women. I charge you, O
women, for the love you bear to men, to like as much
of this play as please you; and I charge you, O men,
for the love you bear to women—as I perceive by your
simpering, none of you hates them—that between you
and the women the play may please. If I were a 16
woman I would kiss as many of you as had beards 17
that pleased me, complexions that liked me, and 18
breaths that I defied not; and I am sure as many as 19
have good beards or good faces or sweet breaths will
for my kind offer, when I make curtsy, bid me farewell. 21

22

Exit.

Date and Text

"As you like yt, a booke" was entered in the Stationers' Register, the official record book of the London Company of Stationers (booksellers and printers), on August 4, 1600, along with *Much Ado about Nothing, Henry V,* and Ben Jonson's *Every Man in His Humor,* all labeled as "My lord chamberlens mens plaies" and all ordered "to be staied" from publication until further notice. Evidently the Chamberlain's men (Shakespeare's acting company) were anxious to protect their rights to these very popular plays. Despite their efforts *Henry V* was pirated that same month. *As You Like It* did not appear in print, however, until the First Folio of 1623. The Folio text is a good one, based seemingly on the theatrical promptbook or on a literary transcript either of it or of an authorial manuscript.

Francis Meres does not mention the play in September of 1598 in his *Palladis Tamia: Wit's Treasury* (a slender volume on contemporary literature and art; valuable because it lists most of Shakespeare's plays that existed at that time). The play contains an unusually clear allusion to Christopher Marlowe's *Hero and Leander* ("Who ever loved that loved not at first sight?" 3.5.82), first published in 1598. Almost certainly *As You Like It* was written between 1598 and the summer of 1600, either before or after *Much Ado about Nothing.*

Textual Notes

These textual notes are not a historical collation, either of the early folios or of more recent editions; they are simply a record of departures in this edition from the copy text. The reading adopted in this edition appears in boldface, followed by the rejected reading from the copy text, i.e., the First Folio. Only a few major alterations in punctuation are noted. Changes in lineation are not indicated, nor are some minor and obvious typographical errors.

Abbreviations used:
F the First Folio
s.d. stage direction
s.p. speech prefix

Copy text: The First Folio

1.1. 105 she hee   **154 s.p. Oliver** [not in F]   **154 s.d. Exit** [at l. 153 in F]

1.2. 3 I were were   **51 goddesses and** goddesses   **55 s.p. [and elsewhere] Touchstone** Clow   **55–56 father** farher   **80 s.p. Celia** Ros   **88 Le** the   **251 s.d.** [at l. 249 in F]   **280 [and occasionally elsewhere] Rosalind** Rosaline

1.3. 55 likelihood likelihoods   **76 her** per   **87 s.d. with Lords &c**   **124 be** by   **135 we in** in we

2.1. 49 much must   **50 friends** friend   **59 of the** of

2.3. 10 some seeme   **16 s.p. Orlando** [not in F]   **29 s.p. Orlando** Ad   **50 woo** woe   **71 seventeen** seauentie

2.4. 1 weary merry   **42 thy wound** they would   **65 you** your

2.5. 1 s.p. Amiens [not in F]   **38 s.d. All together here** [before l. 35 in F]   **41–42 No . . . weather** &c   **46 s.p. Jaques** Amy

2.7. s.d. Lords Lord   **10 [and elsewhere] woo** woe   **38 brain** braiue   **55 Not to seem** Seeme   **87 comes** come   **161 treble, pipes** trebble pipes,   **174 s.p. Amiens** [not in F]   **182 Then** The   **190–193 Heigh-ho . . . jolly** &c   **201 masters** masters

3.2. 26 good pood   **123 a desert** Desert   **143 her** his   **234 such fruit** fruite   **241 thy** the   **340 lectures** Lectors   **354 deifying** defying

3.3. 52 so so   **88 s.p. Touchstone** Ol   **99 s.d. Exit** Exeunt

3.4. 29 a lover Louer

3.5. 105 erewhile yerewhile   **128 I have** Haue

4.1. 1 me be me   **18 my** by   **44 thousandth** thousand   **202 it** in

4.2. 2 s.p. First Lord Lord   **7 s.p. Second Lord** Lord   **10 s.p. Second Lord** [not in F]

4.3. 5 s.d. [at l. 4 in F]   **8 bid** did bid   **143 In** I   **156 his** this

5.1. 36 sir sit   **55 policy** police

5.2. 7 nor her nor   **31 overcame** ouercome

5.3. 15 s.p. Both Pages [not in F]   **18 ring** rang   **24–26 In . . . spring** In spring time, &c [also at ll. 30–32 and 36–38]   **33–38** [this stanza comes before l. 21 in F]

5.4. 25 s.d. Exeunt Exit   **34 s.d.** [at l. 33 in F]   **80 so to the** so ro   **113 her** his   **150 s.p. Jaques de Boys** 2 Bro [also at l. 182]   **163 them** him   **170 were** vvete   **197 s.d. Exeunt** Exit

Shakespeare's Sources

Shakespeare's chief source for *As You Like It* was Thomas Lodge's graceful pastoral romance, *Rosalynde: Euphues' Golden Legacy* (1592). Lodge was indebted in turn to *The Tale of Gamelyn*, a fourteenth-century poem wrongly included by some medieval scribes as "The Cook's Tale" in Chaucer's *Canterbury Tales. Gamelyn* was not printed until 1721, but Lodge clearly had access to a manuscript of it. Although Shakespeare may not have known *Gamelyn* directly, his play still retains the hearty spirit of this Robin Hood legend. (In later Robin Hood ballads, Gamelyn or Gandelyn is identified with Will Scarlet, a member of Robin Hood's band.)

Even a brief account of *Gamelyn* suggests how greatly the original tale is inspired by Robin Hood legends of outlaws valiantly defying the corrupt social order presided over by the Sheriff and his henchmen. Gamelyn, the youngest of three brothers, is denied his inheritance by his churlish eldest brother, John. When Gamelyn demands his rights, John orders his men to beat Gamelyn, but the young man arms himself with a club, or truncheon, and proves a formidable fighter. Later Gamelyn defeats the champion wrestler in a local wrestling match (a lower-class sport befitting the social milieu of this story) and returns home to find himself locked out by his brother. He kills the porter, flings the man's body down a well, and feasts his companions day and night for a week. John feigns a reconciliation and slyly asks if he can bind Gamelyn hand and foot merely to satisfy an oath he has sworn over the death of the porter. Gamelyn trustingly agrees and is made prisoner. After his bonds have been secretly loosed by Adam the Spencer (the steward), Gamelyn pretends to remain bound until the propitious moment for revenge and escape. The moment arrives during a feast of monks who churlishly refuse to help Gamelyn. With Adam's help he overcomes many of them, ties up his brother, and escapes to the woods, where he and Adam are rescued from hunger by a band of merry outlaws. As their chief, Gamelyn becomes a champion of the poor and an enemy of rich churchmen. His brother, now sheriff, brands

Gamelyn an outlaw and manages to imprison him, but Gamelyn's second brother, Sir Ote, stands bail for him. On the day of the trial, Gamelyn frees Sir Ote and hangs the Sheriff and the jury. Gamelyn finally obtains his inheritance and becomes chief officer of the King's royal forests. This story is uninfluenced by the pastoral tradition and contains no love plot. Its Robin Hood traditions are very much present, nonetheless, in Shakespeare's contrasting portrayal of a tyrannical court and of a just society in banishment.

Lodge retains the primitive vigor of *Gamelyn*, but adds generous infusions of pastoral sentiment in the manner of Sir Philip Sidney's *Arcadia* (1590) and sententious moralizing in the manner of John Lyly's *Euphues* (1578). The pastoralism is presented in conventional terms, with none of the genial self-reflexive satire we find in Shakespeare. Psychological motivation is intricate, often more so than in Shakespeare's play. The style is also heavily influenced by Lyly's exquisitely balanced, antithetical, and ornamented prose. For his pastoralism Lodge was indebted not only to Sidney but to the ancient pastoral tradition that included the Greek Theocritus and the Roman Virgil, the Italian Sannazaro (*Arcadia*) and the Portuguese Jorge de Montemayor (*Diana*). Pastoralism by Lodge's time had become thoroughly imbued with artificial conventions: abject lovers writing sonnets to their disdainful mistresses, princes and princesses in shepherds' disguise, idealized landscapes, stylized debate as to the relative merits of love and friendship, youth and age, city life and country life, and so on. Some of these conventions were derived also from the vogue of sonneteering pioneered by Francis Petrarch and can thus be described as the stereotypes of "Petrarchism." Lodge accepts these conventions and gives us typical pastoral lovers even in his hero and heroine, although the elements he derived from *Gamelyn* certainly add a contrasting note of violence and danger.

Selections from Lodge's *Rosalynde* follow. Because its length precludes a printing of the entire novel, however, a summary may be useful to fill in the omitted passages and to highlight what Shakespeare has retained or altered in his play. Lodge's account begins much like that of *Gamelyn*. Saladyne, the envious eldest brother, bribes the champion wrestler to do away with Rosader (Orlando) in the wrestling match. Rosader succeeds instead in killing the wrestler and in winning the heart of Rosalynde, daughter of the banished King Gerismond. When she sends him a jewel, Rosader is not at all tongue-tied like his counterpart in Shakespeare's play; instead, he composes a Petrarchan sonnet on the spot. The usurping King Torismond (who is unrelated to Gerismond and is not, like Duke Frederick, the usurper of his banished brother's title), despite his evil nature, is impressed by Rosader's grace and martial prowess. Rosader returns home with friends, breaks open the door, and feasts his company. Saladyne overwhelms Rosader in his sleep and binds him to a post, but Rosader is untied by Adam and overwhelms his eldest brother's guests as in *Gamelyn*. In this case, however, the guests are Saladyne's kindred and allies, all of whom have refused to help Rosader. The Sheriff tries to arrest Rosader and Adam, but they escape to the Forest of Arden in France. They are saved from starvation by the kindly King Gerismond and his exiled followers. Rosalynde and King Torismond's daughter Alinda have meanwhile been banished from court and have taken up residence in the forest under the names of Ganymede and Aliena. They befriend old Corydon (Corin) and young Montanus (Silvius), who is hopelessly in love with the haughty Phoebe. "Ganymede" poses as a woman to test Rosader in his wooing, and they are joined in a mock marriage. Saladyne, now repenting of his evil deeds, comes to the forest, is saved by his brother from a lion, and falls in love with Alinda (whom he helps to rescue from ruffians). The denouement is much as in Shakespeare, although the triumphant return to society is more complete: King Torismond is slain, Gerismond is restored to his throne, Rosader is named heir apparent, and all the friends are appropriately rewarded.

Despite Shakespeare's extensive indebtedness to this charming romance, there is a crucial difference: Lodge's pastoral world is never subjected to a wry or satirical exploration. Lodge offers no equivalents for Touchstone, the fool who sees the absurdity of both country and city; Jaques, the malcontent traveler; William and Audrey, the clownishly simple peasants; or Sir Oliver Mar-text, the ridiculous hedge-priest. Nor does Lodge tell of Le Beau, the court butterfly. Hymen is a Shakespearean addition, and the conversion of Duke Frederick by a hermit instead of his being overthrown and killed is a characteristically Shakespearean softening touch. Shakespeare's added characters are virtually all foils to the conventional pastoral vision he found in his source.

Rosalynde: Euphues' Golden Legacy
By Thomas Lodge

[*Rosalynde* begins with the death of a knight, John of Bordeaux, and his bestowing a legacy on his three sons. The eldest, Saladyne, receives the manor house and estate, while Fernandyne and Rosader are given certain lands and other gifts. Rosader, his father's darling, is placed in the charge of Saladyne, since he is not yet of age. Saladyne, resentful of his youngest brother, resolves to himself to abuse his authority by oppressing Rosader with an enforced low condition: "Though he be a gentleman by nature, yet form him anew and make him a peasant by nurture. So shalt thou keep him as a slave and reign thyself sole lord over all thy father's possessions."]

In this humor was Saladyne, making his brother Rosader his footboy for the space of two or three years, keeping him in such servile subjection as if he had been the son of any country vassal. The young gentleman bare[1] all with patience, till on a day, walking in the garden by himself, he began to consider how he was the son of John of Bordeaux, a knight renowned for many victories and a gentleman famoused for his virtues; how, contrary to the testament of his father, he was not only kept from his land and entreated[2] as a servant but smothered in such secret slavery as he might not attain to any honorable actions.

"Ah," quoth he to himself, nature working these effectual[3] passions, "why should I, that am a gentleman born, pass my time in such unnatural drudgery? Were it not better either in Paris to become a scholar, or in the court a courtier, or in the field a soldier, than to live a footboy to my own brother? Nature hath lent me wit to conceive,[4] but my

1 bare bore **2 entreated** treated **3 effectual** ardent **4 wit to conceive** intelligence to understand

brother denied me art[5] to contemplate. I have strength to
perform any honorable exploit but no liberty to accomplish
my virtuous endeavors. Those good parts that God hath bestowed upon me, the envy of my brother doth smother in
obscurity; the harder is my fortune, and the more his frowardness."[6]

With that, casting up his hand, he felt hair on his face,
and perceiving his beard to bud, for choler he began to
blush and swore to himself he would be no more subject to
such slavery. As thus he was ruminating of his melancholy
passions, in came Saladyne with his men and, seeing his
brother in a brown study and to forget his wonted reverence,[7] thought to shake him out of his dumps thus:

"Sirrah," quoth he, "what, is your heart on your half-
penny,[8] or are you saying a dirge for your father's soul?
What, is my dinner ready?"

At this question, Rosader, turning his head askance and
bending his brows as if anger there had plowed the furrows
of her wrath, with his eyes full of fire he made this reply:

"Dost thou ask me, Saladyne, for thy cates?[9] Ask some of
thy churls, who are fit for such an office. I am thine equal
by nature, though not by birth, and though thou hast more
cards in the bunch,[10] I have as many trumps in my hands as
thyself. Let me question with thee why thou hast felled my
woods, spoiled my manor houses, and made havoc of such
utensils[11] as my father bequeathed unto me? I tell thee,
Saladyne, either answer me as a brother or I will trouble
thee as an enemy."

At this reply of Rosader's Saladyne smiled, as laughing at
his presumption, and frowned, as checking his folly. He
therefore took him up thus shortly:

"What, sirrah! Well, I see early pricks the tree that will
prove a thorn. Hath my familiar conversing with you made
you coy,[12] or my good looks[13] drawn you to be thus contemp-
tuous? I can quickly remedy such a fault, and I will bend
the tree while it is a wand.[14] In faith, sir boy, I have a snaffle

---

5 art training, skill   **6 frowardness** evil disposition   **7 wonted reverence**
customary show of respect (due an older brother)   **8 is your . . . half-
penny** i.e., is there something special on your mind, some particular
object   **9 cates** delicacies, things to eat   **10 bunch** pack of cards
11 utensils useful possessions   **12 coy** disdainful   **13 good looks**
favorable regard   **14 wand** i.e., sapling

for such a headstrong colt. You, sirs, lay hold on him and bind him, and then I will give him a cooling-card[15] for his choler."

This made Rosader half mad, that, stepping to a great rake that stood in the garden, he laid such load upon his brother's men that he hurt some of them and made the rest of them run away. Saladyne, seeing Rosader so resolute and with his resolution so valiant, thought his heels his best safety and took him to a loft adjoining to the garden, whither Rosader pursued him hotly. Saladyne, afraid of his brother's fury, cried out to him thus:

"Rosader, be not so rash. I am thy brother and thine elder, and if I have done thee wrong, I'll make thee amends. Revenge not anger in blood, for so shalt thou stain the virtue of old Sir John of Bordeaux. Say wherein thou art discontent, and thou shalt be satisfied. Brothers' frowns ought not to be periods[16] of wrath. What, man, look not so sourly! I know we shall be friends, and better friends than we have been, for *Amantium irae amoris redintegratio est.*"[17]

These words appeased the choler of Rosader, for he was of a mild and courteous nature, so that he laid down his weapons and, upon the faith of a gentleman, assured his brother he would offer him no prejudice; whereupon Saladyne came down, and after a little parley they embraced each other and became friends, and Saladyne promising Rosader the restitution of all his lands "and what favor else," quoth he, "any ways my ability or the nature of a brother may perform." Upon these sugared reconciliations they went into the house arm in arm together, to the great content of all the old servants of Sir John of Bordeaux.

Thus continued the pad hidden in the straw[18] till it chanced that Torismond, King of France, had appointed for his pleasure a day of wrestling and of tournament to busy his commons' heads, lest, being idle, their thoughts should run upon more serious matters and call to remembrance their old banished king. A champion there was to stand against all comers, a Norman, a man of tall stature and of great strength, so valiant that in many such conflicts he

15 **a cooling-card** something to cool his ardor   16 **periods** sentences
17 **Amantium . . . est** the quarrels of lovers are the renewal of love
18 **pad . . . straw** i.e., concealed danger.   **pad** paddock, toad or frog

always bare[19] away the victory, not only overthrowing them which he encountered but often with the weight of his body killing them outright. Saladyne, hearing of this, thinking now not to let the ball fall to the ground but to take opportunity by the forehead, first by secret means convented[20] with the Norman and procured[21] him with rich rewards to swear that if Rosader came within his claws he should nevermore return to quarrel with Saladyne for his possessions. The Norman, desirous of pelf—as *Quis nisi mentis inops oblatum respuit aurum?*[22]—taking great gifts for little gods, took the crowns of Saladyne to perform the stratagem.

Having thus the champion tied to his villainous determination by oath, he prosecuted the intent of his purpose thus. He went to young Rosader, who in all his thoughts reached at honor and gazed no lower than virtue commanded him, and began to tell him of this tournament and wrestling, how the King should be there and all the chief peers of France, with all the beautiful damosels of the country.

"Now, brother," quoth he, "for the honor of Sir John of Bordeaux, our renowned father, to famous[23] that house that never hath been found without men approved[24] in chivalry, show thy resolution to be peremptory.[25] For myself thou knowest, though I am eldest by birth, yet, never having attempted any deeds of arms, I am youngest to perform any martial exploits, knowing better how to survey my lands than to charge my lance. My brother Fernandyne he is at Paris poring on a few papers, having more insight into sophistry and principles of philosophy than any warlike endeavors. But thou, Rosader, the youngest in years but the eldest in valor, art a man of strength and darest do what honor allows thee. Take thou my father's lance, his sword, and his horse, and hie thee to the tournament, and either there valiantly crack a spear or try with the Norman for the palm of activity."

[Rosader accepts the proposal with alacrity and hastens to the tourney. Present at the event are Torismond, the usurp-

---

19 bare bore   **20 convented** met   **21 procured** persuaded   **22 Quis . . . aurum** who in his right mind refuses money that is offered. (Adapted from Terence, *Andria*, l. 555. *Pelf* means "money, riches.")   **23 famous** make famous   **24 approved** proved, tested   **25 peremptory** unhesitating

ing King of France, his daughter Alinda, and Rosalynde, daughter of the banished King Gerismond, now living in the Forest of Arden.]

At last, when the tournament ceased, the wrestling began, and the Norman presented himself as a challenger against all comers, but he looked like Hercules when he advanced himself against Achelous,[26] so that the fury of his countenance amazed all that durst attempt to encounter with him in any deed of activity; till at last a lusty[27] franklin of the country came with two tall[28] men that were his sons, of good lineaments and comely personage. The eldest of these, doing his obeisance to the King, entered the list and presented himself to the Norman, who straight coped with him and, as a man that would triumph in the glory of his strength, roused himself with such fury that not only he gave him the fall but killed him with the weight of his corpulent personage. Which the younger brother, seeing, leaped presently into the place and, thirsty after the revenge, assailed the Norman with such valor that at the first encounter he brought him to his knees, which repulsed so the Norman that, recovering himself, fear of disgrace doubling his strength, he stepped so sternly to the young franklin that, taking him up in his arms, he threw him against the ground so violently that he broke his neck and so ended his days with his brother. At this unlooked-for massacre the people murmured and were all in a deep passion of pity; but the franklin, father unto these, never changed his countenance, but as a man of a courageous resolution took up the bodies of his sons without any show of outward discontent.

All this while stood Rosader and saw this tragedy; who, noting the undoubted virtue of the franklin's mind, alighted off from his horse and presently sat down on the grass and commanded his boy to pull off his boots, making him ready to try the strength of this champion. Being furnished as he would, he clapped the franklin on the shoulder and said thus:

"Bold yeoman, whose sons have ended the term of their years with honor, for that I see thou scornest Fortune with

26 **Achelous** a river god with whom Hercules wrestled in order to win Dejanira as his wife   27 **lusty** vigorous   28 **tall** brave

patience and thwartest* the injury of Fate with content in
brooking[29] the death of thy sons, stand awhile and either see
me make a third in their tragedy or else revenge their fall
with an honorable triumph.''

The franklin, seeing so goodly a gentleman to give him
such courteous comfort, gave him hearty thanks, with
promise to pray for his happy success. With that Rosader
vailed bonnet[30] to the King and lightly leaped within the
lists, where, noting more the company than the combatant,
he cast his eye upon the troop of ladies that glistered there
like the stars of heaven; but at last Love, willing to make
him as amorous as he was valiant, presented him with the
sight of Rosalynde, whose admirable beauty so inveigled
the eye of Rosader that, forgetting himself, he stood and fed
his looks on the favor of Rosalynde's face; which she perceiving blushed, which was such a doubling of her beauteous excellence that the bashful red of Aurora[31] at the sight
of unacquainted Phaëthon[32] was not half so glorious.

The Norman, seeing this young gentleman fettered in the
looks of the ladies, drave him out of his memento[33] with a
shake by the shoulder. Rosader, looking back with an angry
frown as if he had been wakened from some pleasant
dream, discovered to all by the fury of his countenance that
he was a man of some high thoughts; but when they all
noted his youth and the sweetness of his visage, with a
general applause of favors,[34] they grieved that so goodly a
young man should venture in so base an action; but seeing it
were to his dishonor to hinder him from his enterprise, they
wished him to be graced with the palm of victory. After Rosader was thus called out of his memento by the Norman,
he roughly clapped to him with so fierce an encounter that
they both fell to the ground and with the violence of the fall
were forced to breathe, in which space the Norman called
to mind by all tokens that this was he whom Saladyne had
appointed him to kill, which conjecture made him stretch
every limb and try every sinew that, working his death, he
might recover the gold which so bountifully was promised
him. On the contrary part, Rosader while he breathed was

29 **brooking** enduring with patience   30 **vailed bonnet** took off his cap
31 **Aurora** goddess of the dawn   32 **Phaëthon** the sun god (whose son is
also named Phaëthon)   33 **memento** musing   34 **applause of favors**
look of approval in their faces

not idle but still cast his eye upon Rosalynde, who, to encourage him with a favor, lent him such an amorous look as might have made the most coward desperate, which glance of Rosalynde so fired the passionate desires of Rosader that, turning to the Norman, he ran upon him and braved him with a strong encounter. The Norman received him as valiantly, that there was a sore combat, hard to judge on whose side Fortune would be prodigal. At last Rosader, calling to mind the beauty of his new mistress, the fame of his father's honors, and the disgrace that should fall to his house by his misfortune, roused himself and threw the Norman against the ground, falling upon his chest with so willing a weight that the Norman yielded nature her due and Rosader the victory.

The death of this champion, as it highly contented the franklin as a man satisfied with revenge, so it drew the King and all the peers into a great admiration[35] that so young years and so beautiful a personage should contain such martial excellence; but when they knew him to be the youngest son of Sir John of Bordeaux, the King rose from his seat and embraced him, and the peers entreated[36] him with all favorable courtesy, commending both his valor and his virtues, wishing him to go forward in such haughty[37] deeds that he might attain to the glory of his father's honorable fortunes.

As the King and lords graced him with embracing, so the ladies favored him with their looks, especially Rosalynde, whom the beauty and valor of Rosader had already touched; but she accounted love a toy and fancy a momentary passion that, as it was taken in with a gaze, might be shaken off with a wink, and therefore feared not to dally in the flame; and to make Rosader know she affected him, took from her neck a jewel and sent it by a page to the young gentleman. The prize that Venus gave to Paris[38] was not half so pleasing to the Trojan as this gem was to Rosader; for if Fortune had sworn to make him sole monarch of the world, he would rather have refused such dignity than have lost the jewel sent him by Rosalynde. To return her with the like he was unfurnished, and yet, that he might more than in his

35 **admiration** astonishment   36 **entreated** treated   37 **haughty** exalted
38 **prize . . . Paris** (Paris awarded Venus the golden apple as the fairest of the goddesses, and receives Helen as his prize.

looks discover his affection, he stepped into a tent and, taking pen and paper, writ this fancy:

> Two suns at once from one fair heaven there shined,[39]
> Ten branches from two boughs, tipped all with roses,
> Pure locks more golden than is gold refined,
> Two pearlèd rows that nature's pride incloses;
> Two mounts fair marble-white, down-soft and dainty,
> A snow-dyed orb, where love increased by pleasure
> Full woeful makes my heart and body fainty:
> Her fair, my woe, exceeds all thought and measure.
> In lines confused my luckless harm appeareth,
> Whom sorrow clouds, whom pleasant smiling
>   cleareth.

This sonnet he sent to Rosalynde, which when she read she blushed, but with a sweet content in that she perceived love had allotted her so amorous a servant.

[Rosader, returning home to an unfriendly greeting from Saladyne, breaks open the door and, with the help of old Adam Spencer, a loyal and trusty servant, provides a hearty welcome for all his friends. He is outwardly reconciled to Saladyne, but the latter is only biding his time to be revenged. Rosalynde, meanwhile, discovering herself to be in love with Rosader, composes a madrigal on the subject of her passion.]

Scarce had Rosalynde ended her madrigal before Torismond came in with his daughter Alinda and many of the peers of France, who were enamored of her[40] beauty; which Torismond perceiving, fearing lest her perfection might be the beginning of his prejudice[41] and the hope of his fruit end in the beginning of her blossoms, he thought to banish her from the court. "For," quoth he to himself, "her face is so full of favor that it pleads pity in the eye of every man; her beauty is so heavenly and divine that she will prove to me as Helen did to Priam;[42] some one of the peers will aim at her

---

39 Two . . . shined (The two suns are Rosalind's eyes, followed in this catalogue of her charms by her ten fingers and two arms, her hair, her teeth, her breasts, etc.)   **40 her** i.e., Rosalynde's   **41 his prejudice** a dislike of him   **42 Helen . . . Priam** (Helen's beauty proved the undoing of Troy, of which Priam was King.)

love, end the marriage,[43] and then in his wife's right attempt the kingdom. To prevent therefore 'had I wist'[44] in all these actions, she tarries not about the court, but shall, as an exile, either wander to her father or else seek other fortunes." In this humor, with a stern countenance full of wrath, he breathed out this censure[45] unto her before the peers, that charged her that that night she were not seen[46] about the court. "For," quoth he, "I have heard of thy aspiring speeches and intended treasons." This doom[47] was strange unto Rosalynde, and presently, covered with the shield of her innocence, she boldly brake out in reverent terms to have cleared herself; but Torismond would admit of no reason, nor durst his lords plead for Rosalynde, although her beauty had made some of them passionate, seeing the figure of wrath portrayed in his brow. Standing thus all mute, and Rosalynde amazed, Alinda, who loved her more than herself, with grief in her heart and tears in her eyes, falling down on her knees, began to entreat her father thus:

ALINDA'S ORATION TO HER FATHER IN DEFENSE OF FAIR ROSALYNDE

"If, mighty Torismond, I offend in pleading for my friend, let the law of amity crave pardon for my boldness, for where there is depth of affection there friendship alloweth a privilege. Rosalynde and I have been fostered up from our infancies and nursed under the harbor of our conversing together with such private familiarities that custom had wrought an union of our nature, and the sympathy of our affections such a secret love that we have two bodies and one soul. Then marvel not, great Torismond, if, seeing my friend distressed, I find myself perplexed with a thousand sorrows; for her virtuous and honorable thoughts, which are the glories that maketh women excellent, they be such as may challenge love and rase[48] out suspicion. Her obedience to Your Majesty I refer to the censure of your own eye, that since her father's exile hath smothered all griefs with patience and in the absence of na-

---

43 end the marriage i.e., achieve her in marriage and thus end the contest as to who will marry Rosalynde   **44 had I wist** if I had only known   **45 censure** judgment   **46 were not seen** be seen no more   **47 doom** verdict   **48 rase** erase

ture hath honored you with all duty as her own father by nouriture,[49] not in word uttering any discontent nor in thought, as far as conjecture may reach, hammering on revenge, only in all her actions seeking to please you and to win my favor. Her wisdom, silence, chastity, and other such rich qualities I need not decipher;[50] only it rests for me to conclude, in one word, that she is innocent. If, then, Fortune, who triumphs in variety of miseries, hath presented some envious person as minister of her intended stratagem to taint Rosalynde with any surmise of treason, let him be brought to her face and confirm his accusation by witnesses; which proved, let her die, and Alinda will execute the massacre. If none can avouch any confirmed relation of her intent, use justice, my lord—it is the glory of a king—and let her live in your wonted favor; for if you banish her, myself, as copartner of her hard fortunes, will participate[51] in exile some part of her extremities."

Torismond, at this speech of Alinda, covered his face with such a frown as[52] tyranny seemed to sit triumphant in his forehead, and checked her up[53] with such taunts as made the lords, that only were hearers, to tremble.

"Proud girl," quoth he, "hath my looks made thee so light of tongue or my favors encouraged thee to be so forward that thou darest presume to preach after[54] thy father? Hath not my years more experience than thy youth and the winter of mine age deeper insight into civil policy than the prime of thy flourishing days? The old lion avoids the toils,[55] where the young one leaps into the net; the care of age is provident and foresees much; suspicion is a virtue where a man holds his enemy in his bosom.[56] Thou, fond[57] girl, measurest all by present affection, and as thy heart loves, thy thoughts censure; but if thou knewest that in liking Rosalynde thou hatchest up a bird to peck out thine own eyes, thou wouldst entreat as much for her absence as now thou delightest in her presence. But why do I allege policy[58] to thee? Sit you down, huswife, and fall to your needle; if idleness make you so wanton, or liberty so malapert, I can quickly tie you to a sharper

---

49 by nouriture by nurture, by adoption   **50 decipher** recount   **51 participate** share   **52 as** that   **53 checked her up** rebuked her   **54 after** to   **55 flourishing . . . toils** youthful . . . nets   **56 holds . . . bosom** i.e., is fearful and suspicious   **57 fond** foolish   **58 allege policy** cite matters of statecraft

task. And you, maid, this night be packing, either into Arden to your father or whither best it shall content your humor, but in the court you shall not abide."

This rigorous reply of Torismond nothing amazed Alinda, for still she prosecuted[59] her plea in the defense of Rosalynde, wishing her father, if his censure might not be reversed, that he would appoint her partner of her exile; which if he refused to do, either she would by some secret means steal out and follow her or else end her days with some desperate kind of death. When Torismond heard his daughter so resolute, his heart was so hardened against her that he set down a definitive and peremptory sentence that they should both be banished, which presently was done, the tyrant rather choosing to hazard the loss of his only child than anyways to put in question the state of his kingdom, so suspicious and fearful is the conscience of an usurper. Well, although his lords persuaded[60] him to retain his own daughter, yet his resolution might not be reversed, but both of them must away from the court without either more company or delay. In he went with great melancholy and left these two ladies alone. Rosalynde waxed very sad and sat down and wept. Alinda she smiled, and sitting by her friend began thus to comfort her. [Alinda promises to remain faithful always.]

At this Rosalynde began to comfort her,[61] and after she had wept a few kind tears in the bosom of her Alinda, she gave her hearty thanks, and then they sat them down to consult how they should travel. Alinda grieved at nothing but that they might have no man in their company, saying it would be their greatest prejudice in that two women went wandering without either guide or attendant.

"Tush," quoth Rosalynde, "art thou a woman and hast not a sudden shift[62] to prevent a misfortune? I, thou seest, am of a tall stature and would very well become the person and apparel of a page; thou shalt be my mistress,[63] and I will play the man so properly that, trust me, in what company soever I come I will not be discovered. I will buy me a suit and have my rapier very handsomely at my side, and if any knave offer wrong, your page will show him the point of his weapon."

---

59 prosecuted persisted in   **60 persuaded** pleaded with   **61 comfort her** take comfort   **62 sudden shift** quickly devised stratagem   **63 my mistress** i.e., the lady I serve

At this Alinda smiled, and upon this they agreed and presently gathered up all their jewels, which they trussed up in a casket, and Rosalynde in all haste provided her of robes, and Alinda, from[64] her royal weeds, put herself in more homely attire. Thus fitted to the purpose, away go these two friends, having now changed their names, Alinda being called Aliena, and Rosalynde Ganymede. They traveled along the vineyards and by many byways at last got to the forest side,[65] where they traveled by the space of two or three days without seeing any creature, being often in danger of wild beasts and pained with many passionate sorrows.

[In the Forest of Arden, Rosalynde and Alinda encounter old Corydon and young Mantanus—the latter hopelessly in love with Phoebe—and overhear a pleasant eclogue between them on the subject of unrequited love. Striking up a conversation with these country folk, Rosalynde and Alinda agree at length to buy a farm from Corydon's master and settle down in Arden. Saladyne meanwhile devises a craven assault on Rosader in his sleep, binds him in fetters, and leaves him for two or three days without food, from which sad condition Rosader is at last secretly rescued by Adam Spencer and assisted in a counterplot. Pretending to be fettered still, Rosader awaits a time during the evening festivities when Saladyne and his guests are fuddled with wine, throws off his chains, and lays about him with a poleax, hurting many and killing some. Now outlaws and painfully aware that the law is on Saladyne's side, Rosader and Adam make a bloody escape from the Sheriff's posse that has come to arrest them.]

But Rosader and Adam, knowing full well the secret ways that led through the vineyards, stole away privily through the province of Bordeaux and escaped safe to the Forest of Arden. Being come thither, they were glad they had so good a harbor;[66] but Fortune, who is like the chameleon, variable with every object and constant in nothing but inconstancy, thought to make them mirrors of her mutability and therefore still crossed them thus contrarily. Thinking still to pass

---

64 from changing from   **65 forest side** edge of the forest   **66 harbor**
place of refuge

on by the byways to get to Lyons, they chanced on a path that led into the thick of the forest, where they wandered five or six days without meat, that they were almost famished, finding neither shepherd nor cottage to relieve them; and hunger growing on so extreme, Adam Spencer, being old, began first to faint and, sitting him down on a hill and looking about him, espied where Rosader lay as feeble and as ill perplexed, which sight made him shed tears and to fall into these bitter terms:

[Adam reflects on the vicissitudes of fortune and the need for patience as the only remedy.]

"Master," quoth he, "you see we are both in one predicament, and long I cannot live without meat; seeing therefore we can find no food, let the death of the one preserve the life of the other. I am old and overworn with age; you are young and are the hope of many honors. Let me then die; I will presently cut my veins, and, master, with the warm blood relieve your fainting spirits; suck on that till I end, and you be comforted."

With that Adam Spencer was ready to pull out his knife, when Rosader, full of courage though very faint, rose up, and wished Adam Spencer to sit there till his return. "For my mind gives me,"[67] quoth he, "I shall bring thee meat." With that, like a madman, he rose up and ranged up and down the woods, seeking to encounter some wild beast with his rapier that either he might carry his friend Adam food or else pledge his life in pawn of his loyalty.

It chanced that day that Gerismond, the lawful King of France banished by Torismond, who with a lusty crew of outlaws lived in that forest, that day in honor of his birth made a feast to all his bold yeomen and frolicked it with store of wine and venison, sitting all at a long table under the shadow of lemon trees. To that place by chance Fortune conducted Rosader, who, seeing such a crew of brave[68] men having store of that for want of which he and Adam perished, he stepped boldly to the board's end and saluted the company thus:

"Whatsoe'er thou be that art master of these lusty squires, I salute thee as graciously as a man in extreme dis-

67 gives me has a foreknowledge   **68 brave** gallant

tress may. Know that I and a fellow friend of mine are here
famished in the forest for want of food; perish we must unless relieved by thy favors. Therefore, if thou be a gentleman,
give meat to men, and to such men as are every way worthy of
life. Let the proudest squire that sits at thy table rise and
encounter with me in any honorable point of activity whatsoever, and if he and thou prove me not a man, send me away
comfortless. If thou refuse this, as a niggard of thy cates, I
will have amongst you[69] with my sword; for rather will I die
valiantly than perish with so cowardly an extreme."

Gerismond, looking him earnestly in the face and seeing so
proper a gentleman in so bitter a passion, was moved with so
great pity that, rising from the table, he took him by the hand
and bade him welcome, willing him to sit down in his place
and in his room not only to eat his fill but be lord of the feast.

"Gramercy,[70] sir," quoth Rosader, "but I have a feeble
friend that lies hereby famished almost for food, aged and
therefore less able to abide the extremity of hunger than myself, and dishonor it were for me to taste one crumb before I
made him partner of my fortunes; therefore I will run and
fetch him, and then I will gratefully accept of your proffer."

Away hies Rosader to Adam Spencer and tells him the
news, who was glad of so happy fortune, but so feeble he was
that he could not go, whereupon Rosader got him up on his
back and brought him to the place. Which when Gerismond
and his men saw, they greatly applauded their league of
friendship; and Rosader, having Gerismond's place assigned
him, would not sit there himself, but set down Adam Spencer. Well, to be short, those hungry squires fell to their vict-
uals and feasted themselves with good delicates and great
store of wine. As soon as they had taken their repast, Gerismond, desirous to hear what hard fortune drave them into
those bitter extremes, requested Rosader to discourse, if it
were not any way prejudicial unto him, the cause of his
travel. Rosader, desirous any way to satisfy the courtesy of
his favorable host, first beginning his exordium with a volley
of sighs and a few lukewarm tears, prosecuted[71] his discourse and told him from point to point all his fortunes: how
he was the youngest son of Sir John of Bordeaux, his name

69 cates . . . have amongst you provisions . . . attack you   **70 Gramercy**
many thanks   **71 prosecuted** continued

Rosader, how his brother sundry times had wronged him, and lastly how, for beating the Sheriff and hurting his men, he fled.

"And this old man," quoth he, "whom I so much love and honor, is surnamed Adam Spencer, an old servant of my father's and one that for his love never failed me in all my misfortunes."

When Gerismond heard this, he fell on the neck of Rosader, and next discoursing unto him how he was Gerismond, their lawful king exiled by Torismond, what familiarity had ever been betwixt his father, Sir John of Bordeaux, and him, how faithful a subject he[72] lived and how honorably he died, promising for his sake to give both him[73] and his friend such courteous entertainment as his present estate could minister, and upon this made him one of his foresters. Rosader, seeing it was the King, craved pardon for his boldness in that he did not do him due reverence and humbly gave him thanks for his favorable courtesy. Gerismond, not satisfied yet with news, began to inquire if he had been lately in the court of Torismond, and whether he had seen his daughter Rosalynde or no. At this Rosader fetched a deep sigh and, shedding many tears, could not answer; yet at last, gathering his spirits together, he revealed unto the King how Rosalynde was banished and how there was such a sympathy of affections between Alinda and her that she chose rather to be partaker of her exile than to part fellowship, whereupon the unnatural King banished them both. "And now they are wandered none knows whither, neither could any learn since their departure the place of their abode." This news drave* the King into a great melancholy, that presently he arose from all the company and went into his privy chamber, so secret as the harbor[74] of the woods would allow him. The company was all dashed at these tidings, and Rosader and Adam Spencer, having such opportunity, went to take their rest. Where we leave them, and return again to Torismond.

[Torismond, desirous of possessing the estate to which Saladyne has become heir, picks a quarrel with Saladyne over his treatment of Rosader and has the elder brother thrown into

72 he i.e., Sir John of Bordeaux   **73 his . . . him** i.e., Sir John's . . .
Rosader   **74 harbor** shelter

prison. Saladyne repents his abuse of Rosader and resolves, when free, to search for him far and wide in order to be reconciled with him.]

Rosader, being thus preferred[75] to the place of a forester by Gerismond, rooted out the remembrance of his brother's unkindness by continual exercise, traversing the groves and wild forests, partly to hear the melody of the sweet birds which recorded[76] and partly to show his diligent endeavor in his master's behalf. Yet whatsoever he did, or howsoever he walked, the lively image of Rosalynde remained in memory; on her sweet perfections he fed his thoughts, proving himself like the eagle a true-born bird, since as the one is known by beholding the sun, so was he by regarding excellent beauty. One day among the rest, finding a fit opportunity and place convenient, desirous to discover his woes to the woods, he engraved with his knife on the bark of a myrtle tree this pretty estimate of his mistress's perfection:

SONETTO

Of all chaste birds the phoenix doth excel,
Of all strong beasts the lion bears the bell,
Of all sweet flowers the rose doth sweetest smell,
Of all fair maids my Rosalynde is fairest.

Of all pure metals gold is only purest,
Of all high trees the pine hath highest crest,
Of all soft sweets I like my mistress' breast,
Of all chaste thoughts my mistress' thoughts are
    rarest.

Of all proud birds the eagle pleaseth Jove,
Of pretty fowls kind Venus likes the dove,
Of trees Minerva doth the olive love,
Of all sweet nymphs I honor Rosalynde.

Of all her gifts her wisdom pleaseth most,
Of all her graces virtue she doth boast.
For all these gifts my life and joy is lost
If Rosalynde prove cruel and unkind.

In these and suchlike passions Rosader did every day eternize the name of his Rosalynde, and this day especially when Aliena and Ganymede, enforced by the heat of the sun

75 preferred promoted **76 recorded** sang

to seek for shelter, by good fortune arrived in that place where this amorous forester registered his melancholy passions. They saw the sudden change of his looks, his folded arms,[77] his passionate sighs; they heard him often abruptly call on Rosalynde, who, poor soul, was as hotly burned as himself, but that she shrouded her pains in the cinders of honorable modesty. Whereupon, guessing him to be in love and according to the nature of their sex being pitiful in that behalf, they suddenly brake off his melancholy by their approach, and Ganymede shook him out of his dumps thus:

"What news, forester? Hast thou wounded some deer and lost him in the fall? Care not, man, for so small a loss; thy fees was but the skin, the shoulder, and the horns. 'Tis hunter's luck to aim fair and miss, and a woodman's fortune to strike and yet go without the game."

"Thou art beyond the mark, Ganymede," quoth Aliena. "His passions are greater and his sighs discovers more loss; perhaps in traversing these thickets he hath seen some beautiful nymph and is grown amorous."

"It may be so," quoth Ganymede, "for here he hath newly engraven some sonnet. Come and see the discourse of the forester's poems."

Reading the sonnet over and hearing him name Rosalynde, Aliena looked on Ganymede and laughed, and Ganymede, looking back on the forester and seeing it was Rosader, blushed. Yet, thinking to shroud all under her page's apparel, she boldly returned to Rosader and began thus:

"I pray thee tell me, forester, what is this Rosalynde for whom thou pinest away in such passions? Is she some nymph that waits upon Diana's train whose chastity thou hast deciphered[78] in such epithets? Or is she some shepherdess that haunts these plains whose beauty hath so bewitched thy fancy, whose name thou shadowest in covert[79] under the figure of Rosalynde, as Ovid did Julia[80] under the name of Corinna? Or say me, forsooth, is it that Rosalynde of whom we shepherds have heard talk—she, forester, that

---

77 folded arms (A sign of melancholy.)   **78 deciphered** written down
79 thou shadowest in covert you conceal   **80 Julia** (19 B.C.–A.D. 28)
granddaughter of Augustus Caesar, banished from Rome. The poet Ovid, thought to have been in love with her, was also banished, though for unknown reasons.

is the daughter of Gerismond, that once was King and now an outlaw in this forest of Arden?"

At this Rosader fetched a deep sigh and said:

"It is she, O gentle swain, it is she. That saint it is whom I serve, that goddess at whose shrine I do bend all my devotions—the most fairest of all fairs, the phoenix of all that sex, and the purity of all earthly perfection."

"And why, gentle forester, if she be so beautiful and thou so amorous, is there such a disagreement[81] in thy thoughts? Haply[82] she resembleth the rose that is sweet but full of prickles? Or the serpent regius[83] that hath scales as glorious as the sun and a breath as infectious as the aconitum[84] is deadly? So thy Rosalynde may be most amiable and yet unkind, full of favor and yet froward,[85] coy without wit, and disdainful without reason."

"O shepherd," quoth Rosader, "knewest thou her personage, graced with the excellence of all perfection, being a harbor wherein the Graces shroud their virtues, thou wouldst not breathe out such blasphemy against the beauteous Rosalynde. She is a diamond bright but not hard, yet of most chaste operation, a pearl so orient that it can be stained with no blemish, a rose without prickles, and a princess absolute as well in beauty as in virtue. But I, unhappy I, have let mine eye soar with the eagle against so bright a sun that I am quite blind; I have with Apollo enamored myself of a Daphne,[86] not, as she, disdainful, but far more chaste than Daphne; I have with Ixion[87] laid my love on Juno, and shall, I fear, embrace naught but a cloud. Ah, shepherd, I have reached at a star; my desires have mounted above my degree and my thoughts above my fortunes, I, being a peasant, having ventured to gaze on a princess whose honors are too high to vouchsafe such base loves."

"Why, forester," quoth Ganymede, "comfort thyself. Be blithe and frolic, man. Love souseth[88] as low as she soareth

---

81 disagreement strife   **82 Haply** perhaps   **83 the serpent regius** a fabulous serpent   **84 aconitum** aconite or wolfsbane, a poisonous plant   **85 froward** perverse   **86 Daphne** chaste nymph pursued by Apollo and transformed at her own request into a laurel tree rather than lose her chastity   **87 Ixion** (As punishment for his crimes, including his presumption in trying to win the love of Juno or Hera, Ixion was bound to a perpetually turning wheel in the underworld.)   **88 souseth** swoops (like a hawk) high: Cupid shoots at a rag[89] as soon as at a robe, and Venus' eye, that was so curious,[90] sparkled favor on polt-footed[91]* Vulcan. Fear not, man. Women's looks are not tied to dignity's feathers,[92] nor make they curious esteem where the stone is found but what is the virtue.[93] Fear not, forester. Faint heart never won fair lady. But where lives Rosalynde now? At the court?"

"O no," quoth Rosader, "she lives I know not where, and that is my sorrow; banished by Torismond, and that is my hell. For might I but find her sacred personage and plead before the bar of her pity the plaint of my passions, hope tells me she would grace me with some favor, and that would suffice as a recompense of all my former miseries."

[At a subsequent meeting, Rosalynde, still disguised as Ganymede, begs Rosader to describe his mistress's charms and is obliged with a "sonnet" or lyric poem. Rosalynde professes to smile "at the sonettos, canzones, madrigals, rounds, and roundelays that these pensive patients pour out when their eyes are more full of wantonness than their hearts of passions," and deplores such "painted lures" designed to beckon maidens to their destruction, but she is flattered for all that. Rosader insists on his sincerity, offering two more "sonnets" as proof.]

As soon as they had taken their repast, Rosader, giving them thanks for his good cheer, would have been gone, but Ganymede, that was loath to let him pass out of her presence, began thus: "Nay, forester," quoth he, "if thy business be not the greater, seeing thou sayst thou art so deeply in love, let me see how thou canst woo: I will represent Rosalynde, and thou shalt be as thou art, Rosader. See in some amorous eclogue how, if Rosalynde were present, how thou couldst court her, and while we sing of love, Aliena shall tune her pipe and play us melody."

---

89 a rag i.e., a person in rags (as distinguished from a person in robes or fine apparel)   **90 curious** fastidious   **91 polt-footed** clubfooted **92 looks** gazes.   **dignity's feathers** i.e., the finery of rank and station **93 nor make . . . virtue** i.e., nor do women bestow their special esteem on wealth lacking in virtue (?)

[Together they fashion a wooing eclogue on the subject of this feigned courtship of Rosalynde by her Rosader.]

All this while did poor Saladyne, banished from Bordeaux and the court of France by Torismond, wander up and down in the Forest of Arden, thinking to get to Lyons and so travel through Germany into Italy; but the forest being full of bypaths and he unskillful of the country coast, slipped out of the way and chanced up into the desert[94] not far from the place where Gerismond was and his brother Rosader. Saladyne, weary with wandering up and down and hungry with long fasting, finding a little cave by the side of a thicket, eating such fruit as the forest did afford and contenting himself with such drink as nature had provided and thirst made delicate, after his repast he fell in a dead sleep. As thus he lay, a hungry lion came hunting down the edge of the grove for prey and, espying Saladyne, began to seize upon him; but seeing he lay still without any motion, he left to touch him, for that lions hate to prey on dead carcasses; and yet desirous to have some food, the lion lay down and watched to see if he would stir. While thus Saladyne slept secure, Fortune, that was careful over her champion, began to smile and brought it so to pass that Rosader, having stricken a deer that, but lightly hurt, fled through the thicket, came pacing down by the grove with a boar spear in his hand, in great haste. He spied where a man lay asleep and a lion fast by him. Amazed at this sight, as he stood gazing, his nose on the sudden bled, which made him conjecture it was some friend of his. Whereupon drawing more nigh, he might easily discern his visage and perceived by his physiognomy that it was his brother Saladyne, which drave Rosader into a deep passion, as a man perplexed at the sight of so unexpected a chance, marveling what should drive his brother to traverse those secret deserts, without any company, in such distress and forlorn sort. But the present time craved no such doubting ambages,[95] for either he must resolve to hazard his life for his relief or else steal away and leave him to the cruelty of the lion. In which doubt he thus briefly debated with himself.

94 desert sparsely inhabited place   **95 ambages** delays

ROSADER'S MEDITATION

"Now, Rosader, Fortune that long hath whipped thee with nettles means to salve[96] thee with roses, and having crossed thee with many frowns, now she presents thee with the brightness of her favors. Thou that didst count thyself the most distressed of all men mayst account thyself now the most fortunate amongst men, if Fortune can make men happy or sweet revenge be wrapped in a pleasing content. Thou seest Saladyne, thine enemy, the worker of thy misfortunes and the efficient cause[97] of thine exile, subject to the cruelty of a merciless lion, brought into this misery by the gods, that they might seem just in revenging his rigor and thy injuries. Seest thou not how the stars are in a favorable aspect, the planets in some pleasing conjunction, the Fates agreeable to thy thoughts, and the Destinies performers of thy desires, in that Saladyne shall die and thou free of his blood, he receive meed for his amiss[98] and thou erect his tomb with innocent hands? Now, Rosader, shalt thou return to Bordeaux and enjoy thy possessions by birth and his revenues by inheritance. Now mayst thou triumph in love and hang Fortune's altars with garlands. For when Rosalynde hears of thy wealth it will make her love thee the more willingly; for women's eyes are made of chrysocoll,[99] that is ever unperfect unless tempered with gold, and Jupiter soonest enjoyed Danae[100] because he came to her in so rich a shower. Thus shall this lion, Rosader, end the life of a miserable man and from distress raise thee to be most fortunate." And with that, casting his boar spear on his neck, away he began to trudge.

But he had not stepped back two or three paces but a new motion struck him to the very heart, that,[101] resting his boar spear against his breast, he fell into this passionate humor:

"Ah, Rosader, wert thou the son of Sir John of Bordeaux, whose virtues exceeded his valor, and yet the most hardiest knight in all Europe? Should the honor of the father shine in the actions of the son, and wilt thou dishonor thy parentage

96 salve assuage   **97 efficient cause** cause that makes things what they are   **98 meed for his amiss** reward for his misdeeds   **99 chrysocoll** chrysocolla, a name of a mineral meaning "gold solder"   **100 Danae** a king's daughter, confined in a tower, whom Zeus or Jupiter contrived to visit in a shower of gold   **101 that** so that

in forgetting the nature of a gentleman? Did not thy father at his last gasp breathe out this golden principle: Brothers' amity is like the drops of balsamum[102] that salveth the most dangerous sores? Did he make a large exhort unto concord,[103] and wilt thou show thyself careless?[104] O Rosader, what though Saladyne hath wronged thee and made thee live an exile in the forest, shall thy nature be so cruel, or thy nurture so crooked, or thy thoughts so savage as to suffer so dismal a revenge? What, to let him be devoured by wild beasts? *Non sapit qui non sibi sapit*[105] is fondly spoken in such bitter extremes. Lose not his life, Rosader, to win a world of treasure; for in having him thou hast a brother, and by hazarding for his life thou gettest a friend and reconcilest an enemy; and more honor shalt thou purchase by pleasuring a foe than revenging a thousand injuries."

With that his brother began to stir and the lion to rouse himself, whereupon Rosader suddenly charged him with the boar spear and wounded the lion very sore at the first stroke. The beast, feeling himself to have a mortal hurt, leaped at Rosader and with his paws gave him a sore pinch on the breast, that he had almost fallen; yet as a man most valiant, in whom the sparks of Sir John of Bordeaux remained, he recovered himself and in short combat slew the lion, who at his death roared so loud that Saladyne awaked and, starting up, was amazed at the sudden sight of so monstrous a beast lie slain by him and so sweet a gentleman wounded. He presently, as he was of a ripe conceit,[106] began to conjecture that the gentleman had slain him in his defense. Whereupon, as a man in a trance, he stood staring on them both a good while, not knowing his brother, being in that disguise. At last he burst into these terms:

[Saladyne speaks to Rosader without recognizing him, thanking him for saving his life. Rosader takes the advantage of his disguise to elicit from Saladyne his life's story, which is told with such earnest remorse that Rosader perceives a true change of heart in his oldest brother. He reveals his identity and the brothers are reconciled. Rosader shows his

102 balsamum balm   103 exhort unto concord exhortation in behalf of concord   104 careless heedless   105 Non . . . sapit he knows nothing who knows not himself   106 was . . . conceit had a ready understanding

brother the forest for two or three days, during which time Rosalynde grows increasingly restive and impatient at her Rosader's absence. When Rosader eventually shows up, Rosalynde is sharp-tongued in her rebuke but finally accepts his explanation of finding his now-banished brother. A new complication arises (in an incident not dramatized by Shakespeare) when Alinda and Rosalynde are nearly abducted by some villains hoping to present her to the lustful King Torismond. Saladyne acquits himself so bravely in fighting off this attack that he wins the love of Alinda, still disguised as the shepherdess Aliena. Saladyne is no less attracted to her. As if to demonstrate that the course of true love seldom runs smoothly, however, the lovers are invited to overhear the unhappy wooing of Montanus for his proud and disdainful Phoebe, who has now fastened her affections on Ganymede. Alinda confesses to having her own doubts about men's constancy.]

Saladyne, hearing how Aliena harped still upon one string, which was the doubt of men's constancy, he broke off her sharp invective thus: "I grant, Aliena," quoth he, "many men have done amiss in proving soon ripe and soon rotten; but particular instances infer no general conclusions, and therefore I hope what others have faulted in shall not prejudice my favors. I will not use sophistry to confirm my love, for that is subtlety,[107] nor long discourses, lest my words might be thought more than my faith; but if this will suffice, that by the honor of a gentleman I love Aliena and woo Aliena not to crop the blossoms and reject the tree but to consummate my faithful desires in the honorable end of marriage."

At this word "marriage" Aliena stood in a maze what to answer, fearing that if she were too coy, to drive him away with her disdain, and if she were too courteous, to discover the heat of her desires. In a dilemma thus what to do, at last this she said: "Saladyne, ever since I saw thee I favored thee. I cannot dissemble my desires, because I see thou dost faithfully manifest thy thoughts, and in liking thee I love thee so far as mine honor holds fancy still in suspense;[108] but if I knew thee as virtuous as thy father or as well qualified as thy

107 subtlety ingenious contrivance   **108 so far ... suspense** so far as my honor, holding passion always in check, will allow

brother Rosader, the doubt should be quickly decided. But
for this time to give thee an answer, assure thyself this: I will
either marry with Saladyne or still live a virgin."

And with this they strained[109] one another's hand, which
Ganymede espying, thinking he had had his mistress long
enough at shrift,[110] said, "What, a match or no?"

"A match," quoth Aliena, "or else it were an ill market."[111]

"I am glad," quoth Ganymede. "I would Rosader were
well here to make up a mess."[112]

"Well remembered," quoth Saladyne. "I forgot I left my
brother Rosader alone, and therefore, lest being solitary he
should increase his sorrows, I will haste me to him. May it[113]
please you, then, to command me any service to him, I am
ready to be a dutiful messenger."

"Only at this time commend me to him," quoth Aliena,
"and tell him though we cannot pleasure him we pray for
him."

"And forget not," quoth Ganymede, "my commendations;
but say to him that Rosalynde sheds as many tears from her
heart as he drops of blood from his wounds for the sorrow of
his misfortunes, feathering all her thoughts with disquiet[114]
till his welfare procure her content. Say thus, good Saladyne,
and so farewell."

He, having his message, gave a courteous adieu to them
both, especially to Aliena, and so, playing "Loath to depart,"
went to his brother. But Aliena, she perplexed and yet joyful,
passed away the day pleasantly, still praising the perfection
of Saladyne, not ceasing to chat of her new love till evening
drew on. And then they, folding[115] their sheep, went home to
bed. Where we leave them and return to Phoebe.

[Phoebe, despairing in her love for Ganymede, composes various epistles to him and commissions Montanus to act as her
messenger. Rosalynde as Ganymede undertakes to cure Montanus of his infatuation by showing him the letters, to which
the faithful lover responds by wishing that Ganymede may
have Phoebe in Montanus's stead; Phoebe's happiness is all

---

109 strained confined, held   **110 he had . . . shrift** i.e., Saladyne had
held Aliena long enough in private conference   **111 an ill market** i.e., a
bad bargain, unprofitable or dishonest dealing   **112 make up a mess**
make up a group of four (as at table)   **113 May it** if it may   **114 feathering . . . disquiet** i.e., allowing herself no contented thoughts   **115 folding** putting in the sheepfold

that Montanus desires. Rosalynde and Alinda resolve to assist Montanus somehow in getting the love of Phoebe. Rosalynde does so by going directly to Phoebe and offering her stern if compassionate advice: hope no longer for Ganymede, but instead seek affection where it can be reciprocated.]

Thus, Phoebe, thou mayst see I disdain not, though I desire not, remaining indifferent till time and love makes me resolute. Therefore, Phoebe, seek not to suppress affection, and with the love of Montanus quench the remembrance of Ganymede; strive thou to hate me as I seek to like of thee, and ever have the duties of Montanus in thy mind, for I promise thee thou mayst have one more wealthy but not more loyal." These words were corrosives to the perplexed Phoebe, that, sobbing out sighs and straining out tears, she blubbered out these words:

"And shall I then have no salve of Ganymede but suspense, no hope but a doubtful hazard, no comfort, but be posted off to the will of time? Justly have the gods balanced my fortunes, who, being cruel to Montanus, found Ganymede as unkind to myself; so in forcing him perish for love, I shall die myself with overmuch love."

"I am glad," quoth Ganymede, "you look into your own faults and see where your shoe wrings[116] you, measuring now the pains of Montanus by your own passions."

"Truth," quoth Phoebe, "and so deeply I repent me of my frowardness towards the shepherd that, could I cease to love Ganymede, I would resolve to like Montanus."

"What,[117] if I can with reason persuade Phoebe to mislike of[118] Ganymede, will she then favor Montanus?"

"When reason," quoth she, "doth quench that love that I owe to thee, then will I fancy him; conditionally, that if my love can be suppressed with no reason, as being without reason, Ganymede will only wed himself to Phoebe."

"I grant it, fair shepherdess," quoth he, "and to feed thee with the sweetness of hope, this resolve on: I will never marry myself to woman but unto thyself."

And with that Ganymede gave Phoebe a fruitless kiss and such words of comfort that before Ganymede departed she

116 wrings pinches   **117 What** i.e., do you mean to say   **118 mislike of** dislike

arose out of her bed and made him and Montanus such cheer as could be found in such a country cottage, Ganymede in the midst of their banquet rehearsing the promises of either in Montanus's favor, which highly pleased the shepherd. Thus, all three content and soothed up in hope, Ganymede took his leave of his Phoebe and departed, leaving her a contented woman and Montanus highly pleased. But poor Ganymede, who had her thoughts on her Rosader, when she called to remembrance his wounds, filled her eyes full of tears and her heart full of sorrows, plodded to find Aliena at the folds,[119] thinking with her presence to drive away her passions. As she came on the plains she might espy where Rosader and Saladyne sat with Aliena under the shade, which sight was a salve to her grief and such a cordial unto her heart that she tripped alongst the lawns full of joy.

At last Corydon, who was with them, spied Ganymede, and with that the clown[120] rose and, running to meet him, cried:

"O sirrah, a match, a match! Our mistress shall be married on Sunday."

Thus the poor peasant frolicked it before Ganymede who, coming to the crew, saluted them all, and especially Rosader, saying that he was glad to see him so well recovered of his wounds.

"I had not gone abroad[121] so soon," quoth Rosader, "but that I am bidden to a marriage which, on Sunday next, must be solemnized between my brother and Aliena. I see well where love leads delay is loathsome, and that small wooing serves where both the parties are willing."

"Truth," quoth Ganymede, "but a happy day should it be if Rosader that day might be married to Rosalynde."

"Ah, good Ganymede," quoth he, "by naming Rosalynde, renew not my sorrows, for the thought of her perfections is the thrall of my miseries."

"Tush, be of good cheer, man," quoth Ganymede. "I have a friend that is deeply experienced in necromancy and magic. What art can do shall be acted for thine advantage. I will cause him to bring in Rosalynde, if either France or any bordering nation harbor her; and upon that take the faith of a young shepherd."

Aliena smiled to see how Rosader frowned, thinking that Ganymede had jested with him. But breaking off from those matters, the page, somewhat pleasant,[122] began to discourse unto them what had passed between him and Phoebe, which, as they laughed, so they wondered at, all confessing that there is none so chaste but love will change. Thus they passed away the day in chat, and when the sun began to set, they took their leaves and departed, Aliena providing for their marriage day such solemn[123] cheer and handsome robes as fitted their country estate and yet somewhat the better in that Rosader had promised to bring Gerismond thither as a guest. Ganymede, who then meant to discover herself before her father, had made her a gown of green and a kirtle of the finest sendal[124] in such sort that she seemed some heavenly nymph harbored in country attire.

Saladyne was not behind in care to set out the nuptials, nor Rosader unmindful to bid guests, who invited Gerismond and all his followers to the feast, who willingly granted, so that there was nothing but the day wanting to this marriage.

In the meanwhile, Phoebe, being a bidden guest, made herself as gorgeous as might be to please the eye of Ganymede; and Montanus suited[125] himself with the cost of many of his flocks to be gallant against that day, for then was Ganymede to give Phoebe an answer of her loves and Montanus either to hear the doom of his misery or the censure[126] of his happiness. But while this gear was a-brewing, Phoebe passed not one day without visiting her Ganymede, so far was she wrapped in the beauties of this lovely swain. Much prattle they had and the discourse of many passions, Phoebe wishing for the day, as she thought, of her welfare and Ganymede smiling to think what unexpected events would fall out at the wedding. In these humors the week went away, that at last Sunday came.

No sooner did Phoebus' henchman[127] appear in the sky to give warning that his master's horses should be trapped in[128] his glorious coach but Corydon, in his holiday suit, marvel-

---

122 pleasant merry   **123 solemn** ceremonial, festive   **124 kirtle . . . sendal** cloak made of a thin rich silken material   **125 suited** outfitted **126 doom** judgment.   **censure** verdict   **127 Phoebus' henchman** i.e., the groom tending the horses of the sun   **128 trapped in** adorned with trappings in the harness of

ous seemly in a russet jacket welted[129] with the same and
faced[130] with red worsted, having a pair of blue camlet[131]
sleeves bound at the wrists with four yellow laces, closed
afore[132] very richly with a dozen of pewter buttons; his hose
was of gray kersey,[133] with a large slop[134] barred overthwart[135]
the pocket-holes with three fair guards[136] stitched of[137] either
side with red thread; his stock was of the own,[138] sewed close
to his breech, and for to beautify his hose he had trussed
himself round with a dozen of new-threaden points[139] of med-
ley color; his bonnet was green, whereon stood a copper
brooch with the picture of Saint Denis; and to want[140] nothing
that might make him amorous in his old days, he had a fair
shirtband of fine lockram,[141] whipped over[142] with Coventry
blue of no small cost. Thus attired, Corydon bestirred himself as chief stickler[143] in these actions and had strewed
all the house with flowers, that it seemed rather some of
Flora's[144] choice bowers than any country cottage.

Thither repaired Phoebe with all the maids of the forest to
set out the bride in the most seemliest sort that might be.
But howsoever she helped to prank out Aliena, yet her eye
was still on Ganymede, who was so neat in a suit of gray that
he seemed Endymion[145] when he won Luna with his looks or
Paris when he played the swain to get the beauty of the
nymph Oenone.[146] Ganymede, like a pretty page, waited on
his mistress Aliena and overlooked[147] that all was in a readi-
ness against[148] the bridegroom should come, who, attired in a
forester's suit, came accompanied with Gerismond and his
brother Rosader early in the morning; where arrived, they
were solemnly[149] entertained by Aliena and the rest of the
country swains, Gerismond very highly commending the fortunate choice of Saladyne in that he had chosen a shepherd-

---

129 welted edged   **130 faced** covered   **131 camlet** costly fabric of wool
and silk   **132 afore** before, in front   **133 kersey** a coarse, ribbed woolen
cloth   **134 slop** loose breeches   **135 overthwart** across   **136 guards**
ornaments   **137 of** on   **138 stock . . . own** i.e., his hose were part of
the slop or breeches   **139 points** tags used to fasten clothing, especially
the hose to the doublet   **140 want** lack   **141 lockram** linen fabric
142 whipped over bound closely with thread   **143 stickler** manager
144 Flora goddess of flowers   **145 Endymion** a shepherd boy whose
beauty as he slept won the love of the moon (Luna)   **146 Oenone** Paris'
wife when he was a shepherd; he deserted her for Helen   **147 overlooked** oversaw   **148 against** anticipating the time when   **149 solemnly**
ceremoniously, festively

ess whose virtues appeared in her outward beauties, being no less fair than seeming modest.

Ganymede, coming in and seeing her father, began to blush, nature working affects by her secret effects. Scarce could she abstain from tears to see her father in so low fortunes—he that was wont to sit in his royal palace, attended on by twelve noble peers, now to be contented with a simple cottage and a troop of reveling woodmen for his train. The consideration of his fall made Ganymede full of sorrows; yet that she might triumph over fortune with patience and not any way dash that merry day with her dumps, she smothered her melancholy with a shadow of mirth and very reverently welcomed the King not according to his former degree but to his present estate, with such diligence as Gerismond began to commend the page for his exquisite person and excellent qualities.

As thus the King with his foresters frolicked it among the shepherds, Corydon came in with a fair mazer[150] full of cider and presented it to Gerismond with such a clownish salute that he began to smile and took it of[151] the old shepherd very kindly, drinking to Aliena and the rest of her fair maids, amongst whom Phoebe was the foremost. Aliena pledged[152] the King and drunk to Rosader; so the carouse[153] went round from him to Phoebe, etc. As they were thus drinking and ready to go to church, came in Montanus, appareled all in tawny,[154] to signify that he was forsaken; on his head he wore a garland of willow, his bottle[155] hanged by his side, whereon was painted despair, and on his sheephook hung two sonnets as labels of his loves and fortunes.

[Gerismond, hearing of Montanus's unavailing passion for Phoebe, orders her to be brought before him in order that he may, like Rosalynde, lecture her on the cruelty of her behavior toward Montanus. She counters by insisting that her case is as hopeless and that Ganymede is no less cruel in his treatment of her.]

Gerismond, desirous to prosecute[156] the end of these passions, called in Ganymede, who, knowing the case, came in

150 **mazer** wooden drinking cup   151 **of** from   152 **pledged** toasted
153 **carouse** drinking of healths   154 **tawny** cloth of tawny color
155 **bottle** leather drink container   156 **prosecute** pursue

graced with such a blush as beautified the crystal of his face
with a ruddy brightness. The King, noting well the physiognomy of Ganymede, began by his favors to call to mind the
face of his Rosalynde, and with that fetched a deep sigh. Rosader, that was passing[157] familiar with Gerismond, demanded of him why he sighed so sore.

"Because, Rosader," quoth he, "the favor of Ganymede
puts me in mind of Rosalynde."

At this word Rosader sighed so deeply as though his heart
would have burst.

"And what's the matter," quoth Gerismond, "that you
quite[158] me with such a sigh?"

"Pardon me, sir," quoth Rosader, "because I love none but
Rosalynde."

"And upon that condition," quoth Gerismond, "that Rosalynde were here, I would this day make up a marriage betwixt her and thee."

At this Aliena turned her head and smiled upon Ganymede, and she could scarce keep countenance. Yet she
salved[159] all with secrecy; and Gerismond, to drive away such
dumps, questioned with Ganymede what the reason was he
regarded not Phoebe's love, seeing she was as fair as the wanton that brought Troy to ruin.[160] Ganymede mildly answered:

"If I should affect the fair Phoebe, I should offer poor
Montanus great wrong to win that from him in a moment
that[161] he hath labored for so many months.* Yet have I promised to the beautiful shepherdess to wed myself never to
woman except unto her, but with this promise, that if I can by
reason suppress Phoebe's love towards me, she shall like of
none but of Montanus."

"To that," quoth Phoebe, "I stand, for my love is so far
beyond reason as it will admit no persuasion of reason."

"For justice," quoth he, "I appeal to Gerismond."

"And to his censure will I stand," quoth Phoebe.

"And in your victory," quoth Montanus, "stands the hazard of my fortunes; for if Ganymede go away with conquest,[162] Montanus is in conceit[163] love's monarch; if Phoebe
win, then am I in effect most miserable."

---

157 passing surpassingly, very **158 quite** requite, repay **159 salved**
soothed, healed **160 the wanton . . . ruin** i.e., Helen of Troy **161 that**
which **162 go away with conquest** win **163 in conceit** in thought

"We will see this controversy," quoth Gerismond, "and then we will to church. Therefore, Ganymede, let us hear your argument."

"Nay, pardon my absence awhile," quoth she, "and you shall see one in store."

In went Ganymede and dressed herself in woman's attire, having on a gown of green with kirtle[164] of rich sendal, so quaint that she seemed Diana[165] triumphing in the forest. Upon her head she wore a chaplet of roses, which gave her such a grace that she looked like Flora perked in the pride[166] of all her flowers. Thus attired came Rosalynde in and presented herself at her father's feet, with her eyes full of tears, craving his blessing and discoursing unto him all her fortunes, how she was banished by Torismond and how ever since she lived in that country disguised.

Gerismond, seeing his daughter, rose from his seat and fell upon her neck, uttering the passions of his joy in watery plaints, driven into such an ecstasy of content that he could not utter one word. At this sight if Rosader was both amazed and joyful, I refer myself to the judgment of such as have experience in love, seeing his Rosalynde before his face whom so long and deeply he had affected. At last Gerismond recovered his spirits and in most fatherly terms entertained[167] his daughter Rosalynde, after many questions demanding of her what had passed between her and Rosader.

"So much, sir," quoth she, "as there wants nothing but Your Grace to make up the marriage."

"Why, then," quoth Gerismond, "Rosader, take her. She is thine, and let this day solemnize both thy brother's and thy nuptials." Rosader, beyond measure content, humbly thanked the King and embraced his Rosalynde, who, turning towards Phoebe, demanded if she had shown sufficient reason to suppress the force of her loves.

"Yea," quoth Phoebe, "and so great a persuasive that, please it you, madam, and Aliena to give us leave, Montanus and I will make this day the third couple in marriage."

She had no sooner spake this word but Montanus threw away his garland of willow, his bottle, where was painted de-

---

164 kirtle cloak   **165 Diana** goddess of the hunt and of the moon
166 perked in the pride dressed in the splendor   **167 entertained**
spoke with, occupied the attention of

spair, and cast his sonnets in the fire, showing himself as
frolic as Paris when he handseled[168] his love with Helena. At
this Gerismond and the rest smiled and concluded that Montanus and Phoebe should keep their wedding with the two
brethren. Aliena, seeing Saladyne stand in a dump, to wake
him from his dream began thus:

"Why, how now, my Saladyne, all amort?[169] What, melancholy, man, at the day of marriage? Perchance thou art sor-
rowful to think on thy brother's high fortunes and thine own
base desires to choose so mean a shepherdess. Cheer up thy
heart, man, for this day thou shalt be married to the daughter of a King. For know, Saladyne, I am not Aliena, but
Alinda, the daughter of thy mortal enemy Torismond."

At this all the company was amazed, especially Gerismond, who, rising up, took Alinda in his arms and said to
Rosalynde:

"Is this that fair Alinda, famous for so many virtues, that
forsook her father's court to live with thee exiled in the country?"

"The same," quoth Rosalynde.

"Then," quoth Gerismond, turning to Saladyne, "jolly forester, be frolic, for thy fortunes are great and thy desires excellent. Thou hast got a princess as famous for her
perfection as exceeding in proportion."[170]

"And she hath with her beauty won," quoth Saladyne, "an
humble servant as full of faith as she of amiable favor."

While everyone was amazed with these comical events,
Corydon came skipping in and told them that the priest was
at church and tarried for their coming. With that Gerismond
led the way, and the rest followed, where to the admiration of
all the country swains in Arden their marriages were solemnly solemnized.

[In the midst of a festive dinner, complete with homely fare
and a song by Corydon, the brother of Saladyne and Rosader
named Fernandyne arrives with news that twelve peers of
France are nearby in arms to restore Gerismond's right by
doing battle with Torismond. The men rush eagerly from the

168 handseled inaugurated with gifts, first experienced **169 amort**
dejected **170 proportion** portion, dowry; shape

dinner to join in the encounter, wherein they put Torismond's army to flight and slay the tyrant. Alinda thus loses
her father but is comforted by her union with Saladyne.]

Well, as soon as they were come to Paris, Gerismond made
a royal feast for the peers and lords of his land, which continued thirty days, in which time summoning a parliament, by
the consent of his nobles he created Rosader heir apparent to
the kingdom. He restored Saladyne to all his father's land
and gave him the dukedom of Nameurs; he made Fernandyne principal secretary to himself; and that fortune might
every way seem frolic, he made Montanus lord over all the
Forest of Arden, Adam Spencer captain of the King's guard,
and Corydon master of Alinda's flocks.

Thomas Lodge's *Rosalynde: Euphues' Golden Legacy* was first published in
London in 1590. The present excerpted text is based on the first edition.

In the following, departures from the original text appear in boldface; original readings are in roman.

p. 108 *thwartest twhartest   **p. 117** *drave drive   **p. 121** *polt-footed pole-footed
p. 132 *months monts

Further Reading

Barber, C. L. "The Alliance of Seriousness and Levity in *As You Like It.*" *Shakespeare's Festive Comedy.* Princeton, N.J.: Princeton Univ. Press, 1959. In the context of his general thesis about the relation of Shakespeare's comedies to popular holiday and festivity, Barber sees the play as an exploration of passion that at once validates the experience of romantic love and exhibits a witty "detachment from its follies." Rosalind embodies and reconciles the two attitudes, alternating between "holiday and everyday perspectives."

Barton, Anne. "*As You Like It* and *Twelfth Night:* Shakespeare's Sense of an Ending." In *Shakespearian Comedy,* ed. Malcolm Bradbury and D. J. Palmer. Stratford-upon-Avon Studies 14. London: Edward Arnold; New York: Crane, Russak, 1972. Barton considers the play the "fullest and most stable realization of Shakespearian comic form," masterfully balancing romantic and realistic views of the world. Unlike *Twelfth Night,* which reveals the instabilities of comedy, the ending of this play reveals a poise and equilibrium witnessing to Shakespeare's faith in the resolutions comedy achieves.

Berry, Edward I. "Rosalynde and Rosalind." *Shakespeare Quarterly* 31 (1980): 42–52. Patiently comparing Shakespeare's play with its source, Thomas Lodge's *Rosalynde,* Berry examines the implications of Shakespeare's alterations, focusing mainly on the figure of Rosalind/Rosalynde, who becomes in Shakespeare's hands "a figure of the playwright himself."

Berry, Ralph. "No Exit from Arden." *Shakespeare's Comedies: Explorations in Form.* Princeton, N.J.: Princeton Univ. Press, 1972. Berry resists romantic readings of the play, finding instead that the romantic ideal is "challenged by the probings of realism, common sense, and satire." In the actions of both the court and the forest, Berry finds unease and the "simple will to dominate." The play's happy ending can be therefore only provisional, relocating rather than resolving the problems that have surfaced.

Bono, Barbara J. "Mixed Gender, Mixed Genre in Shakespeare's *As You Like It.*" In *Renaissance Genres: Essays on Theory, History, and Interpretation,* ed. Barbara K. Lewalski. Cambridge: Harvard Univ. Press, 1986. Examining the play's complex emotional interactions, Bono argues that both Orlando and Rosalind are transformed, as he is led to revise his early idealization of women and she is led, through her efforts to educate Orlando, to "exorcise her own fears about love." The playfulness of these negotiations of gender difference reveals a confidence, which Shakespeare's tragedies later deny, in the possibility of escaping rigid gender definitions and destructive sexual anxieties.

Cirillo, Albert R. "*As You Like It:* Pastoralism Gone Awry." *ELH* 38 (1971): 19–39. Cirillo explores the play's pastoralism, suggesting that Shakespeare undercuts its conventions in order to clarify its heuristic role. The play rejects the idea that pastoral offers "an attainable ideal in life"; rather, the pastoral episode is merely a temporary sojourn in a "second world" that transforms the characters' understanding of their values and experiences.

Erickson, Peter. "Sexual Politics and Social Structure in *As You Like It.*" *Patriarchal Structures in Shakespeare's Drama.* Berkeley, Los Angeles, and London: Univ. of California Press, 1985. In spite of Rosalind's exercise of significant authority, Erickson argues, *As You Like It* merely seduces us into imagining that her actions transform the play's sexual politics. By focusing both upon the implications of the boy actors that played female parts in Shakespeare's theater and Rosalind's actions at the end of the play, Erickson sees that the happy ending is achieved only by reinscribing Rosalind within the structures of male power and patriarchy.

Gardner, Helen. "*As You Like It.*" In *More Talking of Shakespeare,* ed. John Garrett. New York: Theatre Arts Books, 1959. Rpt. in *Shakespeare, The Comedies: A Collection of Critical Essays,* ed. Kenneth Muir. Englewood Cliffs, N.J.: Prentice-Hall, 1965. For Gardner, *As You Like It* is "Shakespeare's most Mozartian comedy," elegant and refined. Through misunderstandings and feigning, characters are led to the truth about themselves and their desires. In the comedy "the world is shown not only as a place where we may find happiness, but as a place where both happiness and sorrow may be hallowed."

Hayles, Nancy K. "Sexual Disguise in *As You Like It* and *Twelfth Night.*" *Shakespeare Survey* 32 (1979): 63–72. Comparing the use of sexual disguise in the two plays, Hayles sees that disguise grants Rosalind a power that it withholds from Viola in *Twelfth Night*. Disguise enables Rosalind to escape Orlando's unrealistic fantasy of her, and, as the play's disguises are finally discarded, the play reveals and resolves the "traditional tension between the needs of the female and the needs of the male."

Jamieson, Michael. *Shakespeare: "As You Like It."* London: Edward Arnold, 1965. After a discussion of the literary traditions and conventions that inform the design of the play, Jamieson's short book contains a scene-by-scene analysis, with special attention to the play's relationship to Shakespeare's other "great comedies." Jamieson views *As You Like It* as generous and affirmative, able to embrace disparate attitudes but finally adopting a romantic view of both courtship and love.

Kuhn, Maura Slattery. "Much Virtue in *If.*" *Shakespeare Quarterly* 28 (1977): 40–50. Kuhn explores the many improbabilities, uncertainties, and conditional assertions of the play, and holds that the experiences in Arden function to effect the suspension of disbelief and validate the evidence of the provisional. By accepting Arden's premises, Kuhn argues, characters "are rewarded with conclusions transcending their expectations."

Leggatt, Alexander. *"As You Like It." Shakespeare's Comedy of Love.* London: Methuen, 1974. Leggatt locates the comic effects of the play in the juxtaposition of its convincing naturalism and obvious artifice, ultimately suggesting that even the commonsense distinction "between ordinary experience and the conventionalized actions of storybook characters" may be a false one. In this play of contrasting perspectives, "no one attitude can be taken as absolute or final"; at the end the audience is invited to share in the mockery of the play's conventions while being permitted to recognize the reality of the love that underlies them.

Montrose, Louis Adrian. " 'The Place of a Brother' in *As You Like It:* Social Process and Comic Form." *Shakespeare*

Quarterly 32 (1981): 28–54, Montrose examines the ways in which the comedy recognizes and resolves social conflicts, especially the rivalry between elder and younger brothers and the tension between female power and a patriarchal culture that must control it. As the play explores these differential social relations, it contains and discharges the tensions that are released, serving not only as "a theatrical *reflection* of social conflicts" but also as "a theatrical *source* of social conciliation."

Nevo, Ruth. "Existence in Arden." *Comic Transformations in Shakespeare*. London and New York: Methuen, 1980. *As You Like It*, for Nevo, is a confident and accomplished comedy, one in which Shakespeare celebrates the principles of his comic art, making them the very material of the play. Rosalind's activities in the forest embody "comic pleasure itself." They serve as "a liberating playful fantasy" that tests her capacities for life and for love as she tests "these same potencies in others."

Park, Clara Claiborne. "As We Like It: How a Girl Can Be Smart and Still Popular." *The American Scholar* 42 (1973): 262–278. Rpt. in *The Woman's Part: Feminist Criticism of Shakespeare*, ed. Carolyn Swift Ruth Lenz, Gayle Greene, and Carol Thomas Neely. Urbana, Ill.: Univ. of Illinois Press, 1980. Park's witty title nicely encapsulates what she sees as the "extent—and the limits—of acceptable feminine activity in the Shakespearean world." She finds Rosalind the most forceful and successful of Shakespeare's women, but though she appealingly extends the possibilities of female behavior, even she keeps her activity confined to traditional domains of action and "gladly and voluntarily" relinquishes her authority.

Young, David. "Earthly Things Made Even: *As You Like It*." *The Heart's Forest: A Study of Shakespeare's Pastoral Plays*. New Haven, Conn.: Yale Univ. Press, 1972. Young explores Shakespeare's skillful use of the conventions of the pastoral in *As You Like It*. The play not only presents traditional pastoral themes, but functions ultimately as a commentary on the pastoral itself. Neither idealism nor satire—the two poles of pastoralism—satisfies Shakespeare, who continually tests one against the other and finally seeks a reconciliation between them.

Ay, now am I in Arden, the more fool I. When I was at home I was in a better place, but travelers must be content.

(TOUCHSTONE 2.4.14–16)

[*Song*]   Under the greenwood tree
Who loves to lie with me . . .   (AMIENS   2.5.1–2)

[*Song*]   Here shall he see
No enemy
But winter and rough weather.   (AMIENS   2.5.6–8)

I can suck melancholy out of a song as a weasel sucks eggs.

(JAQUES   2.5.11–12)

[*Song*]   Who doth ambition shun,
And loves to live i' the sun,
Seeking the food he eats
And pleased with what he gets . . .   (AMIENS   2.5.35–38)

"Thus we may see," quoth he, "how the world wags."

(JAQUES   2.7.23)

". . . And so from hour to hour we ripe and ripe,
And then from hour to hour we rot and rot,
And thereby hangs a tale."   (JAQUES   2.7.26–28)

True is it that we have seen better days.

(DUKE SENIOR   2.7.119)

Thou seest we are not all alone unhappy.

(DUKE SENIOR   2.7.135)

All the world's a stage,
And all the men and women merely players.
They have their exits and their entrances,
And one man in his time plays many parts.

(JAQUES   2.7.138–141)

Sans teeth, sans eyes, sans taste, sans everything.

(JAQUES   2.7.165)

[*Song*]   Blow, blow, thou winter wind,
Thou art not so unkind
As man's ingratitude.   (AMIENS   2.7.174–176)

In respect that it is solitary, I like it very well; but in respect
that it is private, it is a very vile life.
                               (TOUCHSTONE   3.2.15–16)

He that wants money, means, and content is without three
good friends.   (CORIN   3.2.23–24)

O wonderful, wonderful, and most wonderful wonderful!
And yet again wonderful, and after that, out of all whooping!
                               (CELIA   3.2.188–190)

Do you not know I am a woman? When I think, I must speak.
                               (ROSALIND   3.2.246–247)

Men have died from time to time, and worms have eaten
them, but not for love.   (ROSALIND   4.1.101–102)

For ever and a day.   (ORLANDO   4.1.138)

"The fool doth think he is wise, but the wise man knows himself to be a fool."   (TOUCHSTONE   5.1.30–31)

[*Song*]   It was a lover and his lass,
With a hey, and a ho, and a hey-nonny-no . . .
                               (PAGES   5.3.15–16)

O sir, we quarrel in print, by the book, as you have books for
good manners.   (TOUCHSTONE   5.4.89–90)

All these you may avoid but the Lie Direct; and you may avoid
that too, with an If.   (TOUCHSTONE   5.4.95–97)

Much virtue in If.   (TOUCHSTONE   5.4.101–102)

Contributors

DAVID BEVINGTON, Phyllis Fay Horton Professor of Humanities at the University of Chicago, is editor of *The Complete Works of Shakespeare* (Scott, Foresman, 1980) and of *Medieval Drama* (Houghton Mifflin, 1975). His latest critical study is *Action Is Eloquence: Shakespeare's Language of Gesture* (Harvard University Press, 1984).

DAVID SCOTT KASTAN, Professor of English and Comparative Literature at Columbia University, is the author of *Shakespeare and the Shapes of Time* (University Press of New England, 1982).

JAMES HAMMERSMITH, Associate Professor of English at Auburn University, has published essays on various facets of Renaissance drama, including literary criticism, textual criticism, and printing history.

ROBERT KEAN TURNER, Professor of English at the University of Wisconsin–Milwaukee, is a general editor of the New Variorum Shakespeare (Modern Language Association of America) and a contributing editor to *The Dramatic Works in the Beaumont and Fletcher Canon* (Cambridge University Press, 1966–).

JAMES SHAPIRO, who coedited the bibliographies with David Scott Kastan, is Assistant Professor of English at Columbia University.

❖

JOSEPH PAPP, one of the most important forces in theater today, is the founder and producer of the New York Shakespeare Festival, America's largest and most prolific theatrical institution. Since 1954 Mr. Papp has produced or directed all but one of Shakespeare's plays—in Central Park, in schools, off and on Broadway, and at the Festival's permanent home, The Public Theater. He has also produced such award-winning plays and musical works as *Hair, A Chorus Line, Plenty,* and *The Mystery of Edwin Drood,* among many others.